Packing Heat

Nadine's heart was beating fast and she was bristling with excitement. What she had just seen had brought a smile to her face. Her adversary Valerie Neiman had been flat on her back on a desk with Daniel Garsante leaning over her. She had to admit that watching them had turned her on – they were, after all, a good-looking couple.

This wasn't the reason her heart was beating a lot faster than normal, though. What she had seen had given her ideas and, when Garsante had picked up a file and put it in the safe, she had no qualms in memorising the combination.

Other books by the author:

Feminine Wiles

Packing Heat
Karina Moore

BLACK LACE

Black Lace books contain sexual fantasies.
In real life, always practise safe sex.

This edition published in 2004 by
Black Lace
Thames Wharf Studios
Rainville Road
London W6 9HA

Originally published 1999

Printed and bound in Great Britain by Clays Ltd, St Ives PLC

ISBN 0 352 33356 1

Chapter One

Nadine Brookes shaded her eyes and gazed down the slope of the valley towards the orange groves. It was a beautiful sight. Green pastureland rolling gently down to the vineyards and the fruit orchards and all of it bathed in clear, hot sunlight. But Nadine was not basking in the splendour of the view – far from it, every moment she had to spend in the place seemed to drag on for ever. As she stood there, seconds turning into minutes, she felt the familiar coil of resentment tighten inside herself. She needed a release. God, how she needed a release.

She glanced back at the house, pristine white and sparkling in the sunshine. Any moment now, she predicted, they would be sitting down to lunch, expecting her to join them, expecting her to smile and dazzle, to laugh at her uncle's God-awful jokes and play the dutiful niece as they entertained today's group of lunch guests. No, Nadine decided emphatically. She ducked quickly beneath the white wooden fence and began to walk down the gentle slope. Definitely no. She would get around her uncle later. Right now, she needed something else.

She was halfway down the slope when she saw him. Jake or Joey or Jack. Some name like that anyhow. He was at the far end of the nearest orange orchard, stripped to the waist as he hammered a wooden post deep into the soil. Nadine carried on slowly downward. As she reached the entrance to the orchard, she stopped for a moment to watch him. His upper body was tan, an even shade of light mahogany. Smooth muscles in his broad back gleamed with sweat, rippling as he pounded at the post. Nadine smiled at the sight – this was exactly the something else that she needed!

Quietly, she made her way over, purposely walking round behind him until she stood on the far side of the wooden post. It amused her as he suddenly paused mid-strike, arm and hammer aloft, and stared at her strappy-sandal-clad feet. His gaze travelled quickly up to her face.

'Hey,' she said in greeting, trying not to laugh at his arm and hammer caught in a freeze-frame, mid-air. 'Please, Jack, don't hit me. I promise I'm a good girl!'

He dropped his arm, leaning on the large hammer on the ground. 'It ain't too clever to go creeping up on a man like that, miss. Not when he's working with a hammer and all.'

Nadine shrugged carelessly, liking the hint of surliness in his manner, liking even more the scowl on his face. 'Just being polite and saying hello, Jack. There's no need to go biting my head off.'

He lifted his eyes without moving his head and stared off into the distance. 'Jake, miss,' he corrected. 'The name's Jake.'

Nadine bit back a smile. Jake, Jack, who cared? she thought. All she cared was that he surely was about the best-looking workhand she'd ever seen at her uncle's place. Maybe this once she'd break her own golden rule and be nice to the hired help. She decided on her approach. Sweet. She would be sweet as a toffee and pecan pie.

'Hot afternoon, isn't it, Jake?'

Jake dropped his gaze back to her. 'Uh huh.' He

nodded. A tiny bead of sweat trickled along his eyebrow. He flicked it away with his forefinger.

'Even hotter working out here, I bet.' Nadine noticed another bead of sweat trickle down the side of his weather-darkened face. She fought a strong urge to reach up and press her fingertip to it.

'That's right, miss,' Jake replied, squinting up into the azure sky, creasing his eyes against the sunlight.

Softly, Nadine exhaled, brushing her own lower lip with her breath. She began to fan herself with her hand, waving it Southern-belle-like in front of her neck and chest. Much to her annoyance, Jake made a move to continue work.

'Guess I better finish up with this post, miss,' he mumbled, heaving his hammer up from the ground.

As she watched him turn round to do just that, bracing his legs a step apart, she couldn't help but notice the tensed muscles of his long thighs, defined by his dusty jeans. A surge of heat took her by surprise, tearing through her abdomen. She saw the way his longish hair clung to the back of his neck, the way its natural dark-blond colour was stained even darker by reams of sweat. She fanned herself a little faster.

'Why not take a break?' she suggested, rather too quickly.

Jake glanced towards her, surprise softening his sun-induced scowl. 'A break?'

He looked so genuinely bemused that Nadine was amazed. Why ever did he think she was bothering to talk to him – she *never* spoke to the help this way. She could see the sweet approach would work ... eventually, but, Lord, she couldn't wait that long: the coiled-up feeling in her tummy felt as tight as sprung copper wire. Time to be more direct.

'All work and no play makes Jake a dull boy,' she purred, moving her fingertip seductively back and forth along her collarbone.

A trace of a smile appeared on his face. He pursed his lips and nodded. 'I like that,' he muttered.

'My little word-play?' she asked, wondering if he even understood the concept of word-play.

He nodded again. 'Yeah, I like that. The word-play.' He let the hammer drop to the ground and took a step towards her. 'But I like the inference more.'

Astonished, Nadine had to stop her jaw from dropping open. *Inference*. What kind of a workhand used words like that? He took another step forward. 'I can read too, miss,' he added. His voice was heavy with sarcasm but a hint of a flirt made its way through.

'Whole sentences?' teased Nadine, back on track.

'Whole books.'

'Wow.' She breathed out playfully. 'I'm impressed. What else can you do?'

'Whole bunch of things, miss.' He touched the delicate top button of her long summer dress.

'Wow,' she repeated, not so playfully.

Dipping her eyes, she watched him undo the button. He paused as though expecting her to stop him but she kept her eyes fixed firmly downward. He started on the second button, then the third, then the fourth, continuing down the front panel of her dress until all the buttons were undone.

He straightened up from his haunches. 'May I?' he whispered.

'Sure,' she replied, her voice a little throaty, a little lower in tone than normal.

Placing his thumb and forefinger on the edges of her dress, he nudged it ever so slightly apart. Nadine tensed in anticipation as he pushed his hands inside and placed them round her tiny waist. Though he clasped her lightly, she could feel the roughness of his calloused palms and she found herself short of breath – she wanted those rough hands everywhere, touching and feeling her own silken skin. As if reading her thoughts, he began to oblige, working his hands upward, rubbing his thumbs systematically up her ribcage until she felt him stop beneath the underslope of her breasts.

4

'Don't stop,' she coaxed softly.

He didn't answer. Instead, his hands started moving again, over her chest, cupping her breasts through the fine lace of her bra. It felt good. The pressure of his hands on her breasts. So good that she could feel the resentments and frustrations which had built up over the past few days simply trickle away as the heady feelings of arousal took over. Lifting her eyes from her own body, she looked up at the man before her. His face was set, his handsome, suntanned features now fixed in a mask of sexual entrancement. He stared steadily back at her and gently began to rub the heels of his hands over her breasts. Nadine felt her nipples respond, then, as he passed his thumbs back and forth over them, she felt them grow and harden until they strained within the confines of her bra. Quickly she reached behind her back underneath her dress and unclasped the fastener of her bra, freeing her pert, perfect breasts. Straightaway he felt beneath the loosened garment and covered her breasts with his hard, workman's hands. She heard him groan softly under his breath.

'You like feeling my body, Jake?' she asked slowly.

'Your skin's so smooth. So soft,' he answered.

'Wouldn't you like to look at me, too?' she invited, breathless with excitement at the thought. 'Really look at me?'

Jake nodded quickly, wrenching her dress wide open as he did so. He held the front panels of her dress apart whilst she lifted her loosened bra right up to her collarbone. A stab of excitement pierced her belly as she displayed her breasts to him, and she watched him closely as he gazed upon her, his eyelids growing heavy with desire.

'You're so lovely,' he said softly, reaching for her breasts once again, cupping one in each hand. Nadine suddenly felt hot, really hot, unbearably hot ... She lifted off his right hand and pushed it urgently down into the front of her white, lace panties, guiding it straight between her thighs. Whether he was surprised or not she couldn't tell, but he certainly needed no further encouragement and she lost her breath entirely as he pressed up a little and then gently began to massage her sex.

'Is that what you want, miss?' he murmured, moving his mouth close to her ear.

Nadine moaned in assent, her mind starting to float as the pleasures of her body took over. His left hand was still on her breasts, playing with each of her nipples in turn. His right hand was deep in her panties, sending flickers of warmth through her sex and upper thighs.

'Definitely what I want,' she said, opening her legs to accommodate his hand even better. She moved her feet a step apart and, as she did so, Jake crouched down in front of her. Nadine gasped with delight as he suddenly reached for the crotch of her panties and, with one firm wrench, pulled it clear to the side. Jake had bared her entire sex and, holding her panties securely to the side with one hand, he was proceeding to glide the pad of his middle finger back and forth along the nude pink nub of her clitoris.

'Oh yes,' moaned Nadine at the sharp jabs of pleasure leaping up along the seam of her sex. She stared down at his broad, brown shoulders, at the sweat-stained centre parting of his hair, and then suddenly she had to lean forward and grasp at the wooden post in front of them. Jake had quickened his movements, precipitating the onset of her climax. Her legs began to weaken, her stomach began to dance and she jerked back her head as the tide of orgasm started, building, building, from the tiny core between her legs, until she exploded in a sweat of trembling relief.

Clasping the post tightly, she savoured the familiar drained luxury that she always felt after an orgasm of such strength. Fine tendrils of her hair clung damply to the edges of her face and her pulse rate and breathing vied to be the first to recover. It took a few moments before she even realised that Jake had risen to his feet in front of her, but when she did she couldn't miss the exaggerated rise and fall of his chest nor the pronounced swelling at the front of his jeans. Her eyes fell upon his hard, flat belly and, despite the welcome satisfaction of her release, she simply couldn't lift her eyes from that hard, hard stomach, picturing it pressed to her, warm and smooth and slippery with passion. Jake seemed equally absorbed, his gaze fixed firmly on her unfettered breasts, and, as Nadine curled her fingers into the waistband of her panties, he shot his tongue hungrily to the corner of his lips. Slowly, she began to ease her panties down, peeling them over the smooth symmetry of her hipbones.

All of a sudden, out of the corner of her eye, she saw movement.

Dammit! she cursed to herself, flicking her panties back into place.

'What's up?' Jake's voice sounded strained.

In answer, Nadine twitched her head in the direction of the grassy slope. Jake let out a groan of sexual frustration. Then, as if remembering just exactly what he was up to, he stepped away from Nadine in alarm.

'Don't worry,' said Nadine, calmly redoing her bra and dress. 'Just thank God that my uncle's too vain to wear his glasses. He can hardly see further than the end of his nose without them!'

Jake looked doubtful. 'I need this job, miss. Don't think the boss would appreciate me messing with his niece.'

Nadine let out a dismissive sigh. 'I said, don't worry. I can deal with my uncle; he's a pussycat.'

Jake's voice still carried the strain of sexual frustration. He raked his eyes down her now-clothed body. 'Then again,' he added huskily, 'you sure are worth losing a job over, miss.'

'You're a sweet guy,' said Nadine, smiling. 'Hopefully I'll see you later on.'

'Shit, I hope so,' he groaned.

Still smiling prettily, she turned slightly and began to walk out of the orchard, towards her advancing uncle.

'Hey, Uncle Will,' she sang out brightly, meeting up with him midway on the slope.

Her uncle peered at her as she approached, creasing up his myopic eyes in a bid to focus. Willem Brookes was a tall, strong man, handsome despite the visible ravages of too much sunshine, a result of the endless hours he had spent working his fruit farms. Right now, his handsome jaw was set in a firm line of disapproval. 'We missed you at lunch, Nadine,' he reproved sternly.

'Lunch?' Nadine made herself look confused, her clear, green eyes wide with bewilderment. She glanced down at her wristwatch. 'Oh, darn it, Uncle Will,' she said, tapping the face of the watch. 'My watch has stopped. Look!' She waved her wristwatch in front of her uncle as he struggled valiantly to focus on it.

'I see,' said her uncle, clearly not seeing anything at all.

'I'm sorry,' said Nadine, falsely contrite. 'I did so want to be there.'

'Yes, well.' Uncle Willem seemed almost convinced. Then he nodded his head down towards the orange grove. 'What were you doing way down there, right where that workhand is working?'

Nadine followed the line of his gaze. She saw Jake hard at work once again, his young fit torso gleaming. Her tummy lurched with residual sexual excitement at the sight of him and she almost felt like rounding on her uncle for interrupting their highly enjoyable interlude. But that wouldn't be smart. And that was one thing Nadine prided herself on: she was smart.

'Oh, I was just taking a walk down there,' she said by way of explanation.

'I see,' her uncle said again. Nadine thought she saw him narrow his eyes slightly with what could have been a tinge of scepticism. She acted quickly.

'I think I'll go freshen up,' she said, changing the subject. 'Far too hot to be out walking today.'

She graced her uncle with a radiant smile and saw his prickly expression soften. Touché, she congratulated herself. She always could twist him right round her little finger!

With that, she sauntered slowly back up the slope and headed on into the house.

Willem Brookes stayed where he was for a good ten minutes on the pretext of surveying his acres of land. Really, he was mulling over in his mind what to do about Nadine. Whether or not the mistake was genuine, he was more than a little annoyed that she had missed lunch today – he had invited along a number of big names in fruit distribution and Nadine's startlingly pretty face at the table would have gone a long way to softening them up. But, he had to admit it, it was far more than lunch that was bothering him. Nadine's visits here were so few and so short as to be almost an insult. That bothered him. It bothered him a lot. His dead brother's only child, *his* only niece, and she could scarcely make the effort to visit! Absently, Willem slapped at a bug which had settled on his cheek. It wasn't much to ask, he reasoned, a little loyalty in return for the extremely generous allowance he gave her each month. That same allowance that paid for her house and her car and all those fine, fancy clothes.

What to do about Nadine, Willem muttered softly to himself.

Turning the water pressure to low, Nadine stood under the shower and let the water trickle gently down her body. She rubbed soap lazily over the smooth curve of her stomach and her mind drifted back to her encounter with Jake. As she thought of his hard, rough hands upon her, she felt the heavy languor of lust begin to gather and subconsciously moved her hands to her breasts, soaping each firm swell of flesh, loving the luxurious feel of herself. She closed her eyes and touched her nipples, letting her fingertips drift gently.

9

Her nipples were slippery with soap and trickling water and so, so sensitive. She paused a moment whilst touching herself, pressing her forefingers to the hardening tips, and behind her closed eyelids the image of Jake, aroused and erect as he had been, sprang to the fore. Between her legs, tingles of excitement tickled her insides, sharpening as she flicked her fingers back and forth over her nipples. For several moments, she savoured the taut, slightly tense sensation of arousal and, not wishing to relieve it, she removed her hands from her body, stepping out of the shower in a state of heightened sensuality.

She stood still on the bathroom floor, letting droplets of water trickle down her legs and speckle the light-coloured carpet. Naked, her skin warm and damp from the shower, she walked through to her adjoining bedroom, switching off the air-conditioning unit as she passed by it. Almost immediately, the air in the room hung heavy, perfumed by the bathroom fragrance of her long, soapy shower. The still, leaden heat in the room seemed to exacerbate her sharpened level of sensuality and she felt a light sheen of perspiration mingle with the dampness on her skin. Moving over to the mirror, she gazed at her reflection, her green eyes trancelike, as though she were mesmerised by her own beauty. And beautiful she undoubtedly was – light-golden skin flawless and smooth, shimmering dark hair falling below her shoulders, styled in long layers of expensively cut perfection. She was around five foot seven in height, slender, long-limbed, and she moved with a grace that was almost feline.

As she stood there, her hair fell over the tops of her breasts and, to see herself better, she flicked it back behind her shoulders. By any standards, her bared breasts were simply perfect, smallish and high, each firm globe centred by a smooth, pink-brown nipple.

Nadine dipped her gaze to the small, dark triangle of her pubes, neatly trimmed to a light glossy down. She moved her legs a step apart as she had done for Jake and imagined what he had seen when he had crouched down before her and pulled the crotch of her panties to one side. That, coupled with the opening movement of stepping apart, sent a teasing sensation through her sex. Relishing the feeling, she half turned and twisted her head back round to admire the fine line of her back and the lovely, rounded curves of her bottom. This sexually charged contemplation of her own loveliness was a ritual she often enjoyed. She was so caught up in herself now that she did not notice her bedroom door being nudged open and a petite maid, lumbering under a heavy burden of clean laundry, enter the room. It was only when the maid dropped the linen on the bed that they saw one another.

'For God's sake!' snapped Nadine, snatching up a shirt from a nearby chair and holding it in front of herself. 'Can't I get any privacy around here?'

The maid, blushing blood red, was beside herself. 'I'm so sorry, miss. I never thought to knock, I thought you were down at lunch with your uncle.'

'Well, as you can see, I'm not! So if you wouldn't mind . . .' Nadine made a shooing-out movement with her hand.

'Yes, of course,' said the maid, scuttling to the door, head bowed. 'So sorry, miss,' she muttered again as she edged her way out.

Nadine strode over to the door and slammed it shut. The second time in an hour she'd been interrupted. This place was unbelievable – God, she hated it. Nothing here but fields and fruit and more fields and more fruit! And if that wasn't bad enough, she couldn't even find a private moment to relax in the way she loved to relax. That was it, she decided. Enough was enough. She wouldn't stay here a moment longer. She'd make up some excuse for her uncle and she'd get the hell out. Right now.

Decision made, she dressed quickly, buttoning up the same summer dress she had worn earlier. She threw her things haphazardly into her case, snapped shut the

11

locks, snatched up a piece of paper and scribbled down a few words to her uncle. Then, after tripping down the wide staircase to the hallway, she stuck the note plumb in the centre of a large, ornate wall mirror before stepping outside.

It was quiet in the gravelled courtyard in front of the house. Good, thought Nadine, she could slip away without being seen. Her car was parked on the edge of the circular courtyard. She walked over to it, threw her case in the back and slid into the driver's seat. The Mercedes sport's engine purred into life, low and sexy, drowned by the crunching of the tyres on the gravel when she drove round the circle and then down the long, straight driveway. Bye-bye, Unc, bye-bye, San Bernardino, she sang softly to herself.

Before too long she was out of sight of the house. The driveway had been constructed with linear precision between two fruit orchards and stretched for a good mile before it reached the road. Nadine sped along it, tapping her fingers nonchalantly on the wheel as she drove. About halfway along, she happened to glance in her rear-view mirror and her tummy gave a little leap. She had caught a fleeting glimpse of dirty-blond hair and dusty blue jeans. She hit the brake pedal immediately and thought for a moment. Whilst she was certainly in a hurry to get away, she also hated unfinished business. And Jake was definitely unfinished business.

She reversed up the driveway a little, then pulled in to the side and got out. Jake, evidently having heard the car, was looking over. His expression brightened when he saw who it was. Nadine waited by the car.

'Hi there,' he said, strolling over.

'Hi there yourself,' she said, smiling.

'You going somewhere, miss?' he asked, cocking his head towards the car.

Nadine nodded. 'Yeah. I have to get home to Santa Barbara.'

Jake's face fell. 'Oh,' he said softly.

'But,' continued Nadine, 'I wouldn't want to go without saying goodbye . . .' She paused a little before adding, 'Properly.'

'Properly?' Jake raked his fingers back through his hair. 'Does that mean what I think it –'

'Yes it does,' murmured Nadine, aware, whilst she watched his fingers in his hair, of a sweeping warmth through her abdomen. Jake looked to her to be hot and sweaty but decidedly sexy all the same, and she wasn't about to deny herself. She'd spent three days in this godforsaken outback – she more than deserved some pleasure.

Moving closer, she placed her hands familiarly on his smooth chest, feeling the heat of his sun-baked skin. He clasped her slender wrists gently.

'I guess this is my lucky day,' he said in a low, croaky voice.

Nadine drew her palm down his flat stomach, down to his hips, down to the hardness in his groin. She moulded her hand to the considerable swelling in his jeans. 'I guess it's mine too,' she chuckled, pulling at the buttons of his fly. When his jeans were undone, she pushed her hand down into the waistband of his boxers. Jake groaned slightly as she passed her thumb over the smooth, sensitive head of his penis.

His hands were resting on her exposed shoulders. He moved his fingers slowly in towards her collarbone, then, curling his forefinger into the low neckline of her dress, subtly he pulled it forward and glanced inside to her cleavage. In her rush to dress, Nadine had neglected to put on either bra or panties and the delight in discovering this showed on Jake's face. He reached in and cupped her warm, bare breasts. As he fondled her, her stomach flickered and jumped and she continued to roll her thumb round and round his swollen tip, moistening the head with its own clear fluid.

Suddenly Jake dipped and reached under the hem of Nadine's long dress. His hand clasped her ankle, drifting up her sleek calf and her knee until it reached the

13

silken skin of the back of her thigh. When, after a moment, his hand roamed upward and touched her left buttock, Nadine felt a rolling tug of desire pull at her groin.

'Pull up my dress, Jake,' she gasped excitedly.

He did just that, lifting the hem up to her thighs and gazing at her legs.

'Higher,' she urged.

Jake's eyes glittered like gemstones. 'Higher? Here?' he asked hoarsely. 'You sure?'

Nadine nodded, her cheeks flamed with passion.

He bunched the lower part of her dress in his fists and lifted it right up to her waist.

'Holy God,' he groaned, feasting his eyes on her exposed flesh. Nadine gloried in his downward gaze, aware of a heavy dew of excitement dampening her sex. Impatiently, she reached down between her legs and touched herself. Jake groaned again and, still holding up her dress with one hand, he let go with the other and grasped her naked bottom, feeling first one buttock then the other. Nadine pushed back, pressing her bottom to his hand. She couldn't resist the urge to flutter her fingers against herself, and the combined stimuli of Jake's hand and her own was almost too much. Jake was looking similarly tortured, his forehead drawn with furrows, his upper lip sweating. Snatching at his jeans and boxers, he pulled out his penis.

Nadine eyed the long, smooth shaft hungrily. She needed it now, pushing up deep, deep inside her until she could feel her belly ignite with the heat of it.

'Quick, Jake,' she said breathlessly, grabbing her dress herself to free his other hand.

Jake placed his knee between hers, and tapping from one knee to the other he nudged her legs apart. Then, gripping her hipbones for support, he bent his knees and began to ease himself inside her. Nadine delighted in the sensation, the slight tightness of her body being opened by his cock, then the feeling of his hot, hard organ gaining entry, sliding easily upward, filling her completely. She pushed her hips forward a fraction to maximise penetration and almost squealed with delight as he began to move, the moist friction of his movements within making her tingle with pleasure. She could feel him rub his pubic bone against hers and her sex felt alive, warmed and thrilled. He was pressed close to her, gripping her waist now, and she caught the fresh, tangy scent of his sweat. It excited her all the more. That, and his increasingly wonderful movements inside her. She felt her moisture seep to her bottom, tickling and titillating the crease between her buttocks, and as she thought of her actions, her recklessness, making love at the side of the driveway, her dress clutched up at her waist, her legs and bottom utterly exposed to anyone who happened to pass, she was spurred on even further. Her hips joined in with Jake's rhythm, beyond her mind's control. They moved with frenzied energy and she closed her eyes, succumbing to the vibrant, joyful sensations inside. More and more frenzied became their movements. Nadine thought her knees would buckle as she rode the escalating tide. Lord, he must be strong, she thought hazily, knowing his firm grip on her jerking hips was all that was holding her upright.

Abruptly, Jake tensed. He let out such a long, low groan that Nadine opened her eyes. She saw the rapture of climax on his face just a second or so before her own body peaked. Pulsating pleasure ripped through her sex, travelling like a lit fuse to her stomach and bottom.

'Heaven. Pure heaven,' she gasped, leaning heavily against his chest.

'Yeah,' panted Jake.

Nadine could feel his body shaking slightly. The twinned strain of their sex and holding her upright, no doubt. She took pity on him, tugging him with her down to the grass. She had let her dress fall back down to her ankles and she sat demurely, curling her knees beneath her. Jake lay back, his chest shiny with sweat and heaving with the exertion of it all.

Nadine rested back on her arms, tipping back her head and closing her eyes against the sunshine. They stayed like that, just the two of them. No sign of anyone else. Somewhere in the distance, a piece of farming machinery began to whine softly.

A while later, Nadine leant over and kissed Jake quickly on the mouth. 'That was real nice,' she murmured.

Jake's eyes flew open. He lifted his head from the grass and nodded. 'It sure was.' He smiled.

'Well,' said Nadine with a sigh. 'I guess I better go.'

'I guess so,' muttered Jake, sitting up. He rose quickly to his feet then held out his hand to Nadine. She let him pull her up, giggling when he tried to dust down her dress as he walked her over to her car. He held open the door as she settled herself in. After he closed the door, he leant down on the top of it.

'I love the way you say goodbye,' he muttered, still a little husky.

Nadine chuckled lightly. 'And I love your idea of a send-off!'

Despite his short-sightedness, it was the first thing Willem Brookes noticed when he entered the hallway: the pale-yellow scrap of paper stuck rudely in the centre of his favourite antique mirror. Willem strode directly to it and peeled it off. Completely unsurprised, he read the message:

Had to leave in a hurry, Uncle Will. Friend v. sick. I'll call soon.

Nadine

With a resigned look on his face, Willem shook his head. He wasn't happy with Nadine. Not at all.

Chapter Two

A day earlier, in her large house up in a lush, leafy suburb of Santa Barbara, Ashley Ray had a few moments to herself before her personal trainer was due. She sat down at her desk and began to write out 'quickie' invites for the dinner party she intended to host in two days' time. It was short notice she knew, but, when the urge to entertain was upon her, Ashley always acted. If people couldn't make it, they couldn't make it, but Ashley derived a great deal of satisfaction in knowing that people usually shifted around their social calendars to ensure that they could. She pulled out all the stops, short notice or not, and her guests appreciated that. Her parties were always a resounding success.

As she wrote out invitations to both Nadine Brookes and Valerie Neiman, Ashley paused. Sucking thoughtfully on the end of her pen, it occurred to her that maybe she shouldn't invite both to the same dinner – she knew very well how much they disliked one another. But, reasoned Ashley, they were such fun. And besides, there would be several other people there to dilute any atmosphere. And, thought Ashley, her mind made up, she had one hell of a big dining table. She could seat them at opposite ends.

With a smile on her face, she licked and sealed both envelopes just as the doorbell sounded. Ashley walked slowly through to the hallway. No point in wasting valuable energy. She had an hour's workout ahead; she'd expend her energy then.

'Hey, Carlo,' she said, pulling open the door. 'Right on time as usual. Come on in.'

Carlo stepped inside, carrying his fitness equipment effortlessly through to the living room. Ashley followed behind, admiring the cut of his black, sporty shorts. Of course, the backside in them helped, thought Ashley with a silent giggle. Her husband wore designer shorts too, at the country club, but the sight of them clinging to his portly backside didn't do a thing for her.

Carlo set up quickly in the centre of the room. 'Ready to warm up, Ashley?' he asked, his laid-back Californian drawl completely at odds with the intense dark looks of his Cuban heritage.

'Ready,' said Ashley, following his lead in the stretching warm-up. She mirrored his movements exactly, leaning when he leant, stretching when he stretched, twisting when he twisted.

'*Feel* the stretch in those muscles,' said Carlo earnestly.

Ashley was feeling something, that was for sure, but she had an idea it was more to do with Carlo's muscles than her own. Today, for some reason, his smooth, flexing biceps were distracting her from her programme. Concentrate, she told herself, shutting her eyes and increasing her aerobic pace.

'Not yet,' said Carlo. 'Slow down, go with me.'

Ashley opened her eyes. Darn it, there they were again. Distracting, smooth, brown muscles. Flexing. Releasing. Flexing. Flexing.

'Er, Carlo, I'm lost,' she said breathlessly, totally losing her rhythm. On flexed his muscles, as strong as iron, as rich as caramel.

'What's up?' He smiled, springing to an athletic stop.

18

'Don't know,' mumbled Ashley, noticing for the first time his perfectly sculpted jawline.

Carlo stood in the centre of the room, hands on hips, handsome head cocked to one side. He looked at her thoughtfully. 'Something on your mind, Ashley?' he asked.

Ashley shook her head. 'No,' she replied.

'Sure?'

'Uh huh. I'm just feeling a little . . . off today.'

Carlo nodded, still regarding her thoughtfully. 'You know, we could always reschedule. With you feeling a little off and –'

'*No!*' objected Ashley, rather more vehemently than she intended.

Carlo looked like she had slapped him. 'Hey, it was just an idea.'

'Sorry, Carlo,' murmured Ashley, wondering what in the world was wrong with her. 'I didn't mean to snap. I guess I'm a little stressed right now.'

'No problem,' said the ever-amiable Carlo. He flashed a broad grin at her. 'Stressed, huh? I think I have just the thing.'

'Oh, you have,' said Ashley, looking dreamily at his lips. She saw him give her a peculiar look. 'I mean, you have?' she corrected quickly.

'Yeah,' said Carlo. 'Relaxation techniques.'

'Oh,' she murmured, disappointment creeping for some reason through her body.

'True relaxation is an art form,' went on Carlo. 'To destress, unwind, detach yourself . . .'

'I suppose so,' agreed Ashley without much interest.

'In my father's country,' continued Carlo, his voice soft and strangely hypnotic, 'in Cuba, we know how to make a lady relax.' Carlo took a step towards her. 'We know how to make a lady relax completely, detach herself, give herself up to a whole other art form.'

'You do?' whispered Ashley.

'Uh huh,' answered Carlo, so near to her now she could feel the warmth of his breath. 'Do you want to

19

learn, Ashley, how to relax, how to give yourself over to the pleasures of your body?'

'Er, I guess,' said Ashley, not so much concerned with the relaxing part as with the giving herself over to the pleasures of her body.

'OK,' murmured Carlo, placing his hands on her shoulders. 'We'll begin with an upper-body massage.'

'OK,' whispered Ashley.

Carlo looked deep into her eyes. 'Where shall we lay you down?' he asked softly.

'P . . . pardon me?' stammered Ashley, unaccustomed to this new seductive tone in Carlo's voice.

'For the massage?' Carlo smiled.

'Oh yes,' said Ashley. 'The massage.' She glanced around and spotted the chaise longue over by the French doors. 'How about there?' She pointed at it.

'Perfect,' said Carlo, leading her over by the hand.

Ashley kicked off her training shoes and lay across the elongated chair on her stomach. She folded her arms at the top and rested her cheek on her wrists. Carlo, she was acutely aware, was kneeling down to her right. She felt him lift a stray ribbon of hair from her neck and tuck it into her high ponytail.

'Thanks,' she mumbled, thinking how fine his fingers had felt on her neck.

He placed his thumbs at the top of her spine and slowly began to trace downward.

'Mmm,' sighed Ashley, wriggling slightly with pleasure.

Down his thumbs moved, expertly manipulating, stroking down her soft bare skin, down to the low back of her lycra top. His fingers continued downward, moving over the material, trying to massage her through the clinging fabric. After a moment or so, he tutted, plucking playfully at the multicoloured material.

'Excuse me, Ashley,' he said lightly. 'This is in the way. Mind taking it off?'

Ashley thought for a moment. But only for a moment. Then she reached behind, eased her top up her back and pulled it over her head, before resting her cheek back on her crossed forearms.

'Much better,' said Carlo, his hands playing wonderfully over her unencumbered back.

Ashley was feeling odd, so unlike she normally felt during a massage. Instead of relaxing, she could feel charges of excitement electrify her senses; instead of drifting towards sleep, she could feel torrents of energy surging through her body. Carlo's hot, dry fingertips seemed simply magical.

'That's lovely,' she sighed.

'You're lovely,' murmured Carlo, his fingers stopping dead in the small of her back.

Ashley was silent.

'Have I gone too far?' he asked quietly.

Ashley raised her head and glanced back at him. She kept her pretty face straight but there was a smile in her voice as she spoke. 'Not far enough, I'd say.'

Carlo grinned, a grin of relief. 'That's what I was hoping you'd say!' He curled his fingers gently into the tight waistband of her leggings. 'Ready for the full body massage?'

Still glancing back at him, Ashley nodded, feeling her face warm as she watched him begin to peel her leggings over her lower back. Slowly, he eased them down, gradually exposing the pale, firm globes of her buttocks and the milky skin of the backs of her thighs. His hands still in her leggings, he stopped. Ashley watched him. He was looking at her bared flesh, gazing at her with such intensity that she felt herself blush. In three years of marriage, she couldn't remember a time when her husband had gazed at her with such intensity. Carlo caught her looking at him. He smiled slowly.

'Skin like porcelain,' he said quietly, his hands beginning to move again, drawing her leggings down to her knees, her calves, her ankles, and then pulling them over her girly pink ankle socks. She was naked then, except for the socks. And it felt superb.

She rested her head down on her wrists as he placed

21

his hands on her back once again. Slowly, sensuously, he worked his hands, pressing his thumbs and finger-tips into the edges of her waistline. The area was overly sensitive and Ashley instantly felt her skin prickle into goose bumps. She giggled on reflex, bucking up her hips simultaneously.

'Oh, man,' she heard Carlo groan.

Glancing back, she saw him gazing longingly at her wriggling, naked body. She felt a sudden, enormous sting of sensation between her legs and, taken aback by it, she immediately stopped wriggling and pressed her stomach and legs hard down against the chaise longue.

Carlo groaned again, this time touching each of her clenched buttocks. Ashley felt her muscles relax in a kind of relief, although the sensation between her legs only sharpened as he rounded his hands against her smooth bottom. Still twisting around, she watched his lean brown fingers on the pale skin of her bare bottom and she couldn't stop herself from gasping with excitement.

Clearly spurred on by her sounds of enjoyment, Carlo fondled and kneaded until her flesh began to turn pink. He trailed his fingertips down the outside of her thighs. She was still holding her legs tightly together and he drifted his fingers back up along their join. Ashley held her breath. Upward, upward he moved. Up to her bottom once again, skimming the surface of her crease. Suddenly, boldly, he eased her cheeks apart.

'Oh, Lord!' she gasped.

'Mmm,' responded Carlo, gazing once again.

Ashley felt excitement rifle through her stomach. Having him look at her so intimately like this. It was making her dizzy, feverish almost.

'Please, Carlo,' she urged. 'Touch me.'

'Where?' he teased gently.

'There,' she gulped.

'Here?' he said, slipping his middle finger down into her crease.

'Yes! There. Right there.'

'Like this?' continued Carlo, rubbing his finger gently up and down.

'Oh, yes,' moaned Ashley, loving the sensation, her tummy jigging in a curious blend of relief and stimulation.

She let her head drop back on to her arms. She closed her eyes whilst Carlo continued to play with her bottom, tickling her crack, dabbing at her anus. The dry ticklish feeling caused by his teasing fingers soon spread from her crease to each of her parted buttock cheeks, then seeped deliciously to the inside of her abdomen. By that time, Ashley could no longer keep still.

'That's so good,' she moaned, arching her back and pushing up her hips.

'This'll be even better,' grunted Carlo, licking his finger and continuing to stimulate.

Ashley couldn't answer. His newly moistened fingertip was now gliding wonderfully between her cheeks, and with each couple of strokes he relicked his finger, maintaining the silky, lubricated ease of movement. Gradually, the thrill of arousal travelled upward. She began pushing so hard against his finger that she was lifting up her stomach and thighs. Suddenly, Carlo grabbed her upraised hips and pulled her down to the end of the chaise longue until she was effectively kneeling and leaning over the end. She was hot and breathless and smarting with arousal. Yearning for more stimulation, she opened her kneeling legs, displaying herself freely.

Behind her, Carlo murmured appreciatively. The moment she felt him touch her, she sighed with utter relief.

His fingers found her clitoris and he twiddled it gently, pulling exquisitely with little playful tugs. She was losing control. She pressed her breasts into the end seating of the sofa, raising up her bottom and hips as Carlo played with her from behind. As promised, he was tireless in the giving of pleasure, teasing her swelling clitoris with such slow, skilful finesse that she could hardly stand it.

'Please, Carlo,' she moaned deliriously, straining her hips back against his fingers.

Carlo was merciless. He stopped touching her sex and transferred his attentions back to her out-thrust bottom. He began to squeeze each soft, rosy cheek, then began lifting and separating them in rhythmic provocation. Ashley squeezed her eyes shut at the delightful stimulus – one moment her buttocks were being pushed together, the next they were being parted and lifted. Colours began to shift in her mind and still he continued. Squeezing, lifting, parting, arousing . . .

Finally, he was ready. With several rubs on her overworked clitoris, he brought her to her peak. A magnificent, energy-sapping orgasm claimed her, lifting her high into a reeling, flashing orbit. She writhed over the end of the sofa, wave after wave of pleasure rolling within.

'I've never known pleasure like it,' she sobbed eventually as the contractions started to subside.

'I haven't finished yet,' promised Carlo grandly. 'This is just the warm-up.'

Wow, thought Ashley, her body glowing inside and out. Exercise had never been such fun!

Chapter Three

A weak golden sun bathed the wide boulevards, falling in pretty, tree-shaded patterns on to the spotless pavements and the impeccably kept gardens. The air was scented with the fragrance of the flowers and shrubs. Blending with it faintly, now and again, was the fresh salty smell of the nearby ocean.

Nothing like it, thought Nadine, inhaling deeply as she approached her own house and parked her car in her driveway. A world away from her uncle's goddamn fruit farm.

It was early evening and she had been driving for some time. She was so glad to be home that she said so aloud as she heaved her bags out of the car and made the short walk up to her pretty, Spanish-style house with its white stucco walls and red-tiled roof. She put her key in the lock, switched off the house alarm, dumped her bags inside the hallway, then wandered back down the driveway to check her mailbox.

Bills, bills, bills, she thought dismissively, sorting quickly through the clutch of mail. As she came across a pale lavender envelope with a familiar loopy scrawl across the front, she edged one perfectly polished fingernail beneath the corner flap to open it. Dinner, tomorrow night, at Ashley Ray's. Good old Ashley,

25

Nadine thought merrily. Ashley's dinners were always terrific. Just what she needed after three days down in San Bernardino.

Drifting contentedly into the house, she tossed the bills casually to one side and made her way over to the phone to pick up her voicemail. Two messages waiting. She listened to the first: Uncle Willem asking her to please return his call straight away. Fat chance, muttered Nadine, moving swiftly on to the next message.

A laughing voice came on the line, low and sexy and good-humoured. Another request for a call-back followed by a meaningful chuckle. Nadine's tummy gave a little twirl. It always did when she thought of Mark. This time, she made the requested call-back.

'Hey,' she whispered, cradling the phone into her neck. 'I'm home.'

'I'm on my way,' laughed the low, sexy voice.

'Hurry,' she purred.

'I'll hurry,' he affirmed, and they both hung up.

Twenty minutes later, Nadine stood by the window watching Mark Kelton pull into the driveway. She had showered quickly and pulled on a brilliant-white T-shirt that highlighted her golden skin tone and which clung to her breasts and skimmed the tops of her thighs. She smelled soapy and fresh. With her face scrubbed clean of make-up and her hair pulled up into a girlish ponytail, she had a teenage look that belied her twenty-seven years.

Mark Kelton stepped out of his car. He was dressed in a smart, dark business suit, a crisp white shirt, a grey silk tie. Obviously he'd come straight from the office, thought Nadine. Mark worked hard. He played hard too but his position within Garsante Holdings was both demanding and time-consuming. Nadine knew that he was one of Daniel Garsante's most valued in-house lawyers. And as such he had one hell of a lot of responsibility. She watched him stroll casually up to the house. She heard him knock confidently at the door, a rat-at-at-at kind of melody. The cockiness of the knock made her smile. She wanted to race to answer but she made herself wait to the count of thirty before she adopted Mark's casual demeanour and strolled to the doorway. She opened the door wide and leant nonchalantly against it. He stood on the doorstep. He let his eyes travel lazily down her body. She dropped her gaze reciprocally from his face to his groin. Their eyes swung back to each other's face. He grinned. She smiled.

Like lightning, he moved, jerking her roughly into his body, pressing his mouth hard on to hers. Their tongues darted hungrily together.

'What kept you?' she gasped breathlessly when they broke for air.

'I was in a meeting,' he said, covering her lips again, his tongue hot and hard against the roof of her mouth. 'Jesus, I've missed you,' he said when they broke apart a second time.

She chuckled. 'How much?'

'This much,' he said, kissing her ear as he pressed himself against her. The hardness in his groin was like rock.

'That much, huh?' she joked, pressing the heel of her hand to his crotch. His cock jerked at the contact.

'C'mon,' he said, nudging her into the hallway. He reached out and closed the front door softly, then took her by the hand and led her to the staircase. He climbed the stairs slowly. Nadine followed silently behind, watching his tall figure in front. Clasping her fingers lightly, he reached the landing and headed directly across to her bedroom. The early-evening sun filtered through the windows at an angle, settling obliquely on the white carpet and the rosewood furniture. Mark walked her over to a patch of sunlight at the edge of her large double bed.

'Hands up,' he murmured.

Nadine obliged, holding her hands up high in the air.

Without further preamble, Mark took hold of the bottom of her T-shirt, swept it up her body and over her head. He tossed it carelessly to one side. Nadine stood still, totally and gloriously naked. She let her arms drop down. Mark took a step back, regarding her. The beam of sunlight fell upon her like a spotlight. Her pert, out-thrust breasts began to swell in the warmth and, with Mark's eyes locked upon them, she felt them tingle with excitement. She arched her back slightly, pushing her breasts outward and, as she did so, she caught sight of her nipples, smooth, swollen, rose-tinted. She ached to have him touch them and she glanced hungrily towards him.

He held up his forefinger and circled it in the air, indicating she should turn. Nadine half twirled, letting him contemplate her back view. The longer he studied her, the more aroused she became. She could feel herself getting wet. She parted her legs slightly, letting air to her moistness, but the movement served only to increase her fervour. Urgently, she turned back round. The excitement in Mark's expression mirrored her own. Looking steadily at her all the while, he undressed, slipping out of his clothes item by item until he stood, tall, lean and naked, a step away from her.

Nadine looked across at him, at his broad square shoulders and smooth, brown chest, at his taut, flat stomach, at his long, muscled legs liberally dusted with sun-kissed, golden-brown hairs. No man made her feel the way Mark did – he made her pulse race, he made her knees weak, he made her insides literally shiver with excitement. Next to herself, she loved him best of all.

Mark's blue eyes were bright with lust. 'Want me to show you how much I've missed you?' he asked, moving towards her.

Nadine sucked in her full lower lip. 'If you want,' she teased.

'Oh, I want,' said Mark gruffly.

He joined her in the patch of sunlight, their bodies

close but scarcely touching. The very tips of her nipples only skimmed the surface of his skin but the sensation was enough to send thrills through her chest. She reached up and ruffled her fingers through his wavy brown hair and he stood compliant as she did so. She was aware of his penis, his wonderful penis, close to her stomach but not touching. She reached down and stroked it, loving its heat, its hardness, its energy.

Mark was silent, licking his lips as though they were dry. After a moment or two of her feeling him, he eased her hands to her sides, then he trailed the back of his fingernail down her smooth, hot stomach until he reached the tiny mound of her mons. Lightly, he brushed the backs of his fingers across her small, springy nest of hair.

Nadine sighed. Mark moved his hand down further, pushing between her thighs and cupping the whole of her sex. He sighed too, letting her wetness soak his fingertips. Then, without removing his hand, he eased her backward until she felt the backs of her knees press against the side of the bed. He kept on easing her backward until there was nowhere else to go. Her knees sort of buckled against the mattress and she had no alternative but to sit down.

Perching on the side of the bed, she sat upright, locking her arms behind her. Mark sank to his knees on the carpet in front and, placing his hands on the lower part of her inner thighs, he pushed her legs widely apart. He whistled softly.

'Beautiful,' he murmured, almost under his breath.

He was virtually eye level with her sex. Nadine held her breath as he moved his head closer . . . an inch away from her . . . half an inch away, a quarter, yet still not touching. Nadine opened her legs even wider, until she felt the strain along her inner thigh.

'Good girl,' he approved softly.

A moment later, she sensed his lips on her clitoris, kissing so lightly it was barely discernible. He kissed a little harder, then began to suck on the crinkly flap of skin, drawing it wholly into his mouth. A sensation of warmth travelled through to her thighs. He twirled his tongue around her bud, teased it with little darting flicks, sucked again until she felt weak. He moved down, licking gently round her sweet moist opening before drifting back upward once again. Placing his thumbs on the peach-fuzzed lips of her labia, he eased them apart, opening her up entirely. Her sex glistened deliciously, her clitoris standing out in the centre like a rich, dewy rosebud. With his tongue flat, he began to lap at her sex, licking up her juices, sending her dizzy. She thrust back her shoulders and tipped back her head until her ponytail tickled the centre of her back. Warm bolts of pleasure kept jolting her sex. She strained even harder to open her legs wider as sensations darted from Mark's flicking tongue.

'Oh God, oh yes,' she moaned as the tightness began to gather behind her mons, tightening magically, tightening up exquisitely into a taut knot of pleasure. She tensed her muscles automatically, her body and mind monopolised by the pulsations of her sex and, as she tensed, her head filled with the image of their love-making and her climax began, creeping steadily from between her legs, the tightness releasing, the pleasure spreading slowly, steadfastly through her chest, and the very peak of it making her back arch.

Mark pushed her fully on to the bed. He kissed her voraciously. Through the rapture of orgasm, she devoured his mouth, tasting the sexy scent of herself on his tongue. He lowered himself on to her, his penis pressing on to her succulent sex. With a swift, easy thrust he was inside her.

Nadine moaned in delight. She bent her legs up at the knee and he pushed in further until he was entirely enclosed. Straight away, he started to move, each deep, upward thrust thrilling them both.

'Yeah, baby, yeah,' groaned Mark, resting his hands on the pillow, one to each side of her head. Simultaneously he raised up his shoulders and chest. The action relieved the pressure of his weight atop her yet made the contact of their hips all the more intense. Their urgency increased. Mark moved quicker, his huge, swollen penis whetting her within.

She raked her hands down his smooth back and grasped hold of his pumping buttocks. She pressed down hard, pulling him inside as far as she could. Mark moved faster – shorter, sharper thrusts now which electrified her sex. She pulled her legs upward, resting them over his shoulders so that she was almost bent double, and she felt each of his movements so acutely that she could only moan at the pleasure of it all. He moved faster still and she felt, very suddenly, the tugging onset of release. Her orgasm made her sweat; it made her moan and cry out. After several exquisite moments, it drained her completely of any residue of strength.

Mark too was bathed in sweat, his eyes tightly closed as he collapsed down to his elbows. With a final thrust, he came. Nadine flung her arms around his neck as he climaxed, dragging his face to hers. He kissed her as he came, passing his groans of ecstasy straight into her mouth.

'Well,' gasped Nadine, out of breath. 'That surely was worth coming home for!'

Mark laughed softly. He eased off her and twisted over on to his back. After a moment or so, he asked, 'And how were things out in fruit country?'

'Fruity,' giggled Nadine. 'Uncle Willem's as pernickety as ever. But at least I've done my duty visit. Shown my face and all. That should keep him happy for a while.'

'Keeps me happy,' said Mark, turning his head on the pillow to gaze at her. 'That pretty face of yours.'

'Why thanks,' said Nadine, turning too on the pillow and gazing back at him.

'The rest isn't bad either,' he joked, letting his forefinger drift across her chest towards her left nipple. He

31

rubbed around the smooth areola, causing the halo of skin to pucker.

'Nice,' murmured Nadine, watching. After a moment or so she leant across him and rested her head on his chest. He stroked her hair gently.

'And how was your week?' she asked.

'Been a good week for business,' he said quietly.

'Yeah?'

'Yeah. We cleaned up on the takeover bid for Feller.'

'Mmm?' Nadine hummed the question.

Mark nodded. 'In the end, they were practically begging us to buy them out.'

Nadine laughed. 'Garsante's company is like some great big fish. Swallowing up all the little ones.'

'Better to be one of the big fish then, sweetheart.'

'True,' she murmured drowsily. 'So true.'

Chapter Four

*I*t was way past 7.15 and Valerie Neiman was running late. She leant across her dresser towards the magnifying mirror and carefully outlined her lips before applying a subtle matt-rose shade of lipstick. She grabbed a tissue, blotted her lips quickly, then stood and smoothed down her dress. It was her favourite dress of the moment, a long, clingy halter-neck. Black, of course. Valerie walked barefoot over to the long wall mirror, placed her feet into a pair of black wedges she had left there, fluffed up her hair a little, then appraised her appearance. The dress embraced her slender curves, moulding to the contours of her high full breasts and falling in a flattering, clinging line to her ankles. A masterpiece of simplicity, this dress, Valerie decided. It complemented everything – her blonde hair, her rich brown eyes, her light summer tan, even the freckles on the tip of her nose. Satisfied, she turned on her heel, plucked up her evening purse from the bed and left.

Only ten minutes late, she thought, eyeing the clock on the dashboard as she turned into the exclusive suburb where Ashley Ray lived. She had known Ashley since high school. They had remained close friends ever since, meeting up regularly to chat and gossip and shop, just like in school. The only difference was,

Ashley was rich now. Rich and married. And Valerie, very definitely, wasn't either.

Still, thought Valerie as Ashley's bullish, red-faced husband appeared in the doorway, Ashley deserved some compensation. Being married to him and all. Rich, he may be. Lovable, definitely not.

'Look who it is,' Ashley's horrible husband boomed out, a drunken slur already in evidence. 'Come on in and join the party.'

He shifted just a fraction in the doorway so that Valerie was forced to squeeze past his ample stomach to get by.

'Thataway,' he said, his hand locating her bottom to guide her through. Though she tried to wriggle free, his hand remained clamped like a vice to her buttocks. It was Ashley who came to her rescue, bustling over to greet her. She grabbed Valerie's hand and, with a move that was both skilful and discreet, she manoeuvred Valerie free of her groping husband.

'Take it as a compliment, Val,' Ashley whispered jovially. 'He only handles the prettiest butts!'

Valerie guffawed – Ashley's good humour was irrepressible and contagious.

'You look as stunning as ever,' said Ashley.

'So do you,' replied Valerie. She did too. There was a new kind of sparkle in Ashley's eyes and her auburn hair shone like a glossy extension to her flame-coloured dress.

'Exercise,' quipped Ashley with a wink. 'I've got a new personal trainer. He's working wonders.'

'I'll say,' said Valerie, taking a sip of the champagne Ashley had plonked in her hand. Over the rim of her glass, she looked around the room. In the far corner, deep in conversation, was a tall, dark man Valerie didn't know. Only his profile was visible to her. But oh what a profile, thought Valerie. Dark swarthy skin, high angular cheekbones, strong straight nose. She tried not to stare and continued to look around the room, but found her eyes repeatedly drawn back to this profile.

'Who is *that*?' she whispered to Ashley.

'You don't want to know,' answered Ashley ominously.

'Oh I do, I do,' said Valerie in an undertone. 'Tell me.'

Ashley swivelled round so that her back was to the person in question. She spoke very softly. 'His name is Daniel Garsante. He owns Garsante Holdings. He's my husband's biggest client.'

Valerie inched her mouth close to Ashley's ear. 'And why don't I want to know him?'

'Because, sweetie, I've heard he's one hard S.O.B. Charming as hell on the surface, but underneath? Hard, hard, hard.'

'I see,' murmured Valerie, continuing to stare over Ashley's shoulder. Suddenly, with the reflex action of one who is aware of being stared at, he turned. For a split-second, Valerie met his black-eyed gaze, then swiftly she slid her eyes to the side.

But her move had not been swift enough – she could see through her peripheral vision that the tables had been turned, that he was the one watching her now.

'O–oh,' she mouthed to Ashley as he initiated a move towards them. Ashley, ever the graceful hostess, turned as he approached.

'Daniel,' she said, faultlessly polite.

'Ashley,' he responded, correspondingly polite though his eyes were still fixed firmly on Valerie. It was clear he expected an introduction. It was equally clear he wasn't going to ask for one. It was equally, equally clear that Ashley was caught in an unenviable situation: she was wavering, torn between offending her husband's biggest client or involving her best friend in an unwanted introduction.

But looking at the face before her, surpassing even the profile, Valerie wasn't at all sure that the introduc-

35

tion *was* unwanted. Besides, she reasoned, she didn't like to see Ashley uncomfortable.

'Valerie,' she said softly, holding out her hand. 'Valerie Neiman.'

He took her hand and shook it steadily. 'Pleased to meet you, Valerie Neiman. I'm Daniel Garsante.'

'Pleased to meet you, Daniel Garsante,' she mimicked lightheartedly.

A flicker of amusement sparkled in his eyes. 'You will be,' he said confidently.

Valerie was silent, unsure whether he was continuing the joke or whether he was serious. Something in his manner indicated the latter. He had kept a hold of her hand and his wonderful, dark eyes were locked on hers. Close beside her, Ashley cleared her throat as if to break the moment. Still he held on to her hand. She felt herself flush. Should she pull away? Should she leave her hand in his? Ashley cleared her throat more noisily, patently trying to help, but still he held on to her hand. Uncharacteristically, she began to feel a little flustered, a little too warm for comfort, until suddenly the well-timed commotion of more arrivals succeeded where Ashley's throat-clearing had failed, distracting them all simultaneously.

Valerie lifted her eyes to the living-room doorway. To her horror, she saw that one of the new arrivals was none other than Nadine Brookes. Valerie shot Ashley an accusing look – Ashley knew very well that she and Nadine hated the sight of one another. All Ashley did was shrug apologetically, mouth a quick sorry, and look helplessly towards the doorway. And as Valerie glanced back in that direction, even she was forced to smile when she saw that Nadine was being shepherded towards them by Ashley's errant husband, his beefy hand stuck firmly to Nadine's perfect bottom. Following close behind was Nadine's handsome lover, Mark Kelton.

Daniel Garsante had turned at the commotion. 'Evening, Mark,' he said as Mark Kelton approached.

36

'Evening, Daniel,' replied Mark, thrusting forward his hand.

Daniel shook briefly then clasped his hand on Mark's shoulder in a familiar gesture. 'Good work on the Feller takeover.'

Mark smiled. 'Thanks.'

'Mark,' continued Daniel, addressing the little group, 'is one of those rare commodities – a lawyer I actually like! And sharp too. Sharper than a shark's tooth. Good thing he works for me.'

Mark laughed affably. 'Thanks again,' he said, grinning. 'I think!' He batted Ashley's husband's hand off Nadine's backside and then eased her forward slightly to effect an introduction to Daniel. 'Daniel, meet Nadine.'

'Exquisite,' said Daniel, kissing Nadine's fingertips.

What a creep, thought Valerie, wondering why on earth she felt a little stab of jealousy in her tummy. It eased off almost immediately as Daniel switched his attention smartly back to her. 'And what do you do, Valerie Neiman?' he asked smoothly.

'I'm a dancer.'

'Really, where?'

'Shows mostly. I'm between jobs right now.'

'Ever thought of lap dancing as a filler?' piped up Nadine, a smirk plastered to her beautiful face.

'Ever thought of working at all?' shot back Valerie.

Ashley's husband tittered but everyone else was silent. The silence stretched on embarrassingly. Even Ashley's husband had shut up. Daniel and Mark studied their shoes. Ashley flushed an uncomfortable-looking pink. Valerie cursed herself: why oh why did she always let Nadine get to her? Only Nadine appeared entirely unfazed, the smirk still plastered gluelike to her face.

Within moments, Ashley-the-hostess sprang into autodrive. She glanced around the room, clearing her throat yet again. She held up her glass and clinked her fingernail against the side. 'Well,' she announced with determined good cheer. 'I think it's about time to go on through. I can assure you that the caterers have outdone themselves tonight. Everybody's hungry, I hope . . .'

Past midnight, under the silvery light of the street lamps, Nadine and Mark giggled their way up the driveway. Mark took Nadine's keys from her hand and opened up the door.

'Phew,' he breathed as they stepped inside. 'Safe.' Jokingly, he checked around the hallway and behind the door, then nodded. 'Yep, safe. Strictly a Valerie-free zone!'

Nadine giggled some more.

'Tell me,' said Mark, drawing her to him. 'What is it with you and Valerie? Why do you detest each other so much?'

Nadine shrugged. 'Always have. Always will.'

'Can't argue with a valid, genuine reason like that, can I?' chuckled Mark.

'And you a lawyer too,' teased Nadine softly. 'I thought lawyers could argue anything?'

'I know better than to argue with you,' said Mark, letting his hands drift down her spine and settle in the small of her back.

'Mmm,' murmured Nadine, snuggling against him. She tilted her face up to him. 'Fancy a nightcap before bed?'

'Sure,' he answered, his loins stirring as he gazed down at her. The fresh perfection of her face never ceased to amaze him, her clear green eyes drawing him in with fascinating sorcery.

She eased away from him and moved into the living room. He followed, taking in the splendid, subtle swaying of her hips. Quickly, his penis began to harden.

Nadine, handing him a large snifter of brandy, noticed his condition and chuckled wickedly. 'For me?' she asked, those feline green eyes shining with naughtiness.

'Who else?' said Mark, knocking back his drink.

Nadine moulded her hand to his trousered crotch, running her fingers up and down the hardening shaft. With her other hand, she brought her glass to her lips and took several small sips. Mark watched the way she edged the fine glass rim between her smooth, full lips, the way the golden-brown brandy moistened her mouth as she drank. She continued to fondle him for a while, then pulled away and wandered over to the French doors on the far side of the room. She flicked a switch to the side of the doors and suddenly the rear area of the house was illuminated. Underwater lights lit up a small, oval swimming pool, the blueness of the pool contrasting sharply with the blackness of the night sky. A few steps up from the pool led to a Jacuzzi, as blue and bright as the pool and built into a dark-wood surround.

Nadine opened one of the French doors and stepped out on to the patio. She gazed up into the night then turned to Mark.

'It's a wonderful night, Mark,' she said.

Mark walked out to join her, staring out into the hot summer night.

'I think,' she continued, nudging down the straps of her dress, 'that a half-hour in the Jacuzzi would be nice.'

'Good idea,' Mark murmured.

Nadine's straps hung flimsily on her slender arms. She eased down the side zipper of her dress and let the light garment slip from her body. Mark's groin tugged as he watched her kick the dress away with one slim, golden foot. The simple kicking gesture had made her small, firm breasts jiggle and he yearned to reach out and cover them with his hands, to feel her nipples harden into small red berries against his palms. She was pulling down her black lace thong now, bending as she eased it down her legs. The outside light shimmered on the smooth skin of her back. She bent over further, ostensibly to push her panties over her ankles and feet, but Mark knew from the slight shifting of her body angle that actually she was affording him a magnificent view of her perfect bottom. As she clearly intended, her firm flawless buttocks were directly in front of him. She leant over further, trailing the ends of her long, dark hair on the patio flags and, as she did so, she glanced round to him, her eyes flashing with excitement. She bent her knees ever so slightly to pull her panties off completely, and in that moment Mark caught a glimpse of the gorgeous, plump lips of her sex, pouting prettily at the base of her silky bottom crease. At once, he took a stride towards her and pushed his hand between her legs to cup her lovely, soft sex. She felt delightful, the feathery hairs tickling him, the faint suggestion of moistness dampening his skin.

She moaned slightly as he rounded his hand to her sex.

'Open your legs, honey,' he coaxed, his voice all of a sudden a hoarse whisper.

She opened her legs wider, leaning further forward to rest her hands on the ground in front of her. In so doing, she had thrust her bottom further outward and pressed her sex into his hand.

'Like that?' he heard her gasp from somewhere near the ground.

'Exactly like that,' he managed to say.

With the flat of his hand, he began to caress her, tempting himself with the lightness of his strokes when really he wanted to press his hand tight to the whole of her sex, capture her sexual essence. Instead, he grazed the down on her mons with his fingertips, gliding his palm simultaneously across the smooth lips of her labia. His hand soon became wet with her sex dew and he rubbed his fingers hungrily through the special moisture before easing his finger gradually up into the crack of her bottom. Gently, he pressed the length of his finger to the velvet stretch of skin between her vulva and her anus. It felt wonderful.

'Jesus!' he exclaimed, looking down at her beautiful back and the rounded curves of her bottom. He wanted to take her there and then, release his jutting cock from the prison of his trousers and slide it inside the warm wetness of her body. Nadine, however, had started to straighten up. She turned round, her face gloriously flushed, her hair tumbling in a dark, shimmering mass around her naked shoulders.

'Not yet, honey,' she said breathlessly. 'I want us all hot and naked in the Jacuzzi first.'

With that, she grabbed the waist of his trousers and began furiously unbuckling his belt. She worked with amazing speed. In no time at all she had his belt unbuckled, his trousers undone, his shirt unbuttoned. He shrugged off the rest of his clothes whilst she turned on her heel and walked to the steps of the Jacuzzi. She climbed each step slowly, her lithe body illuminated by the outside lights. She knew only too well the devastating effect she had on him; he could tell that from the knowing expression on her face as she turned to look at him. It was the same expression she often wore during their lovemaking, an expression almost of arrogance, of extreme confidence in her hold on him. And, strangely enough, it always turned him on even more.

She had reached the edge of the smallish tub now. She stooped to the side and pressed the button and immediately the water sprang into life, bubbling and frothing into a swirling, white mass. She sat down briefly on the side, then stretched her body and slid into the tub.

'You are,' said Mark, climbing up the steps and slipping in beside her, 'just about the most beautiful woman I've known.'

'Really?' cooed Nadine. She perched on the underwater seat, stretching her arms out wide on the edge of the tub.

'Really,' he confirmed, sitting opposite and adopting the same position. The water whirled between them, massaging their bodies with the warm, swirling eddies.

41

Nadine tipped back her head and closed her eyes. Strands of her hair, damp with humidity and splashes of water, clung to her long, stretched-back neck. Through the bubbling translucence, Mark caught glimpses of her golden breasts, her nipples reddened from the friction of the water. Christ, she's sexy, he muttered to himself. Too sexy. He rose in the tub and moved silently over to her. Half-crouching, the water churning at his chest, he pushed his hands through the current until he found her waist. Her eyes flew open in surprise as he grabbed her.

'Jesus, Mark!' she cursed. 'You scared me!'

'Don't be frightened, pretty baby,' he said, letting his hands wander up to her breasts. He cupped them hungrily as he had wanted to all night.

'Oh OK,' she murmured, dipping her eyes to watch. 'So long as you play with them for ages.'

And play he did. First he squeezed lightly, relishing the round firmness of her high breasts. Then he teased her nipples, drifting the backs of his fingers to and fro, to and fro, across them until Nadine arched her back forcefully, pushing herself on to him.

'Harder,' she urged.

Mark saw her eyes, iridescent with the glaze of arousal. Beneath the water, his crotch burnt, but now he savoured the sensation – he wanted to send her wild from his foreplay before he took his own pleasure.

'Touch me harder, Mark,' Nadine urged again.

He scissored her nipples between his fore and middle fingers, pulling on them gently.

'Harder,' she insisted, arching her back again.

He pulled harder, jerking the pearls of her nipples forward and then abruptly releasing. Time and again he repeated this and Nadine's moans of pleasure grew both in length and volume. Her nipples were so hard and aroused that each time he touched them she thrust her chest forward. He cupped her breasts again, massaging more and more vigorously. Desperately, Mark checked his own level of excitement, though his balls were aching furiously with arousal. He took his hands from Nadine's breasts and, fumbling beneath the water, he found her thighs on the seating. More roughly than he intended, he pushed her legs apart. Nadine lifted herself slightly so that he could push his hand partly underneath her and cup the whole of her sex. He began to stimulate, massaging her sex through the water with the same kind of vigour as he had massaged her breasts. Nadine wriggled joyously on the seat, breathing in short, sharp bursts as he pressed his fingers round and round her sex. She cupped her breasts, tweaking her nipples and pulling at her own mounds of flesh. Mark watched, completely transfixed. Beneath the water, he could feel her lips and clitoris swell; he could feel the rhythmic movements of her hips. He knew she was near to a climax and, with a sudden idea, he pulled her off the seating and on to his lap. With the weakness of sexual enthral, she offered no resistance, neither helping nor hindering. He turned her round so that her back was to his chest, then, on his knees, he manoeuvred them both until they faced the side of the tub.

'What're you doing?' asked Nadine, her voice a little slurry.

'This,' explained Mark, carefully lining Nadine up with one of the swirling, underwater jets. With one swift movement he opened her legs wide.

'Oh my God!' exclaimed Nadine, jerking her head back on his shoulder. Mark kept her legs wide open, loving her long moans of excitement, loving her arching her back, loving her pressing her bottom hard against his cock.

'Is that good, sweetheart?' he murmured into her ear.

'So . . . good!' she gasped, her words disjointed.

'Describe it to me,' coaxed Mark, his voice tight with excitement.

'Oh God,' she moaned. 'It's . . . I'm . . .'

'Come on, honey,' he urged, blowing softly into her ear. 'Tell me how it feels.' He moved his hand over her sex to give her a moment's respite from the jet of pleasure. The water gushed against the back of his hand.

'It feels,' said Nadine shakily, 'like paradise. I'm so hot, I'm on fire. I need more. Give me more, Mark.'

Mark pulled his hand away, letting the water once again stimulate her sex. She squirmed on his lap and he pressed his hands hard against the insides of her thighs, keeping her legs wide, wide apart. She threw her head back against his shoulder and began once again to massage her breasts, flicking her hard pointed nipples with short polished nails.

Suddenly, she ground her head back against his shoulder, panting feverishly and, in spite of the fact that he was holding her thighs, she managed to raise her legs until her ankles and feet were right out of the water, her toes pointing skyward with balletic poise. He felt her body shudder for several glorious seconds, then she twisted round and slumped against him with a satisfied sigh.

'Good?' asked Mark, stroking her back.

'Amazing,' she murmured.

He dropped his hands and began to squeeze her bottom.

'Mmm,' she breathed. 'That's lovely.'

'Yeah,' agreed Mark, acutely aware of his own urgent need now. He carried on squeezing her satin-smooth buttocks, hazily aware of her moving slightly. Next thing he knew her hands were in his lap, stroking his balls and penis.

'Oh yes,' he groaned, and, unable to withstand it any longer, he stood in the centre of the tub, hoiking Nadine up along with him. Quickly, he spun her round, leaning her over the edge of the tub, her bottom perched tantalisingly before him. He grabbed her hips.

'No,' objected Nadine.

'No?' gasped Mark, utterly confused.

'No,' she confirmed, play-wrestling him round until he was the one sitting on the side of the tub, his feet resting on the underwater seating. In an instant, she had herself in position, kneeling on the seating, her head and shoulders level with his crotch. With a wicked little smile, she moved between his open knees and inched her head forward.

Mark felt his whole body react as she stuck out her tongue and began to flick at the end of his penis. A wonderful frisson ran from her tongue through his penis and balls and up through his stomach and chest. She flicked and teased at his cock and balls until he felt himself break out in a torturous sweat.

He glanced down at her beautiful, bowed head. She met his gaze and he pleaded with his eyes and then watched with relief as she opened her mouth and took him inside. Skilfully, she started to suck, simultaneously working her fingers and thumbs up and down his rock-hard shaft. She took him in further, her warm, moist mouth wrapped around him like a silky cocoon, her damp hair slapping gently against her shoulders as she bobbed her head back and forth. She pulled on his length, increasing her rhythm, working her lips and tongue until every ounce of blood and energy in his body seemed to be coursing magically between his legs.

With superb clarity, Mark felt the onset of his orgasm, the exact moment of subtle change, when his balls lifted, when the pleasure intensified and charged towards that magnificent peak. The sensation rushed from his toes to the backs of his knees and then up through the rest of his body. He threw back his head and his mind became woozy. Such was the force of it all, he even thought he heard bells ringing in his ears . . .

Inside the house, bells of a kind were ringing. The phone rang on and on until eventually the answermachine clicked on, a low voice spoke briefly, and the house was once again silent.

* * *

At home in San Bernardino, Willem Brookes listened as Nadine's answerphone clicked on. Wearily, he left another message requesting a call-back. Willem had thought that at this late hour he might just have got hold of his niece. He desperately wanted to talk with her, to discuss what she was doing with her life – his brother would have expected no less from him. The Brookes family were workers, always had been workers, and their money was hard earned: years of rising at dawn and working a fifteen-hour day. So Nadine's laziness confounded Willem and her self-absorption was a real source of worry.

Perhaps she would call tomorrow, he thought. But, deep down, he knew that she wouldn't. He knew he was clutching at straws. In his heart of hearts he knew, had done for some time, what he would have to do to make her sit up and take note.

The name was like the man, handsome, intriguing, innately masculine. And Latin. Very, very Latin. Garsante. Daniel Garsante. Valerie rolled the name around her mouth. It felt strange, like a foreign delicacy that one knew was expensive and delicious, all the more so for its unfamiliarity.

He was one of the rarer Latin types too. Not the short, stocky version that would always run to fat. No, Daniel Garsante was tall and lean, and Valerie knew for sure that, beneath the dress shirt and dinner suit he had worn, she would have found fine, hard muscles and not an ounce of fat anywhere.

Valerie lay in her bed, gazing up at the ceiling. She couldn't sleep, her mind far too active for the luxury of sleep. And Daniel Garsante was playing a lead role in her mind's fevered activity – the only role if Valerie was honest with herself. Why? Ashley had warned her off, told her the kind of man he was. Why, then, was she so fascinated? She played out the evening, scene by scene, in her head. Daniel, seated near Mark and Nadine at the far end of the table, catching her eye too frequently to pass for coincidence. Later on, his attempts to engage her in conversation, over the heads of other dinner guests. Finally, his goodbye. Taking her on one side, kissing her fingertips and asking for her card. Valerie smiled. Like she had a card! She'd given him her home number instead. He hadn't written it down though, she recalled. Most likely, he wouldn't remember it. Most likely, he wouldn't call.

But what if he did? she mused, her stomach warming oddly. She let her hands wander over the tiny T-shirt she was wearing. Imagine his hands doing this, she thought, reaching the tops of her thighs. Imagine his strong, hard fingers stroking her thighs like she was doing now. She began to feel mildly aroused, closing her eyes to try to picture Daniel's face. Immediately, it sprang to the fore behind her closed eyelids, as clearly defined as a photograph. The warmth in her stomach began to seep downward. She moved her hands idly up and down her thighs, finding her fingers gradually drawn to the area of warmth. She touched herself, feeling the firm mound of her pubic bone through her panties. Her tummy zigzagged with darts of excitement and she pressed her hand down on the light cotton fabric.

Daniel's dark eyes swam in her mind, watching with knowing insolence as she slipped her fingertips into the high waistband of her panties and skimmed the warm, velvety skin of her stomach. She pushed down further, down to where the light fluffy hair of her pubis tickled her fingertips. She was feeling slightly light-headed now – extraordinarily relaxed with the unique mix of heaviness and excitement that arousal of the mind and body engendered.

For a while, she simply let her fingertips drift over her mons, enjoying the texture of her trim nest of hair. Then a stronger sensation kicked in, pulling her insides into tight bands of excitement. She kicked back the sheet and lifted her hips slightly and began to ease off her panties.

Her lower body naked now, she lay in the centre of the large double bed. She ran her hands sensuously over her hips and stomach and, when she couldn't resist it any longer, she parted her legs. A warm night breeze drifted in through an open window and Valerie could feel the light current float across her body, meandering between her parted legs. With Daniel's face imprinted so vividly in her mind, it wasn't hard to imagine that the breeze was his fingertips, stroking her body, caressing her intimately.

As the wisps of air continued to kiss her flesh, she moved her hand down, twisting her fingertips lightly through her soft pubic hair. She traced the tendons at the edges of her groin and scratched her fingernails gently along the insides of her long, sleek thighs until her teasing became too much and her sex began actually to ache for stimulation. With something approaching relief, she slid her middle finger into the centre of her sex, her touch immediately evoking flickers of pleasure between her legs. Twirling her finger around her clitoris, she savoured the feel of herself, the smooth, moist softness of her bud. Soon she felt it begin to harden and swell, and, as she toyed with it, it seemed literally to push itself out from her labia. She fingered herself slowly until the heat of excitement rose luxuriously from her sex, trickling to her abdomen and thighs. At that point, she opened her legs wider, bending them up at the knee. Automatically, her fingers fluttered over her clitoris, faster, faster, the heat and the pleasure relentlessly rising. She could hear her own breaths, sharp and quick now, cutting through the darkness of her bedroom. She could feel the sweat break out on her body and dampen her T-shirt. And then, suddenly, it wasn't her own hand between her legs. It was Daniel's. Daniel Garsante's strong, masculine hand, exploring her, rubbing his fingers round her moist, swollen core. It was Daniel Garsante who was watching her, watching the movements of her body, the sexual tension in her muscles. It was he who made her tug wildly at her T-shirt, lifting it high to expose her breasts, and he who lifted her legs in the air so that the mad, glorious throbbing of her sex intensified. Oh God! she cried out in the darkness as a rush of gratification swept down her body and her internal muscles contracted with seeming abandon.

Oh, the power of the mind, she marvelled, and she slowed her hand down between her legs, the sensations too much now, the nerves too raw. She lay back drained and utterly fulfilled. Her body tingled all over. Moments later, she sat up in bed, pulled her damp T-shirt over her head and tossed it to the floor. Then she arranged the sheet back over herself. Curling on her side, she sighed contentedly and felt herself drift off to sleep. And for the first time since the dinner party that evening, the image of Daniel Garsante began to fade away.

Chapter Five

Garsante Holdings occupied a prime, some would say the finest, piece of office real estate in the city, and Daniel Garsante, as befitted the founder and owner of the company, occupied the finest offices within these fine rooms.

Daniel gazed out now at the ocean, leaning his head back into the soft leather of his chair. Behind him, round the long, highly polished board-table, the success of the Feller takeover was being discussed with considerable enthusiasm. Indeed it was something of a coup, and under normal circumstances Daniel would be leading the way in self-congratulations. Today, however, he couldn't be bothered. It wasn't that he wasn't pleased. He was. His team had excelled themselves as usual. But, quite simply, today his mind was elsewhere and for Daniel that was a rarity.

He could recall her telephone number exactly and for Daniel that too was a rarity. When had he ever remembered a girl's number like it was written in ink inside his head?

He could recall the exact colour of her eyes. Rare also.

He could recall every detail of her superb dancer's body. And the way that soft cloud of blonde hair seemed to hug the nape of her neck.

He had to see her again. The mere thought of that aroused him physically then and there, and that's when Daniel knew he had problems. Usually, he liked the games of seduction, the anticipation of conquest, the chase. Once the goal was reached, he invariably began to lose interest. With this girl, none of that seemed to matter. He had to have her and have her he would – and to hell with anticipation!

Staring out at the glittering, jewelled surface of the sea, deep in lustful thought, Daniel realised his hard-on was getting harder. He eased his legs apart, the adjustment making things a little more comfortable, and as he did so he decided on the time and the place he would see Valerie Neiman again. At his forthcoming annual dinner banquet. As all the formal invites had long since gone out he would call her up personally. Making a mental note to do that straight after the meeting, Daniel gradually became aware of silence in the room. The criss-cross of voices across the table had ceased. He spun his chair back round.

Several faces looked at him expectantly.

'Any other business?' asked Daniel quietly.

A disjointed chorus of no's responded.

'Fine,' he continued, tapping the tabletop with the flats of his hands. 'Let's wind this up for today then.'

'Actually,' broke in a confident voice as Daniel made to stand up.

He looked to the speaker. 'Yes?'

'There is just one item – the marketing strategy for Delaney?'

Daniel smiled patiently, unlike the rest of those present, who rounded on the speaker like a bunch of grumpy schoolkids, moaning and tutting as though the lesson bell had sounded.

Unperturbed, the speaker ignored her detractors and continued. 'I think it needs some discussion. It's just not working and –'

Daniel held up his hand. 'Maybe you're right, Nikki.'

Nikki smiled smugly.

'But I don't think we need keep everybody back right now,' continued Daniel. 'This meeting is adjourned.'

Much exuberant chair-shuffling signalled the end of the session. Nikki's smug smile dwindled into nothingness. Daniel waited a few moments until she had collected her papers.

'Nikki,' he called softly.

She looked up, pursed her lips and strode towards him. 'Daniel,' she began, 'I really do think this merits discussion.'

'Do you?' asked Daniel, pressing his forefinger thoughtfully to his lips.

'Yes,' she replied, clearly encouraged. 'As I said –'

'Fine,' said Daniel, cutting her off. 'Step across to my office now and you can tell me your concerns.'

Daniel walked across the inner hall, pausing as he passed by his assistant's desk to collect his messages. He entered his office. The room had several large windows and the same panoramic ocean view as the boardroom. Daniel sat down at his huge, leather-topped desk, gesturing for Nikki to take one of the two seats opposite. She smoothed down her skirt as she did so.

Daniel had been aware of Nikki for some time. A young woman in her late twenties, fond of power suits and pin-prick high heels. Very pretty and very ambitious. Today, she wore her ash-blonde hair up, stylishly pinned with fine tendrils teased out around her face and neck. Her make-up was skilfully applied to look almost natural, cheeks blushed a light tawny-brown, lips a nude, matt pink.

'So?' invited Daniel. 'Delaney?'

'Yes, Delaney's marketing strategy,' Nikki said, and proceeded to outline her ideas. Daniel listened, noticing vaguely that all the time she spoke she kept slowly crossing and uncrossing her legs and each time she did so the short skirt of her black business suit rode up a little higher. By the time she had finished speaking, the skirt had ridden so far up her thighs he could see the lace tops of her stay-up stockings.

'I had Helen type up these notes,' said Nikki, plucking a sheet of paper from her file. 'If I could leave it with you,' she added, pushing it across the desk towards him.

Daniel eyed the paper but didn't move to take it. 'You're well prepared,' he said slowly.

Nikki smiled, that same smug smile from the boardroom. Daniel wasn't sure whether he liked it or not. She stood up and made a show of smoothing down her skirt. She had long, toned legs and he was fairly sure he liked those.

'Anything else?' he asked.

She shrugged ever so slightly and for a second let the tip of her tongue touch her top lip. 'No ... other business,' she said softly. It was stated in a lilting, open kind of way.

Daniel nodded. She was drawing her finger absently across her collarbone, lingering in front of him. Thoughts of Valerie during the meeting had left him highly aroused and now he found himself stirring once again.

'Any other kind of business?' he asked, searching her eyes. They were shining, hot and hungry.

'Yes,' she said simply, croakily.

Daniel dipped his head once in assent, unsurprised. Nikki, he had gleaned, was a girl who liked to be direct. He leant back in the chair, resting his hands on the armrests.

Nikki leant her hip against the front of his desk. She was toying idly with the top button of her jacket. She had slender, graceful hands and smooth, long nails, painted the same nude pink as her lips. The button nestled just above her cleavage.

'Take off your jacket,' Daniel said, his voice low and deep.

Nikki's eyes flickered brightly. 'Just the jacket?' she

asked huskily, her slender fingers already working their way deftly through the buttons.

'For now,' murmured Daniel.

She opened up the jacket, slipped it off her shoulders, then eased her hip off his desk to lean forward and place the jacket on the chair she'd vacated. Daniel liked the movement. He could see the fine curve of her spine and the smooth skin of her back.

She straightened up and faced him, very confident, very sure of herself. She wore a full-cupped black silk bra that covered the whole of each breast. Her short skirt fitted snugly around hips that looked slender. For a moment or two, Daniel studied her, trying to envisage her without the bra and skirt. Very soon he would see but first he wanted to savour these few precious seconds, like she was a gift he was getting the feel of before he actually unwrapped it. He could see her ribcage rise and fall sharply and her obvious excitement pleased him. He smiled his encouragement.

Placing the heels of her hands against the edge of the desk, Nikki leant forward across it. Somehow she seemed to squeeze her breasts together as she did so and Daniel caught a delicious glimpse of cleavage over the top of the full bra cups. The move half amused him but physically it did a whole lot more – the lower part of his belly pitched and he felt a familiar heavy drag in his balls.

Without speaking, he eased forward himself and casually hooked his forefinger around the small black bow at the front of her bra. The bow concealed a fastener and, with a deft manoeuvre of his finger and thumb, Daniel flicked it open.

Her breasts were surprisingly full, much fuller than they had appeared when covered.

'Beautiful,' murmured Daniel virtually under his breath.

Nikki looked down at her own breasts as he spoke then glanced up sharply towards him. Her eyelids were heavier now, heavy with passion. Holding his gaze, she shrugged off the bra, letting it slip to the top of the desk. Daniel dropped his eyes to her chest. She arched her back slightly.

'I think,' said Daniel, getting up from his chair, 'that right·now we have a great deal of business to attend to.'

Nikki chuckled, her breasts jiggling in accompaniment. 'I agree.'

'Good,' said Daniel, walking round the desk until he was standing behind her. Gently, he looped his arms beneath hers and felt for her breasts in front. As he cupped one in each hand, Nikki sighed.

'Do you like that?' whispered Daniel into the nape of her neck.

'Mmm, I've waited so long for this,' she answered, wriggling slightly so that her breasts moved within his loose grip.

'Do that again,' he commanded gently, and she did, her nipples brushing against his cupped palms. Her breasts were very full, very firm, filling Daniel's hands as he squeezed. He moved his middle fingers to her nipples, dabbing at the hardening centres, then flicking gently with the backs of his fingernails. Nikki moaned even louder.

Daniel moved a tendril of hair from the side of her neck then nibbled gently on her earlobe. 'As I said,' he whispered, 'you're very well prepared.' He paused momentarily to tease the very tips of her nipples. 'But there's something you should know about me. In business, I am very well prepared, and I do not take kindly to criticism.'

'I don't understand,' said Nikki, finishing the statement on a gasp as Daniel blew into her ear.

'Delaney's my personal baby. I devised the marketing strategy myself.'

Nikki let out a little wail. 'I had no idea.'

'I know,' crooned Daniel against her ear.

'I'm sorry,' she gasped.

'I know,' he purred, 'but I don't think I can let it go unpunished, can I?'

Nikki glanced back at him, a little uncertain now.

'I could fire you,' he said, circling her nipples so, so gently.

She gulped.

'Or we could go with a more hands-on punishment,' he went on.

With that, he moved his hand to the back of her skirt and pointedly let it rest there. Nikki looked back at him steadily, keeping up with him every step of the way. 'Yes,' she replied, her voice tight with excitement. 'We could go with that.'

Daniel let his hand creep underneath her skirt. He felt the sheer smoothness of her silk stockings, the rougher texture of their lacy tops, then the inimitable satin feel of warm, sleek flesh. Moving up further, he touched material again, silk and luxurious and brief. Pinching his fingers into the fabric, he pulled it slowly downward, dropping his gaze until he saw the tiny scrap of silk appear from under her skirt. He pulled for another inch or two, leaving her panties mid-thigh.

Placing Nikki's hands on the hemline at each side of her skirt, Daniel stepped back and began to list his requirements in a very soft voice.

'Now, Nikki,' he commanded, 'very, very slowly, start to pull up your skirt.'

Nikki curled her fingers around the hem and began to ease her skirt upward.

'Don't look back,' instructed Daniel. 'Keep your eyes facing forward.'

She did as he told her, keeping her eyes steadfastly forward, sliding the skirt up her thighs. The cream-coloured lace of her stocking tops appeared, then a lightly tanned strip of flesh.

'Carry on,' coaxed Daniel.

The gentle curve of her buttocks now. Slowly coming into view.

'Stop there,' he ordered, as she revealed the lower half of her bottom. 'No looking back,' he reminded her.

He was not in a hurry; he took his time surveying her. Fair hair still pinned up perfectly; slender, naked shoulders and back; arms down at her hips holding up the back of her skirt; the lovely teasing sight of bare flesh beneath.

'OK,' he murmured after a while, 'carry on.'

Her skirt moved higher, more flesh revealed. More lovely, silken, naked flesh.

'Good girl,' he muttered when her skirt was finally bunched round her waist, little more now than a creased black tyre of material.

Nikki stood waiting, dutifully holding on to her skirt, the rapid fluctuations of her back and shoulders the only visible signs of her excitement.

'I mustn't work you hard enough,' said Daniel.

'Why's that?' answered Nikki, clearly confused.

'This tan line,' he explained, running his finger up the fine line of paler skin along the join of her buttocks.

Nikki exhaled sharply as he touched her. 'Sundays on the beach.' She chuckled throatily.

'Ah, I see,' he said, not removing his finger. 'You have a beautiful ass, Nikki,' he continued almost conversationally, spreading his hand across it now.

Nikki didn't answer though her back and shoulders rose and fell a fraction more rapidly. But, as he drew back his hand and smacked her bare cheeks, she let out a low, sustained, excited 'yes'.

'You like that, don't you?'

'Mmm, yes,' she answered.

Daniel spanked her again and again, working into a kind of rhythm. Not too hard, not too soft. The clear slapping sound of flesh upon flesh, loud enough to turn them both on. Daniel watched her bottom quiver deliciously each time he brought his hand down and his crotch began to ache with arousal. Nikki was quite obviously worked up, a fine sheen of perspiration glazing the skin of her back. She was pushing her bottom

57

furiously outward, straining back to meet his hand. Quickly, Daniel turned her round to face him. What he saw made his belly pitch again.

Her face was shining, her cheeks flushed pink beneath her tawny blush. Her bare breasts swelled magnificently, tips very red and hard. Her navel was hidden beneath the creased wreck of her skirt but her slender hips and groin were completely, wonderfully, naked.

Daniel noticed her panties, tight and redundant, pulled down to her thighs.

'Take them off,' he said gruffly.

Nikki wriggled out of them, breathing hard and fast.

Daniel eyed the small, sparse tangle of fluffy hair between her legs; he couldn't drag his eyes from it. He reached forward and cupped his hand over it. Nikki jerked joyously, immediately bending her knees outward to open herself up.

'Yeah,' muttered Daniel appreciatively, feeling everything.

'That's so good,' moaned Nikki as he rubbed her smooth, damp sex. She moved her body in gentle undulations as he felt her, her breasts quivering with each movement. He continued to tease, flicking his finger over her clitoris until she seemed so short of breath she was almost panting.

She began to fondle her own breasts, rolling her nipples between her fingertips whilst pushing her hips rhythmically forward. Daniel's forbearance was almost nil, his cock so hard that he had to reach down and undo his zipper to release it. Nikki shot her eyes downward.

'Give it to me, Daniel,' she pleaded. 'All the way!'

'Soon, honey, soon,' he teased, twisting her away from the desk and leading her to one of the nearby chairs.

Prompted by him, she climbed on the chair forward, positioning her knees on each of the wide, low armrests. Then she leant her upper body over the back of the chair, so that her bottom was thrust tantalisingly before him and her breasts swung downward over the chairback.

'Christ, yes,' muttered Daniel in admiration.

He stood to the side, over her, clasping her bottom in one hand and her breasts with the other. Nikki closed her eyes and tilted back her head. Daniel could see her swallow hard as he caressed her. She squirmed in her precarious position, wriggling both her breasts and her bottom in his hands, seemingly unable to decide which needed the stimulus more. Daniel decided for her, spanking her pert bottom hard – much, much harder than before.

Nikki let out a desperate moan, arching her back as far as she could. Flashing open her eyes, she twisted her head round, watching as he spanked her. He could tell she wasn't far from orgasm. She seemed to be in a kind of robotic trance, watching herself being punished. Soon she moved her hand between her legs and started to stroke herself. Gradually her movements quickened, becoming almost frantic. From his position above her, Daniel could just about see the furious motion of her wrist and it spurred him on to spank her harder.

'Oh yes, yes,' she moaned, eyes dancing deliriously.

She jerked back her head, stretching her neck and shoulders. Daniel stilled his hand on her bottom and could feel the trembling, conclusive rush of her climax, the heat of ecstasy bathe her whole body.

'Fantastic,' she sighed, slumping forward over the chairback.

'Yeah,' agreed Daniel, scarcely waiting a moment before grasping the crease of her skirt round her middle and pulling her backwards on to her feet.

'Fantastic,' he repeated as he sunk himself inside her and reaped his pleasure within the hot, moist depths of her body.

Chapter Six

Nadine lay back on the cushioned sunlounger by the side of the pool and gently trailed her fingers through the water. Absently, she watched the water drip from her fingertips like tiny, translucent pearls. Inside the house the telephone rang. Nadine heard it but did not move a muscle. Whoever it was could leave a message, she thought lazily. The phone rang off. Then started again. Nadine ignored it, closing her eyes beneath her dark shades and drifting gently off to sleep.

She woke up twenty minutes later. Warm and woozy from her nap, she adjusted slowly to being awake, stretching her long, sun-drenched limbs. She had had a dream about Mark, a very sexy kind of a dream, and now she felt pleasantly heavy and aroused. While she lay there, enjoying the familiar sexual glow at the base of her stomach, she remembered the phone ringing earlier. In particular, she remembered the persistence of the caller. Could have been Mark, she thought hazily. Ringing to say he could slip away for an hour. Ringing to see if she was there. Goddamn, she muttered, instantly wide awake. She swung her legs over the side of the lounger and charged into the house. She could do with an hour of Mark, an hour of sex and sweat and fun and games. Now she would have to wait until tonight. Why hadn't she just answered the phone?

When she reached the telephone, the message light was flashing. Waiting to hear Mark's deep, smiling voice, she listened. There was no smile in the voice that she heard. The voice was deep but it wasn't Mark's. Uncle Willem, recognised Nadine, preparing to cut the message off. Something stopped her however, some strange inflection in his voice, some mixture of weariness and sadness weighing down each of the words. He was talking clearly and slowly, making sure there was no ambiguity. And yet the words still didn't sound clear to Nadine. She hadn't heard them right, that was all. With a trembling finger she replayed the message and listened again. She felt a cold grip of fury clutch at her insides. She pressed the button and listened again.

'No,' she said tightly. No. No. No.

She jabbed at the button and listened again.

No! He couldn't do this to her. He would not do this to her. Not Uncle Willem. Uncle Willem doted on her, adored her. She had always been able to get him to do anything for her.

Then she had a thought. An enormous wave of relief washed over her. She knew what this was. A bluff. A goddamn bluff. He just wanted some attention was all. Poor Uncle Willem just wanted her attention.

Weak with relief she took several deep breaths to compose herself. Then, with a rock-steady finger, she punched in Uncle Willem's number. Humming softly to herself, she listened to the old-fashioned ring of Uncle Will's telephone. As she waited for Uncle Will to pick up, she glanced at her wristwatch and began to plan her evening with Mark. Dinner first, somewhere special, somewhere smooth, romantic, expensive. Then a long, hot night of love. The glow returned deliciously to the pit of her stomach.

Willem Brookes gazed out of the parlour window, a look of determination set upon his face. Belinda, his housekeeper, beetled into the hall, towards the ringing telephone. As Belinda spoke into the mouthpiece, each word of the one-way conversation drifted through to the parlour. No, Willem wasn't available. No, she didn't know where he could be reached. No, she didn't know when he'd be back. Yes, she'd be sure to pass the message on – phone Nadine as a matter of urgency.

Quietly, Belinda replaced the receiver.

'Thank you, Belinda,' said Willem gravely. 'Not a nice job having to cover for someone, I know.'

Belinda smiled and kept her mouth tightly zipped. She would love to tell her adored employer that really it was her pleasure, that it was about time he put Miss High and Mighty Nadine in her place and stopped letting her run roughshod over him. Instead, Belinda buttoned her lip. Willem looked drawn and sad, she thought. His strong shoulders seemed to sag. Belinda longed to hug him to her, cushion his head on her ample bosom and tell him not to take on so. Tell him that Nadine was spoilt and ungrateful and not worthy of such agonising. Belinda wondered how she might cheer Willem up. Food, she decided with conviction, and bustled off to the kitchen. She would tell Cook to put together his favourite tonight, a prime piece of rib with all of the trimmings then sugared apple tart and double-rich cream.

Nadine had been calling on the hour, every hour. By late afternoon, her mood of calm optimism had vanished. She was fuming, consumed with rage. For the seventh time, she hit redial. Belinda answered yet again. Like before, Belinda was immovable, patiently heading off her demands like some goddamn rosy-cheeked brick wall!

'Belinda,' demanded Nadine. 'Will you please tell me where Uncle Will is?'

'I honestly couldn't say, miss,' answered brick-wall Belinda.

'He's there, isn't he?' accused Nadine, finally snapping. 'Just put him on the line.'

'I really can't do that,' said Belinda. 'But I will be sure and tell him you called.'

Nadine heard a gentle click followed by the dial tone. She stared, incensed, at the receiver. Belinda had hung up on her. That apple-cheeked, do-gooding busybody had only gone and hung up on her!

She slammed down the phone, realisation hitting her like a slap in the face. Uncle Will meant it.

Suddenly the phone started to ring, making her jump. She grabbed for it instantly.

'Uncle Will,' she began, breathless. 'I knew you couldn't mean it. I knew you'd call me –'

'Whoa,' soothed Mark, like he was reining in a runaway horse. 'Steady now.'

'Mark,' sighed Nadine, deflated.

'I don't usually have that effect on you,' said Mark. 'What's up?'

'Everything,' she snapped. 'Everything's up.'

'So tell me.'

'My darling uncle has only gone and stopped my allowance. He called today, left a message saying it stops as from the end of the month.'

'Wow,' whistled Mark. 'Why?'

'He said he didn't like my attitude. He said it didn't do me any good to rely on him. He said I needed to go out and make my own way. Get a job.'

'Sure had a lot to say, this uncle of yours.'

'Yeah,' muttered Nadine. 'And all of it goddamn bullshit! What should I do, Mark?'

'Phone him. Sweet-talk him.'

'I tried that already,' moaned Nadine. 'The old coot won't even take my calls.'

'Sounds like he means business.'

'Oh he means business all right.'

'Don't sweat it, baby,' said Mark lightly. 'He'll come around and I'll take care of you until he does.'

'This isn't a joke, Mark,' said Nadine tersely. 'I have bills. Lots of them.'

'He'll come around,' assured Mark.

'I don't think so.'

Mark was silent. 'Then we'll deal with it,' he said seriously.

'Oh sure,' said Nadine, dripping with sarcasm.

'Look,' said Mark brightly. 'Don't think of it right now. We've got Daniel's party in two days, the perfect place to schmooze. We'll get you a job in no time.'

'I do not want a job,' she hissed. 'I want my goddamn allowance!'

And she slammed down the phone for the eighth time that afternoon.

'I'm sorry,' she whispered, calling back moments later. 'I'm stressed and I'm hurting. D'you forgive me?'

Mark didn't answer.

'Please, baby,' she pleaded. 'I need you. I need you so much.'

'I forgive you,' Mark answered softly.

Chapter Seven

*T*he old lady placed a weary foot on the bottom stair and grabbed at the railing. She stared up at the long flight of steps. Dismay was etched clearly on every line of her leathery, heavily made-up face.

'Darn elevator,' she grumbled, turning to a small, equally leathery man standing by her side. 'You should get the Super in, Dean. How many times did that elevator break down? How many times did I say you should get the Super in?'

'You're right, Phyllis,' said her husband, staring, if possible with more dismay than his wife, up at the long flight of stairs.

In total unison they took a deep sigh, put their heads down, and began to climb up to their apartment.

Suddenly, out of nowhere, came a whirlwind. The old woman flung herself back to the railings with all the drama of a Broadway actress. Her husband, slightly less dramatic, pinned himself against the wall.

'Whoops, sorry,' shouted Valerie – the cause of the whirlwind being her rapid downward pace. She hurtled between them, seemingly unable to slow down her speed. 'Sorry, Mrs Phelps, sorry, Mr Phelps,' she shouted back gaily, tripping eagerly down the stairs and racing out of the lobby.

'Youngsters!' said Mrs Phelps, shaking her head so vigorously that the large gold hoops in her droopy earlobes clanked against her jaw. 'Crazy!'

'You're right, Phyllis,' said Mr Phelps.

'Must be a guy,' she said. 'No girl runs like that but for a guy.'

'You're right, Phyllis.'

With another deep sigh in total unison, they put their heads down and resumed their climb.

Valerie landed out on the street and hopped into her second-hand Honda. She drove jerkily out of her parking space, nudging the bumper of the car in front. She was so excited that she did not even notice.

'OK, now calm down,' she told herself, doing anything but. With one hand on the wheel, she rummaged round the glove compartment until she found her meditation cassette. Inserting it into the tapedeck, she prepared to listen and be calm.

If anything it worked too well. By the time she reached Ashley's, her equilibrium was well and truly restored but her eyelids were dropping and she was driving in the middle of the road. She parked askew on Ashley's long driveway and wandered up to the house.

Ashley appeared in the doorway, questions written all over her face.

'Hey,' said Valerie in a mellow, chilled-out kind of way. 'Guess what? Daniel Garsante called me.'

Ashley's face fell.

'Ashley, I need a favour,' continued Valerie, not noticing Ashley's response. 'I need to raid your wardrobe. I need an amazing dress.'

'Onward and upward,' said Ashley, gesturing Valerie inside.

Eight dresses later, Valerie stood in front of the mirror in the corner of Ashley's large bedroom.

'This is the one,' decided Valerie, cocking her head on one side. It was a beautiful, white Jackie-O-style dress with a wide scooped neck and short, flattering sleeves. The fabric was light, sheer and hellishly expensive.

'Yep.' Ashley nodded.

'Not too much leg?' asked Valerie. Because she was three inches taller than Ashley, Ashley's dresses were always a little bit shorter on her.

'Nope,' said Ashley.

Ashley sounded uncharacteristically subdued. Valerie looked in the mirror across at her. She was perched on the edge of her bed, half-hidden behind the mountain of dresses they had pulled out. Valerie caught her eye.

'You really don't like him, do you?' she asked quietly.

Ashley shrugged slightly. 'Dislike isn't the word. He's devilishly attractive, he's totally charming.'

'But?'

'But, like I told you before, there's something very different underneath. Something steely and hard.'

'So, I like a man hard,' joked Valerie.

Ashley barely cracked a smile. 'Just take care, Val,' she warned. 'Don't go getting hurt on me.'

'Me, hurt? Nah,' said Valerie, twirling round and winking. 'I can take care of myself.'

Ashley smiled, a fraction happier.

'Besides,' said Valerie, 'he's not exactly luring me to the gates of hell. It's a party invite to one of the glitziest parties in town. And you'll be there.'

'You're right,' grinned Ashley, waving her hands airily around. 'It's just a party. Not even a proper date really.'

'Right,' agreed Valerie. 'Not a proper date at all.'

But when she recalled Daniel's smooth, low voice proffering the invitation, her stomach leapt with riotous butterflies. She couldn't help but wish that maybe it was just a teeny bit like a date.

By the time Valerie left, Ashley was back to being her usual bubbly and vibrant self. She just had time to throw on a two-piece lycra work-out outfit, pull her long copper hair up into a ponytail and gloss her lips lightly to a clear pink lustre. She was dabbing scent on the back of her neck when she heard a vehicle outside.

Ashley danced downstairs and pulled wide the front door before Carlo even had a chance to ring the doorbell.

'Hey, Carlo,' she said brightly.

'Hi, Ashley,' he answered with a smile.

My, my, what a smile, thought Ashley, her tummy looping in response. His teeth looked very white against the dark olive-tint of his face, his short black hair was boyishly ruffled and his chocolate-brown eyes shone with energy and mischief.

'I seriously need a work-out today,' said Ashley, leading him through to the living room.

'Me too,' winked Carlo, his eyes more mischievous than ever.

'No, really,' giggled Ashley. 'I have a party on Saturday night, and a dress that I'm going to have to be sewn into. Even a suggestion of wobble will show.'

Carlo eyed her theatrically back and front, then ran his hands slowly down the sides of her stomach and hips. 'Ashley, sweetheart,' he began, 'there is not a single suggestion of fat anywhere. You are firm, baby. Firm.'

Ashley fluttered her eyelashes playfully. 'You really think so?'

'Yeah,' said Carlo, moving behind her and pulling her back against him. 'Though I shouldn't really say that or you'll think you don't need a personal trainer any more.'

'If I'm so firm, then maybe I don't,' giggled Ashley. She twisted round, went up on tiptoe, and kissed him lightly on the lips. 'But I do need you,' she added quietly.

'And,' smiled Carlo, 'just because you're firm, that doesn't mean we don't need to work up a sweat today.'

'No,' agreed Ashley. 'It doesn't.'

She leant back against him whilst he ran his hands gently down the front of her body. Soon the hardness in his groin began to press into the small of her back. Ashley pushed against it, loving it.

'Today,' murmured Carlo, 'I have something special in mind.'

'You do?' asked Ashley dreamily.

'Uh huh,' said Carlo. 'One moment, I have to get something from the van.'

He was gone for less than two minutes, returning into the room with an enormous plain glass mirror. The muscles in his upper arms bunched as he carried it through but his breathing was smooth and even. 'Visual stimulation,' he said, placing the huge mirror against a wall, 'is so good for the body and mind.'

He held out his arm and beckoned her over with his fingers. Ashley, her mind floating with the delights which lay in store, wandered to his side.

Carlo curled her into his arms, then placed his forefinger under her chin and tilted her face towards the mirror.

'Look,' he said softly.

Ashley looked. There was something very sensual about the image of the two of them. Carlo, strong, dark and tall, the bare flesh of his arms and legs showing the fit, trained musculature of an athlete. Herself, petite and slender, her skin pale, her hair the colour of rich autumn leaves. What a contrast, she thought, spellbound. Like night and day.

Carlo edged his fingers beneath the elastic of her short lycra top. He pulled it a little, up over her breasts. Silently, she held up her arms and he pulled her top over her head. He moved to her shorts, easing them down her hips, her legs, her ankles. Crouched on his heels, he slowly untied the laces of her training shoes. He slipped each shoe off in turn. Finally, he removed her small white ankle socks, caressing her feet as he did so.

'Now look,' he whispered, standing up beside her.

Ashley tilted her face back to the mirror. She saw herself in profile, naked next to Carlo. He placed his forefinger on the column of her neck and lightly began to trace downward. He moved down her chest, reaching the swell of her high white breasts. She watched him trace the upperside of her left breast. As he reached the smooth pale halo of her nipple, he paused. Then he began to finger her nipple, dabbing and touching until she could see the centre stand out like a proud little nib.

She gasped as he let his finger drop beneath her nipple. Very lightly, he began to stroke the full under-slope of her breast, then traced down her ribcage and stomach. With slow, firm movements, he caressed her navel.

'Keep looking, Ashley,' he whispered, nudging her round until she faced the mirror.

'Yes,' she murmured, barely audible.

He was standing behind her now, gazing over the top of her head, staring as steadfastly as she at their reflection. His hands still rested on her navel. Apart from that, every inch of her nudity was on display.

'Look how lovely you are,' murmured Carlo. 'Look at your breasts, see how your nipples come alive when I touch them.' And he touched the very tips again, teasing until Ashley felt sharp pulls of desire in her groin.

'And here,' he said, stroking the smooth, milky skin of her stomach.

'And here,' she breathed, pushing his hand on to the red-gold curls of her pubes.

Watching him weave his fingers through her nest of soft hair made her belly flutter deliciously. Gradually, he worked his hand between her thighs, cupping the whole of her sex.

'Mmm, you're so wet,' he murmured, pulling his hand away and putting it to his mouth. She saw his fingers glisten with her moisture before he began licking it slowly from his fingertips. Her stomach swam with heat at the gesture and hurriedly she turned to him, pulling at his clothing.

Moments later he was naked, the smooth muscles of his chest feeling like sun-warmed satin as she ran her hands over them.

Looking back to their reflection in the mirror, she felt no shame at all in standing there nude, in the middle of her living room, in the middle of the day. She saw only the way they appeared in that mirror, their bodies close, their smooth limbs twined together, and all she could think was how erotic the sight was.

Carlo was crouching down now, lifting her right leg and balancing her foot on his shoulder. The movement opened up her legs.

'Oh man,' muttered Carlo, gazing into her open sex.

Ashley felt weak. She could see exactly what he was seeing, her down-coated lips parted, the succulent pink core within.

She shivered with pleasure as he pressed his finger to the length of her clitoris. The pleasure intensified instantly as he vibrated his finger from side to side.

'Keep looking,' urged Carlo, needlessly because her eyes were glued to the mirror, to their bodies, to Carlo's magnificent attentions.

As he flicked his finger skilfully from side to side, the warmth of arousal spread through her sex, reaching the tops of her thighs. She watched her body's response, the way her breasts seemed fuller and her chest coloured to a pretty, pale-pink flush. All the time, her sex was swelling, glistening and wet, and seeing that turned her on even more.

Carlo moved lower, skimming the pulpy skin around her opening. She began to yearn for penetration and, as though sensing this, Carlo deftly popped his finger inside.

Ashley moaned, trying to sink downward, and Carlo pushed in further, burying his finger up to the knuckle. Gently he stimulated, up and down, up and down, until she felt tiny flutters flare throughout her abdomen.

He brought out his finger, trailing it back up to her clitoris, moistening her bud with her own special juices.

She curled her foot around his hot shoulder, wanting to open herself up even more. He was still concentrating on her sex, rubbing wonderfully round her core, and though Ashley wanted to stay in that position, to carry on watching and feeling simultaneously, her legs were becoming a little shaky.

Reluctantly, she dropped to her knees – and she found herself face to face with Carlo, his chocolate-brown eyes bright with passion, his dark skin dotted with beads of perspiration. He trailed his fingertips across her lips, letting her taste herself, letting her catch the tangy scent, and it made her heady and hot and almost unaware of what she was doing. Cramming his fingers into her mouth, she licked and sucked with a hunger she hadn't known before.

It sent them both wild. Pulling her over him, Carlo lay back, positioning her above his engorged penis. Ashley dropped happily down on it, loving the intimate decisive moment of penetration. Kneeling down completely, she felt the wonderful fullness of his cock inside her. And then the need to move and stimulate overtook her. She moved up and down, her body responding instantly to her rhythm, Carlo groaning with pleasure beneath her. She rode him like a cowgirl and the ache and strain of her pumping thighs only added to the glorious pleasure of it all.

'Oh yeah, oh man,' moaned Carlo, as she bucked upon him, her bottom cheeks slapping against his upraised, sweat-slicked thighs. She leant down over him, her nipples brushing lightly on his chest. His balls felt so hard, so slippy, and she could feel them jig against the outside of her sex. Her mind was a whirl, trying to keep pace with her body, and then she felt her orgasm begin, a tight little furl somewhere deep inside starting to unwind and travel. She glanced quickly back to the mirror. Kneeling over Carlo, her thighs spread wide, her hips glued to his. Too much. Too much now.

She came on a reeling wheel of sensation, writhing and sweating, then clamping her knees to his hips in a frozen clasp of sheer delight.

Carlo, underneath her, rocked his hips a little more. Then he bucked up his thighs and buttocks and jerked up his head. Grasping her thighs hard, he groaned out a long, low rush of satisfaction.

When he sank back to the carpet and she slumped exhausted on his heaving chest, she cast a final look into the mirror. Beautiful, she thought, seeing the fulfilment on their faces, the glow and the rosiness, the sweat shining on their skin.

As ever, Carlo was right, she mused happily. Visual stimulation was amazing. So good for the body and mind.

Chapter Eight

*T*all lofty trees ran along the sides of the dark sweeping driveway, their branches sparkling with tiny luminous pinpricks of brilliance. The fairy lights were so numerous, festooned and yet hidden amongst the leaves and branches, that it looked simply magical.

Through the trees, beautifully manicured gardens, lit by the moonlight, seemed to stretch endlessly towards the ocean, the blue-black expanse of water in parts glazed silver by the benevolence of the moon.

Over the past few years, Valerie had travelled to, visited and worked in places and cities of beauty. Lord knows, she even lived in one of the loveliest places in the world. But this, she thought, fighting hard not to press her nose to the car window in child-like awe, this, just a few miles from her apartment, was truly something else. Like a fairytale land. Daniel Garsante lived in a fairytale land.

Ashley, sitting next to her, squeezed her hand. 'Like it?' she stage-whispered in Valerie's ear.

'What do you think?' whispered Valerie back.

'Hey, what's all this whispering?' boomed out Ashley's pork-chop of a husband, peering round from the corner of the limousine. 'Bet you've never been anyplace like this before, have you, Val? Like Cinders going to the ball.'

74

Ashley and she exchanged looks. Ashley smiled a resigned apology, clearly for her husband's habitual lack of tact.

How did she manage to put up with him, wondered Valerie, eyeing Bradley Ray III with something approaching revulsion. Already beet-faced from a pre-party attack on a bottle of bourbon, he was now leaning forward into the liquor cabinet, merrily helping himself. He had a neck just like a bullfrog, she decided, noticing the unattractive way the white collar of his shirt cut into the porcine, spongy skin of his neck.

Ashley squeezed her hand again. 'Look,' she said, pointing outwards.

Valerie turned back to the car window. She saw that they were now approaching the house itself, a huge mansion, stonework cloaked with trailing foliage and climbing wild rose, enormous Georgian windows ablaze with light. The large rectangular courtyard to the front of the house was a highly orchestrated hive of activity: cars and limousines crawling slowly around; guests resplendent in designer dress alighting and making their way to the entrance.

Valerie found her door opened by a polite, pretty-boy valet attendant in a purple waistcoat and black bow tie. She and Ashley got out. Bradley insisted on slurping a final gulp of alcohol before following. He inserted himself between them – not an easy feat since he already appeared to have difficulty walking straight. Clamping his octopus hands to their bottoms, he ushered them forward. Gritting her teeth, Valerie suffered the indignity in silence and allowed herself to be ushered.

The three-inch heels of her strappy sandals sank rather wonderfully a fraction or so into the light, cushiony gravel of the courtyard. Everything, even the gravel, seemed to be designed for maximum comfort she thought, and as they neared the open entrance to the house, as if to confirm her opinion, she heard the perfect strains of classical music. She saw why as soon as they went inside. Glass doors at the rear of the foyer were wide open and out on the lawns, below a stone terrace and wide staircase, was an orchestra.

Valerie stood still, capturing the mood, the enchanting ambiance. Naturally it was Bradley Ray who wrenched her back into reality.

'Looky over there, see who's here,' he boomed, releasing his hold on their bottoms, if only to propel them forward by pushing his hands into the small of their backs.

'Oh my,' muttered Ashley.

'Oh shit,' said Valerie. 'Does she get everywhere?'

'She's here with Mark Kelton,' explained Ashley apologetically, as though she herself were personally responsible. Clearly, she hadn't forgotten her recent dinner party faux pas.

Valerie looked across at Nadine, who was wearing an exquisite ankle-length dress, green to match the colour of her eyes, and, although Valerie would rather have undergone torture than admit it out loud, she saw that Nadine looked absolutely stunning.

'She looks good,' mused Ashley.

'You think?' answered Valerie bitchily.

Ashley cast her a sidelong glance. 'You know, Val, I've never truly understood what it is with you two. Why do you dislike each other so much?'

'There's no great hidden reason,' muttered Valerie. And there wasn't. She almost wished there were, just to give some credence to this mutual dislike. Maybe it was jealousy, maybe they were jealous of each other. Who knew? Who cared? 'Just two girls who don't get along,' she finished rather lamely.

'Two beautiful she-cats more like,' chuckled Bradley. 'Boy, would I like to see you both fight it out!'

This time, Ashley looked at her husband with something approaching revulsion.

Valerie, meanwhile, saw that Nadine had spotted them. Mark Kelton, looking extremely handsome and relaxed, was standing by Nadine's side. Nadine said something to him and they started to walk over.

'Oops, time for me to mingle I think,' quipped Valerie. And she sidestepped neatly out of harm's way.

It took her five minutes to locate him. She was admiring the gold-carpeted expanse of a fine reception room when she saw him. Right there, in the centre of a small group of party guests.

She had wondered whether Daniel Garsante in the flesh could possibly live up to the Daniel Garsante she'd had in her head ever since the evening of Ashley's dinner party. Now she had her answer. He did. Oh, how he did! Dark hair combed back, swarthy skin smooth over lean, angular features, black eyes flashing with a hint of danger. He wore a dazzling white dress shirt and a jet-black dinner suit, amongst a sea of white shirts and black suits, but to Valerie he and he alone stood out.

She wavered for a moment in the doorway, wondering whether to approach. Saved by a passing waiter, she helped herself to a glass of champagne, downed it in three swift gulps, then, before she could prevaricate any more, she began to walk over. At precisely that moment, he lifted his eyes towards her. With a slight nod of the head, he appeared to excuse himself from his guests.

'Valerie Neiman,' he said, voice as smooth as Swiss chocolate.

'Daniel Garsante,' she responded evenly.

He smiled. 'You look beautiful.'

She had taken hours to get ready, teasing every strand of her mussy, bobbed hair till it was exactly right, applying her make-up with utter precision. At least it hadn't been for nothing.

'Oh, this old thing,' she joked, glancing down at her borrowed couture dress. She prayed Ashley wasn't anywhere nearby or she'd never lend her anything again!

'I didn't mean the dress,' said Daniel softly.

Valerie smiled slightly, accepting the compliment. The champagne was working – she was flirty yet calm and, since she was currently in the throes of the most powerful attraction she had ever known, she decided that flirty yet calm was possibly the best state to be in.

There was a momentary silence. Not uncomfortable but full of something. Valerie felt positive that, if she reached out right now to touch him, she would get an electric shock.

'I love your house,' she said, mostly for something to say.

'Would you like me to show you around?' he asked.

'What about your guests?'

'They're grown-ups,' he said flippantly, 'they can cope for a while.'

'In that case,' she laughed, 'I'd love for you to show me around.'

The house was a revelation: the rooms, the ornate ceiling designs, the staircases, the balustrades. She did her very best to appreciate it, truly she did, but it was so difficult to concentrate with Daniel walking by her side, pointing things out in that deep, sexy voice.

'It's magnificent,' she said, as they strolled along a wide landing on the second floor.

Daniel dipped his head in almost objective acknowledgement.

He led her through an archway, down two steps and on to a landing once again. There was a single oak door off the landing. Without speaking, he opened the door and then stepped back to enable her to enter before him.

'My office,' he explained, following her through.

She walked right into the room and looked about her.

'Lovely,' she breathed, vaguely aware that the room was indeed lovely but rather more aware of the fact that Daniel was standing just behind her. So close. She could even catch, very faintly, a whisper of a scent.

Sandalwood or something smooth and similar. She inhaled deeply, trying to appear as though she wasn't.

'Why the sigh?' he whispered, so close behind her.

Valerie shrugged, unable to think of a witty answer.

He touched the nape of her neck, very, very softly. So softly it felt unreal.

'I think that's why,' she answered.

Then his lips were on the nape of her neck, brushing lightly against her skin. She felt goosebumps prickle all over her body. He lifted a strand of her hair and kissed behind her ear.

'Mmm,' she sighed again and turned round to face him.

He dipped his head, butterfly-kissing the sides of her neck. Tremors ran right down her spine and she lifted up her chin, giving him the slender column of her throat.

'Thank you,' he murmured, kissing upwards.

'Don't mention it,' she breathed, tilting back her head for more. He kissed beneath her chin.

A frisson of pleasure ran down her body. She felt unsteady, leaning back for support against something. She felt something sturdy and flat. A desk, she thought. Possibly. His hands were round her waist now, lifting her. Then she was sitting, perched upright. Must be a desk. She could feel cool, hard leather beneath her thighs and fingertips.

He kissed her on the lips. Just as well she was sitting, she thought hazily, else surely her legs would have given way. The feel of his lips on hers, smooth and sweet and just a tad forceful. The inside of his mouth, fresh and hot. His tongue, flicking, teasing, and dancing with hers.

She moved her hands up to his face, cupping his cheeks as they kissed, then moving them to the back of his head, twisting her fingers through his thick dark hair.

He pressed his body to hers and she loved it. She had imagined this scene every night, wondering how his body and mouth would feel. She pulled him to her and mouths still joined, they began to ease down on to the top of the desk. She started to feel the weight of him, the heat of him, and still they kissed and soon she was leaning back fully on the desk and Daniel was leaning on top of her. In seventh heaven, she rested her head down, letting Daniel push his mouth harder on hers.

'Ouch,' she cried, hitting something hard on the desk.

'What is it?' asked Daniel.

'I hit my head on something,' she said, feeling rather foolish.

Daniel looked beyond her head. He appeared distracted for a moment, then straightened up.

'Excuse me for a moment, Valerie,' he said, husky with passion. He reached round her to take hold of something. Valerie saw that it was a business box file of some kind.

'Something important I forgot to put away,' he said, carrying it over to a rich mahogany cabinet against the wall. When he opened the cabinet, Valerie recognised the large, grey metal door of a safe within.

'Excuse me, Valerie,' he repeated, glancing back at her.

'Oh yes, of course,' she said, understanding. She turned her head discreetly away, admiring an oil on the opposite wall. Behind her, she heard the unmistakable seven digit click of a combination. A minute later, she heard the door of the safe snap shut.

'Where were we?' murmured Daniel, back in front of her.

Valerie looked up into his dark, simmering face. Far from being broken, the moment was still very much alive, the attraction between them so vital, so sharp, it seemed electric, hanging in the air like waves of red-hot current.

'I think,' she said, gesturing back to the top of the desk, 'somewhere just about there.'

'Ah, that's right,' he said, moving forward.

'Shouldn't we get back to the party?' she whispered, staring longingly at his lips.

'We should,' he said, staring back at her lips. 'In a while.'

And then he was kissing her again, hungry this time, eating at her lips and mouth. She lost herself in the hot, sweet pleasure of his mouth. He pushed forward again and she leant back again, resting her head unhindered on the desk top.

He leant over her, placing his hands to the sides of her face.

'Come closer,' she urged, reaching round his back to pull him down, feeling his hard body through the beautiful cloth of his dinner jacket.

He pressed himself down further and she felt the huge, hard swell in his groin. Her own body was a teeming, rolling mass of sensation. She needed him desperately, his hard, hard cock inside her, stretching, appeasing her, quenching this sudden blaze.

They were of the same mind. His breath was like fire as he drew back from their kiss and eased his hand straight down between her legs.

'Yes,' she moaned, arching up her back as he found the lacy gusset of her panties and pulled it roughly to one side. She felt him touch the lips of her sex. She knew how wet she must be, she could sense his fingers sliding in her juice. Opening her legs wider, she was aware of him holding her panties to one side still. Waiting for his next move now, her head pounding with excitement. She heard nothing at all, no sound of a zipper, no fumbling of clothes, but when she felt the head of his penis against her, her blood raced like a freight train in her veins.

He nudged the smooth bulbed end against her, like a teasing, exquisite form of torture, then, carefully, he guided himself inside, filling her every bit as wonderfully as she could ever have hoped.

He began to thrust gently, each movement stroking her insides and stoking up the fire raging in her

81

stomach. She joined in his rhythm, lifting her hips, the pressure to climax building gloriously. Wrapping her legs around his trousered buttocks, she held on tightly to his shoulders. Their hips gyrated in rhythmic union, their mouths pressed together again, and gradually Valerie's mind began to shift dimensions. She was diving into a pool of lights, silvers, blacks, golds, whites. The heat between her legs was immense, throbbing, pulsating, somehow connected to the galaxy of light swimming in her head.

It was almost too much. The raw, shuddering peak. She tried to stop the cry before it could escape but the force of her orgasm took her by surprise and her cry sounded so loud to herself she was sure the entire house must have heard it.

Through a furnace of pleasure, she heard Daniel groan. A loud groan, as loud as her own cry of ecstasy. That made her feel good somehow.

'Christ!' he said, locking his arms and gazing down into her face in amazement.

'I know,' she murmured, reeling from it all.

She was in a state of drugged intoxication, a sexual high. She had just had sex with Daniel Garsante. Real sex, not imagined. Real.

What happens now? she wondered as the distant, clinking, chit-chatting sounds of the party filtered in through the partially open door.

Behind a corner on the second-floor landing, Nadine pressed herself back to the wall. She risked a quick glance around the corner. Timed just right – she saw the backs of Daniel Garsante and Valerie Neiman making their way down the wide staircase. Fortune is certainly raining down on me tonight, thought Nadine, smiling a slow, secret smile.

She watched the two of them disappear down the stairs. They looked very proper, not a hair out of place, and walking with a good four inches between them. Unlike ten minutes ago, thought Nadine wryly. When she had seen them through the doorway of the study, bodies pressed close, Valerie Neiman had been flat on her back on a desk, Daniel Garsante leaning over her.

Nadine wasn't sure what she expected when she had seen the two of them disappear upstairs and curiosity had compelled her to follow. She had to admit it, she had felt a little turned on. Watching them. They were good-looking people after all. But that wasn't the reason why her heart was now beating a lot faster than normal. Not at all.

The reason her heart was beating faster and she was bristling with excitement and she couldn't wipe the smile from her lovely lips all had to do with a minor incident played out in the middle of the couple's love-making, when Daniel Garsante had picked up a box file, carried it to a cabinet, and placed it in the confines of a safe inside that cabinet. The reason her heart was beating faster was that she, unlike Valerie, had had no qualms about watching, about memorising Daniel's combination.

The reason her heart was beating faster was because of what she had seen inside the safe.

Chapter Nine

M oney!
      Lots of it. Right when she needed it. Right when Uncle Willem had cut off her allowance and told her to fend for herself.

Nadine edged out from the corner. There was no one else about. She was two floors up from the party and the landing was quiet save the party sounds filtering up from below. Daniel and Valerie had long since disappeared. The landing was empty. She was sure she was alone.

She moved silently along the landing, thick carpet swallowing the sounds of her footsteps. Her dress swished quietly around her ankles as she moved but there was no one to hear it and it didn't bother her at all. She reached the archway she had passed through before. Down the same two steps. On to the circular landing once again.

She faced the fine oak door off the landing. It was closed now. Did she dare do it? she asked herself, staring at that big, closed door. All that she needed, wanted, lay behind that door. And here she was in front of that door, alone and quiet, with the means at her disposal to take just what she wanted.

She took a deep breath. She was thoughtful. Her

heartbeat had slowed to normal. She felt cool, in control. She was icily calm.

Yes, she decided without qualms. She could do it.

The door knob was smooth and rounded, cold when she touched it. It turned so easily, a tool of complicity, aiding and abetting in its silent simplicity. She opened the door a crack, slid through it, closed it again. Daniel had switched off the lights, the room was dark now. She stayed by the wall, giving her eyes time to adjust to the darkness. Gradually, shapes and images came into view – she could make out the desk near the centre of the room and the large dark cabinet against the wall.

Taking her time, edging carefully around the night-shrouded furniture, she moved purposefully towards the cabinet. Nearer and nearer, while it waited patiently for her. Another friend, silent and welcoming.

She bumped her hip against the corner of the desk. Damn, she cursed, rubbing at the spot, glaring malevolently at the not-so-friendly desk.

She was there now, in front of the cabinet. She knelt down, lifting the hem of her dress, careful not to catch it with her shoes. A gentle pull and the cabinet opened. A door behind a door, the second a muted silver-grey.

'Now, sweet honey,' she purred under her breath, reaching to the rounded black dial a quarter of the way down the door. Touching it lightly between her forefinger and thumb, she prepared to twist. Thank God her uncle's short-sight didn't run in the family, she thought, praying that she had seen the numbers correctly when Daniel had used the combination. It had been a strain – she had had to screw up her eyes to see properly and concentrate for all she was worth. Then she'd had to memorise the numbers, playing them through her mind even whilst she watched Daniel and Valerie, even as she'd finally crept away and bided her time in that corner. If this worked, she more than deserved it, she thought. All that hellish concentration.

She twisted forward, she twisted backwards. Seven little digits, in the right sequence, all that stood between her and her future. Computer-like, she recalled the numbers. Click, click, click . . .

'OK, sweetheart,' she murmured at the final twist.

The final number and the lock released. Like a dream the door clicked ajar.

Thank you. Oh Lord, thank you, she mouthed silently, slipping her finger inside the inner edge of the door, tapping it to open it.

She wanted to squeal with delight. Instead she bit her smiling bottom lip. She had never seen such a beautiful sight. Such a neatly stacked-up, beautiful sight. Bundles of bank-new dollar bills, bound with rubber bands, arranged at the forefront of the shelf.

For a moment she looked at them, taking in the sight. Then she picked up one of the packs, the feel of the crisp, clean banknotes sending a shiver of pleasure down her back. She picked up another one, then two more, then more until her hands were full of these bound-up bundles of bills. It was almost erotic, holding this much money in her hands. No more kowtowing to Uncle Willem, no more boring duty visits to the fruit farm. With this, she could have anything she wanted, go anywhere, do anything.

Methodically, she began to remove the money from the safe, stacking it up on the floor by her side. When she had finished, she closed both doors, carefully wiping anything she had touched with the hem of her dress. She wasn't sure why, some faint thought about fingerprints.

As she looked at the money stacked on the floor, a thought occurred to her somewhat belatedly. How in hell was she going to get it out of there? Her evening purse barely had room for her lipstick. Useless, she thought, snapping her purse shut impatiently. Her mind began to tick over, calculating, thinking, resolute. Still kneeling, still thinking, she played her eyes over the dark carpet. Something bright by the leg of the desk caught her eye. Like a panther stretching out in the darkness, she leant over to investigate. It was sparkly.

She leant even further to pick it up. It was an earring, bright and pretty, like a diamond but not quite. A whitish, cut-glass imitation; Nadine could spot the difference a mile off. Her smile grew wider – only one person here tonight who couldn't afford diamonds, that same person who had been writhing in ecstasy on the desk not more than half an hour ago. Valerie Neiman.

An idea was forming in Nadine's mind even as she was trying to solve the problem of transporting the money out of the house. The seed of the idea was already there when her perfect vision picked out an item leaning innocuously against another leg of the desk. It looked like a briefcase. It was a briefcase.

Grabbing it, Nadine began quickly to pile the money inside. As she triumphantly flipped the locks shut, every dollar safely ensconced inside the case, that seed of an idea began to grow to fruition. It was Valerie's earring that she had found, Nadine was sure of it, and it was Valerie who had been in the room with Daniel when he had opened up the safe. If she placed the earring very close to the safe, it would be Valerie that Daniel would think of when he found the money gone. Naturally, therefore, Valerie would be his first suspect.

Perfect, Nadine thought, casually dropping the earring just by the cabinet. How entirely perfect.

She stood up straight, the briefcase firmly in her hand, and found her way back to the door.

Only one final obstacle and then the deed was done, to get outside to the car without being seen and to hide the money away.

Nadine glided smoothly out on to the terrace. A very faint flush tinged her high cheekbones and the hemline of her dress was slightly ruched from where she had been kneeling and wiping down fingerprints. There were no other outward signs of what she had just done.

Accomplished, Nadine would have preferred to have it called. No other outward signs of what she had successfully accomplished.

It had all been so painfully easy. She had made it to Mark's car without seeing anyone, slipping the brief-case in the back before wandering innocently back into the party.

Now she was euphoric. She had pulled it off – she was dizzy with excitement. She wanted to celebrate, she wanted a drink, and she wanted Mark.

He wasn't on the terrace. She went back inside. Weaving through the party guests to find him, she caught sight of Daniel not far away. Valerie was standing next to him. Valerie looked radiant, her light-blonde hair framing her face in that short, tousled bob she favoured. Every so often, Nadine noticed, Daniel and Valerie caught each other's eye and exchanged an intimate knowing kind of look. Nadine also happened to notice Valerie's right earlobe sparkled brightly whilst her left earlobe, very definitely, did not. Thinking of that other earring, lying in front of a certain cabinet, sent a little thrill through Nadine's body. She smiled prettily at no one in particular and moved on to find Mark.

She found him at last. He was standing around, sipping champagne, looking effortlessly sexy. Boy, was he handsome, she thought, trying to look at him as though he were a stranger.

Mark Kelton was indeed a handsome man. He had those crinkly, bright blue eyes that beckoned and enticed, promising the world, a wicked, wicked world. His hair was shortish, light brown, with the slightest of waves which always gave it the air of being ruffled. Mine, Nadine thought with a buzz, my Mark.

Her Mark was not standing alone, she observed. A tall, skinny Scandinavian girl was hovering close by his side. A little too close, reflected Nadine. Under normal circumstances she would have been annoyed, waltzing up to Mark and cutting off the Scandinavian's advances with a comment as sharp as barbed wire. But nothing could dampen her excitement now nor detract from her achievement; she had solved her financial crisis in the blink of an eye and not only that, she had done her very best to lay suspicion firmly at Valerie's door. What more could a girl ask of an evening out?

'Hey, baby,' she said softly to Mark.

Mark flashed an irreverent smile. 'Where were you?' he asked. 'I've been scouting all over.'

Nadine leant towards him, accidentally jabbing the Scandinavian hard in the ribs with the tip of her elbow. 'Tell you later,' she purred in Mark's ear.

Mark looked at her, raising an eyebrow in query.

She pressed her forefinger to her lips in a shushing gesture of conspiracy and Mark took the hint. He shrugged his shoulders, flashed another smile, and slipped his arm around her waist.

The Scandinavian, nursing a bruised ego as well as bruised ribs, teetered off in search of some solace.

'The silver Lexus,' said Mark, pointing out the car and handing his car keys to one of the parking valets.

'It's just over there by that tree,' muttered Nadine, 'why don't we get it ourselves?'

Mark glanced sideways at her. She sounded strangely jittery, not like herself. 'What's the problem?' he asked.

'No problem,' she said tightly.

A minute later, their car appeared in front of them. Nadine still seemed edgy, and remained so the whole time while they got in the car and drove off down the wide, tree-lined driveway. When they were well on their way on the road, she reached round to the back of his seat and appeared to feel around on the floor of the car. Only then did she appear to relax.

'Lost something?' asked Mark.

'No,' she answered quietly. She turned to him with a slow, stealthy smile. 'No,' she repeated again, as if to herself.

Mark looked to the front, driving steadily. He was puzzled. For the better part of the evening, ever since Nadine had rejoined him after disappearing on her own for a while, she had been acting a little strange.

Excited, worked-up. And she had been so eager to leave the party, checking the time constantly as though marking time until it was a decent hour to go. Then just now, whilst they waited for their car, she had been like a cat on hot bricks.

'Everything OK, honey?' he asked, a touch of concern in his voice.

'Better than OK,' she answered, putting her hand on his thigh. She let it rest there and they drove on in silence for a while.

Gradually, Mark became aware of her moving her hand gently, rubbing her palm round and round on his thigh.

'That's nice,' he murmured.

Her hand began to wander upward, kneading at the join of his thigh and groin. A pleasant band of warmth wound its way around his crotch. She slipped her hand between his legs, feeling for his balls. The more she felt him, the hotter he became, the band of heat tightening like a belt around his groin. His cock grew harder and he felt tiny pleasant tugs deep inside his balls.

'Oh yeah,' he encouraged, spreading his legs slightly wider.

Nadine didn't speak. He felt her pull lightly at his fly, open the buttons on his undershorts ... and the next thing he felt was freedom. Hot night air caressing him, gentle fingers caressing him. He glanced down into his lap. She had pulled out his cock and his balls. She was cupping his sac in her right hand, clasping his penis in her left. She was squeezing and stroking in skilful alternation. And the warmth got steadily warmer. He shot his eyes back to the road.

'Christ,' he groaned as she worked on him, the heat getting out of control now, spreading like a forest fire. It felt like molten rock pumping between his legs. Flames began to lick at his lower belly. In total contrast, his lips were dry. He ran his tongue over them, trying at the same time to concentrate on driving.

His hands were shaking on the wheel. The road was

wide and dark, no other cars around. He licked his lips again and tasted the saltiness of sweat along his upper lip. Concentrating on the dark, dark road ahead. Exquisite fingers in his lap. His lips dry. The salt of sweat.

'Have to,' he gasped, swerving into the side, 'I have to pull in!'

'So pull in,' said Nadine smoothly, her green eyes clear and shining in the darkness. She did not stop what she was doing for a second.

Mark pulled on the handbrake whilst Nadine pulled on his penis.

'That's so good,' he coaxed, leaning back in his seat, stretching out his legs in front. He wanted to stretch back, he wanted more leg-room, so he reached for the handle and slid his seat back. Or rather, he tried to slide his seat back. Something prevented it, something solid and obstructive behind his seat.

'What the hell – !' he began, turning his head.

Nadine pressed her finger to his jaw, coaxing his face back around to face the front. 'Don't get distracted, honey,' she murmured in a soft, cracked voice, working her hand firmly to the tip of his cock. She passed her thumb over the sensitive head, and darts of pleasure ran up the shaft.

'Don't get what?' he muttered, resting back his head and closing his eyes and giving in totally to delicious temptation.

They arrived back at Nadine's house about forty-five minutes later. By then, Mark had recovered his energies, and he was feeling very genial, floating on a cloud of post-orgasmic bliss. Nadine, on the other hand, still seemed to be simmering, as though a tide of excitement was just waiting to explode from inside her.

They entered the living room. Nadine went right in, tossing her evening purse carelessly on the sofa. She walked past the light switch, not bothering to flick it on. Mark didn't either. He followed her in quietly. Her manner was starting to affect him, her tightness, her excitement. Something was going on, he could sense it, something in the air between them, and the more he sensed it, the more insidious it became, working its way under his skin until a kind of taut excitement crept inside him too.

They stood in silence in the darkness. Mark could see the silhouette of a palm tree outside, the palm fronds high and shadowy against the night sky. A gentle breeze must have got up because the fronds wavered slightly, casting flickering shadows into the room.

'Nadine?' he said softly.

She was a foot or so away from him, staring out of the window. Her face was in profile, still and reflective and beautiful, her eyelashes lowered, her long, dark hair tumbling to her shoulders and then lost to him in the shadows.

'Nadine?' he said again, wondering if she had heard him the first time.

'I think there's a storm getting up,' she said quietly.

He looked out to the pool. She was right. The breeze was picking up, blowing ripples across the surface of the water. It seemed to fit somehow. It seemed to fit the mood in the room, the hot, sultry mix of tension and excitement.

She turned to him. 'Make love to me, Mark,' she said, her voice low and urgent. 'Make love to me.'

He took hold of her hands, gazing into her lovely face, and as suddenly as the storm whipping up outside, she reached up to his mouth, devouring him like a hungry lioness. He kissed her back, sucking the excitement from inside her mouth. He felt her dig her fingernails into the backs of his hands. Little racks of pain that exacerbated his passion.

'Over here,' he said gruffly, pulling her over to the fireplace.

He pushed her in front of the fireplace. He was far stronger than she was and maybe a little rough, but that didn't matter because he knew by instinct this was exactly what she wanted. She was loving every moment, he could tell.

She faced the fireplace, he stood behind her. Their breath cut through the air with quick, sharp incisiveness.

Mark swept her hair to one side and then felt for the tongue of the zipper at the back of her dress. Quickly, he pulled down the zipper and pushed the straps of the dress off her shoulders. It fell to her waist, baring the upper part of her back. She wriggled her hips as Mark curled his fingers into the garment, wresting it down her hips and legs. When the dress lay crumpled round her ankles, she kicked it hurriedly away.

She had not been wearing any panties. She was nude now, except for high, narrow-heeled sandals with fine black straps round her ankles.

Mark lifted her arms and spread them wide. She grabbed a hold of the high mantel for support. He rearranged her hair over her shoulders and back and then let his knuckles play down the length of her spine. She looked magnificent, arms spread high, slender back gleaming.

He dropped his hand to the curve of her bottom, spanning it over her smooth rounded cheeks. Her skin felt hot, slightly moist.

'Open up your legs, baby,' he said hoarsely.

She stepped apart, and he was able to see the space between the tops of her legs. Very lightly, because he was teasing himself as much as he was her, he touched between her legs, feeling the trim fissure of hair along her cleft, the velvet nudity in between.

Nadine twisted her head round, her eyes flashing like jags of emerald.

'Lick me, Mark,' she said, that note of strange excitement still hovering in her tone.

'Lean forward,' he said breathlessly.

She leant forward a bit while he knelt down behind her. His face was on a level with her bottom. By leaning over slightly, she had curved her bottom outwards and

93

Mark was all but lost in the sight that was in front of him. Eagerly, he clasped her buttocks in his hands and pressed his nose to their silken join, breathing in the faint delectable scent of her, that heady mix all of her own, of soap and freshness and special tang of sex. It rocked him right through to his toes and he pushed his tongue into her crease, craving her taste.

She caught her breath as he did this. Up her bottom crease he pushed his tongue, squeezing her firm smooth cheeks at the same time. Down her crease he brought his tongue, savouring every moment, taking his time.

Nadine jerked her shoulders and sighed. 'Oh honey,' she said over and over.

Mark withdrew his tongue for a moment, teasing, all the time teasing.

'Don't stop,' Nadine urged.

'I won't,' he promised, rubbing his thumbs up the insides of her thighs.

He glanced up at her. She had tipped her head back slightly, and ribbons of her shiny, dark hair swept across her shoulders and upper back. Her body was lithe and toned, her waist minuscule, her bottom pert and pretty. He couldn't drag his eyes from her – desire seemed to tighten in his chest as he looked.

'Nadine,' he said croakily, keeping his hands on the insides of her long, supple thighs. 'I want to see you, every inch of you.'

The look in her eyes, knowing and desirous, made his stomach twist.

'Mmm,' she answered, already dropping her arms and taking her hands off the high mantel.

Lower down, there were two small recesses inlaid in the marble to either side of the fireplace. Nadine bent forward and pushed her hands on these to support herself. Then she moved her legs wide apart.

Mark sighed appreciatively. 'Oh yeah.'

He leant back on his heels for a moment. By leaning over further, Nadine had arched her back and curved her bottom right out, by stepping so widely apart she had opened herself up entirely. Mark was transfixed, barely aware of the low dull ache in his groin that the sight of Nadine was exacting. Her bare bottom was parted now, the lovely, intimate seam exposed, pale pink and shiny and with her tiny roseate anus just peeking out to him. Below, her sex, succulent and rich, fringed towards the front with neat, dusky down.

Mark placed his finger gently on her clitoris. She was already swollen. He drew his finger backwards, Nadine's small gasps of pleasure acting like a musical aphrodisiac, making his semi-hard cock stir into life.

Her dew collected on his fingertip as he touched her, and, as he dragged it carefully backwards up her bottom crease, he could see for himself, despite the opaque shadowy light, the way her crease began to glisten with moisture.

He pressed his finger suddenly to the mouth of her bottom and she flinched delightedly. He rubbed her moisture round a little, wetting and playing with the dry little opening, then letting his fingers drift back to the plumper, wetter area of her sex.

Nadine was moaning quietly, bending her knees and dropping herself down on to his fingers. He swirled his finger round her clitoral bud, watching her sway her hips to an inner sexual beat, watching her bottom move in identical rhythm. It was more than he could stand. Not taking his hand from between her legs, he pressed his mouth to her buttock cheeks and began to kiss each satin globe. He swirled his finger on, round and round her sex, feeling the hardness at her centre and the smooth, wet softness round about and at the same time his lips caressed her cheeks, nibbling, kissing, naturally drawn to the glossy line in between.

'Oh God,' she murmured, as he flicked at her bottom opening with the tip of his tongue.

Still his fingers massaged between her open legs and the more he flicked at her bottom with his tongue, the more she seemed to press her sex down and thrust her hips gently backwards and forwards.

Outside, the breeze was getting stronger, the shadows in the room now jumping and dancing, criss-crossing over them like prancing figurines. Droplets of rain began to pat at the windows and the air in the room was humid and hot. But Mark was oblivious to it all.

He was centred on Nadine, on her movements, her sounds, her scent. Where his hand rested on the outside of her thigh, he could feel the sizzling hotness of her skin. It contrasted with his other hand, working between her legs, feeling her moistness, and with his tongue flicking at her bottom, making her wet.

She tried to bend her knees a bit more and, as she did so, Mark suddenly pushed his tongue inside her tight, petalled bottom. She thrust back instantly, moaning loudly, and, before she had time to move again, he popped his middle finger up into her sex. This time she jerked forward. Quickly, Mark achieved a dual kind of rhythm, working his finger and tongue simultaneously, stimulating her both front and back.

'So good,' she moaned. 'Mmm, yes, baby, so good . . .'

Her voice trailed off as she lost her breath, panting and sighing and dipping her knees.

Between her legs she was very swollen, very aroused – her sex felt delicious, like the succulent flesh of a soft ripe peach. There was perspiration on her thigh now, hot and damp.

'More,' she was saying. 'Don't stop, please, don't stop.'

Mark had no intention of stopping. He worked his finger and tongue in skilful partnership. Up and down. Gentle, steady, shallow penetration.

'Yes,' moaned Nadine, forcing herself on to him, pushing her bottom backwards, pressing her sex downward. She couldn't keep still, writhing in obvious delight, nudging herself deliriously against him.

96

He knew when she was coming. He felt the sudden sweet rush on his finger and the lovely, fluttery spasms round his tongue. She bucked with unbridled joy, gripping the shelves and crying out loud, so clearly utterly consumed by it all. He kept her going, pulling his finger from her sex and rubbing her clitoris with quick, deft strokes and pushing his tongue further into her bottom, milking every ounce of ecstasy from inside her.

'Oh God, Mark,' she sighed eventually, glancing round at him.

Her face was radiant, glowing with pleasure. He could sense her legs were beginning to tremble and he let her slip down to the floor beside him.

'That was unbelievable,' she murmured.

The shadows in the darkness still twisted and moved and the rain was patting harder at the windows. It was very, very hot in the room. Mark felt the heat, and it intensified the burning sense of arousal in his groin. But he chose for the moment to ignore it. Instead he traced his finger down Nadine's bare upper arm. She turned to look at him, tendrils of long hair tousled round her face, eyes bright, shining with secrets.

'Now, sweetheart,' he said, his voice hushed, 'how about you tell me exactly what's going on . . .'

Chapter Ten

She stood up slowly. Without a word, she disappeared upstairs, returning in a matter of seconds. She had put on a violet silk wrap and, standing in front of him, tying the belt, she still said nothing. Her face was inscrutable, her expression bland, but the fervent gleam in her eyes was enough. Grabbing his car keys, she went out the front door.

Mark sat down on the sofa and waited. He heard the sounds of the storm through the open doorway, the rain lashing to the ground, the hot wind rushing through the palms and bushes.

The door slammed shut and she was back beside him. Her hair was slick with water and her damp wrap clung like a translucent film to the curves of her body. She placed something on the carpet between them.

'There,' she said softly.

Mark looked down. He saw a black briefcase, the leather fine and smooth and clearly very expensive.

'What's this?' he asked, shrugging his shoulders.

'Our future,' she purred. 'Our lovely, lazy future, baby.'

Mark was gazing at the briefcase. He was getting an uneasy feeling, something about the case seemed familiar in some way. And Nadine's cryptic words were strange; her lyrical tone was strange. He knew this was something big and he was getting spooked. He was definitely getting spooked.

As he looked harder at the case, suspicion came down on him like a swooping bird of prey. And then he saw the two initials, inlaid in gold on the side of the case, and there was no further need for conjecture. The initials read D.G. Who else but Daniel Garsante. His boss.

Nadine was kneeling by the side of the case, letting her fingers drift seductively over the end. A triumphant half-smile played on her lips.

'What the hell have you done?' asked Mark, fearing her answer. His voice sounded raspy even to himself.

'Opportunity came a-knocking,' she replied. 'And I answered.'

'And what exactly does that mean?'

'It was like a gift, Mark. Honestly.' As if to vindicate herself, she flicked up the clasps and pulled the case open.

'Jesus!' he cried, surveying row after row of pristine dollar bills. Bills of all denominations. Filling the case, just like in a movie.

He raked his fingers back through his hair, staring fixedly at the money. 'Nadine,' he said earnestly, 'what is this? What did you do?'

'I did what I had to do,' she said lightly, still smiling that smile of triumph. 'I've dealt with my financial situation, and on top of that I've got us everything we could ever want.'

Mark looked at her in disbelief. 'What did you do?' he repeated, stopping after each word in a jumpy, staccato-type beat.

'I stole it,' she said softly. 'I took it from a safe in Daniel Garsante's office. I put it in a briefcase I found there, and then I hid it away behind the seat in your car.'

'You stole it,' Mark nodded, not sure he was taking

this in right. 'You actually stole this amount of money from Daniel Garsante?'

'Yes.'

'At the party tonight?'

'Yes.'

'You little fool,' he whispered.

Nadine glanced up at him sharply, the smile frozen in place on her face. 'Take a good look at this money,' she said tightly. 'And then dare to call me a fool.'

Mark pushed his hands against his outspread knees and leant forward. 'You really have no concept of what you've done, do you? You don't know what you're dealing with. You have stolen from a man that you shouldn't look crossways at, never mind steal from. Don't forget he's my boss, I know the man, I know how he works, I know what makes him tick. In business, I've seen him break people, powerful people, and throw them to the wolves without a second thought.'

For the first time, Nadine's smile faltered a little. Then she lifted her chin, a glint of steel in her eyes. 'He won't find out, Mark,' she said calmly. 'I was so careful, it was perfect. He'll never know it was me.'

'Don't you believe it,' muttered Mark. 'The man has a long, long reach, and I guarantee he won't stop until he finds out who did this.'

'But he *won't* find out, I made sure of that,' insisted Nadine. 'I tell you it was perfect. I covered every single, itsy-bitsy one of my tracks. I've done all the hard stuff, now all we have to do is to take this money, bank it somewhere safe away from here, and then lie back and enjoy the rest of our lives.'

Mark slumped against the back of the sofa and blew out a heavy sigh. He shook his head gently. The rain had stopped and the wind had eased and the increasing quiet in the room seemed to bind itself to the humidity, closing in around him like a heavy cloud of smog. He undid another button at the neck of his shirt, pulled off his tie, and tried to stay calm, to straighten out his thoughts. Nadine was still kneeling at his feet, watching him.

'Think of it, Mark,' she whispered. 'We can do whatever we want. You'll never have to work for someone else again. With this sort of money, you can give up work. Or work for yourself.'

Her voice was enthralling, hypnotic. He palmed his hand down his face, and looked at her curled at his feet, guarding her spoils by her side.

'Look,' she urged, lifting the case up in front of him. 'See it all. Whatever we want, Mark. Whatever you want.'

There was such a lot of it. How in God's name had she got away with it, piled it all up and hidden it away in the car?

'Look, Mark,' she whispered again, her words floating wonderfully in the air, making him want to look. He did look. So much money. So many possibilities. All there in that case. He thought for a moment, shutting out everything, trying to think rational thoughts. His whole life he'd worked hard; he had put himself through college, worked his way through graduate school, endured endless nights of waiting tables and tending bar and then studying on through the night. There had been times when he thought sleep was a gift other people got, not him. No, sir, it hadn't been easy, no college trust fund set up for him, no moneyed parents to bale him out – his parents barely even had a dime to call their own. But the struggle had been worth it, he had achieved his goal. He was a lawyer and a goddamn good one at that. He was very well paid and he was respected; in short, at age thirty-one, he had made it.

Or had he?

He pressed his fingertips to his temples, easing the pressure that seemed to be building behind his eyes.

Had he made it? Who really benefited when he pulled off a deal? When he worked late into the night, unravelling the web of corporate law, picking his way through the legal minefield and searching out the loophole that would take the company forward, who really got the credit for all that? Not him, not Mark Kelton. Sure, he got a pat on the back and a nice fat paycheque and he even got a vicarious kick when the company closed in for the kill. But who really got the credit? One man, and that man's company, that's who.

Mark looked into the case again. Now here was that man's money, looking so fine in the bottom of the case, probably money that Mark's expertise had earned him in the first place.

'Whatever we want, Mark.' Nadine's soft voice broke into his thoughts. He glanced at her. She was so beautiful, with her wet hair framing her face and her smooth bare legs curled beneath her. She was sitting at his feet holding forth the money, like a lovely handmaiden proffering a gift. She was being so generous and he had called her a fool. She was offering to share the money and enjoy it together and he'd had the ingratitude to call her a fool. She had acted alone when she took it; nothing to stop her from keeping it all to herself. He would have been none the wiser. She could have disappeared into the night and he would never have known where or why.

There was so much of it and it was so tempting.

'How can you be sure he wouldn't find out who took it?' asked Mark, clutching at a reason not to go along with this.

She looked at him from beneath lowered eyelashes, so calm and self-assured in her reply. 'I know because I took care of it,' she said.

There was just so goddamn much of it. She had done all the hard part and she was so sure it was perfect and she was so gorgeous and generous and, hell, he'd probably earned the money for Garsante anyway.

He smiled slowly down at her. 'When do we leave?' he asked quietly.

She smiled back. 'First thing in the morning,' she said, leaning up to kiss him.

'I think we should celebrate, don't you?' he murmured against her mouth.

'I surely do,' she answered back, climbing astride his lap and shrugging off her damp robe. A rustle of silk and it fell to the floor. Then the celebrations began in earnest.

The following morning was bright and dry, the sky was cloudless, the sun was dazzling, leaves and lawns shone with polished lustre. There was a certain freshness about everything, as though the storm of the night before had literally washed the air clean.

Mark hadn't slept much. He had lain with Nadine curled against his side, sexually exhausted the two of them, but restful sleep had eluded him. There was just one thing on his mind – the money, and the more he tried to ignore it, the more it dug its stubborn heels into his mind. He wasn't torn in any way; he had made his decision and he was more than happy with it. No, the reason he could not sleep was because his thoughts were now revolving around a positive plan of action. Where to go and how to get there? And perhaps most important of all, how not to arouse suspicion?

By 5.00 a.m. he had it all worked out and he drifted off into a dreamy slumber. An hour later he was wide awake again, hands laced behind his head, staring restlessly up at the ceiling. He raised his head slightly to look at the clock on the nightstand: 6.00 a.m. Time to be on the move.

'Nadine,' he murmured.

'Mmm?' She stirred sleepily.

'C'mon, honey. We've got a lot to do.'

She lifted her head off his chest, pushing her hair out of her eyes. 'Yeah,' she said, sitting up in bed and stretching gracefully. Then she turned to look at him, her face flushed with anticipation. 'Like what exactly?'

'Like getting on out of here. We'll pack a couple of suitcases and head for Nevada. We'll drive through Saticoy and Santa Clara and pick up the main route across the desert where practically no one will see us and, for sure, no one will know us.'

'My, my,' she said, smiling. 'You've been doing some thinking.'

'I figured I should do my part.' He grinned. 'After all, you did yours. If anyone sees us as we're leaving, we'll make like we're going away on vacation. I've got some vacation days long overdue so tomorrow I'll phone the office and tell them I've decided to take them to head on out and visit my folks. Then we'll find somewhere suitable to bank the money, drive back here, and that will buy us enough time to pack up properly and take off once and for all.'

Nadine nodded in agreement. 'Sounds good to me, lover.'

As she nodded, strands of her hair flicked over her small breasts. Her smooth, pink-brown nipples kept showing in a now-you-see-them-now-you-don't way and Mark found his attention was beginning to wander. Nadine seemed to notice.

'Oh no. For once we have to stay focused,' she said, slipping out from under the sheet and gliding into the bathroom. At the bathroom door, she paused and turned. 'At least until we're on the road,' she added cheekily.

'Yes,' agreed Mark, throwing back the sheets and trying to ignore what was happening in his groin.

Chapter Eleven

*A*t around the same time on Sunday morning that Nadine and Mark were driving out of Santa Barbara, suitcases packed and houses locked up, Daniel Garsante, having breakfasted in his room, was making his way downstairs in his huge seafront home.

Staff were milling about in the ground-floor rooms, clearing away the party debris, carrying out buffet tables, cleaning and polishing and generally putting things back where they belonged. The windows were open to air the rooms and there was a buzz and bustle of activity about the place that Daniel wanted no part of.

He stepped out on to the back terrace. He had dressed in a black cashmere sweater and black jeans, and, though it was early morning, the heat from the sun already seemed intense, his dark clothing absorbing the rays, the resulting heat burning through to his skin. He stepped back into the comfort of the shade and whistled for his dogs.

Seemingly from nowhere two sleek, lean Dobermann pinschers appeared, their glossy black and tan coats shining with health and vitality.

'Hey, fellers,' said Daniel, patting their handsome heads and tugging gently at the short hair around their necks.

They smiled a white-toothed canine smile, and looked besotted up at their master, nuzzling their heads against his legs.

'Come on, boys,' said Daniel, patting his thigh. 'Let's walk.'

He moved off at a brisk pace across the lawns, dogs trotting obediently at his side. They walked for a long while before reaching some steps that led down to the beach, then they walked some more, across a wide stretch of fine pale sand. The dogs bounded happily in and out of the ocean, keeping Daniel within their sights at all times, and, when he whistled sharply and turned round, they were back at his side within moments.

As he neared the house, Daniel glanced down at his watch, surprised to find he had been walking for almost two hours. The dogs flopped down on the terrace, panting and hot. He smiled fondly at them and let them be, then wandered back into the house.

The rooms were no longer teeming with people nor were there any signs there had been a party there at all. Everything gleamed.

Daniel felt good after his walk. The slight post-party headache he had been suffering from had disappeared and the briskness of his long walk had left a pleasant weak ache in his leg muscles.

Ready to deal with a few pressing business matters, he made his way up to his study. It was only when he was seated at his desk, his hands on the smooth, olive-green leather of the desk surface, that he finally let himself think about Valerie. She had really got to him last night; and it wasn't just their lovemaking he was thinking of, it was the whole of the evening after that. They had tried to stay apart. It was, after all, Daniel's largest party of the year, a function designed fundamentally to marry business and social contacts. Valerie clearly understood the importance of his position as host, at times disappearing to the extent that Daniel felt strangely compelled to go and find her, and introduce her to one set of guests after another. After their initial, most intimate encounter, it had been difficult to talk and be alone together but, by using these introductions as a pretext, it had at least given him the excuse to keep her close by. When Valerie had approached to say good-night, that Ashley and Brad were ready to leave and she was travelling home with them, Daniel had found it impossible to shake off a group of business associates in order to say good-night properly. That, for some reason, had annoyed the hell out of him, and thereafter he had found himself being sharp and resentful to his guests when he should have been gracious and entertaining.

He sat at his desk now, wondering about her. Who exactly was she? He knew she was a dancer. He knew she was a good friend of Ashley Ray, who in turn was the wife of his chief financial adviser, Bradley Ray. Apart from that he knew very little, other than she was decidedly attractive, she was confident and direct, the sexual energy between them was phenomenal and, during their short, frenzied lovemaking she had given him the most powerful orgasm he could remember.

What else did he need to know? he thought, frustrated with himself, frustrated that each time he saw her, she piqued his interest further.

Intent on clearing Valerie from his mind, he diverted his attention to those pressing business affairs. He got up from his desk and went to the safe in order to retrieve the box file he had placed there last night.

It was the very first thing he noticed when he opened up the safe. Of course it was. His money had gone. The box file was there, untouched, unopened. But on the shelf below there was nothing. Where there should have been money, plenty of it, there was nothing.

Quite calmly, Daniel rested his hand on top of the heavy metal door, gazed into the safe, and surveyed the emptiness. His mind ticked over. Methodically, he began to calculate when the robbery must have occurred. How it had been done, he would devote time to later.

And when the culprit or culprits were caught, only then would he show any anger. In Daniel Garsante's book, it was not a question of if they were caught, it was when. Daniel had no doubts whatsoever about that.

The money was in the safe early last evening, that left the later part of the evening, the rest of the night, and this morning. He recalled the number of people passing in and out of the house that morning, many of them nameless, faceless people from outside caterers and cleaning agencies. Then he thought of the similar number of people working at the party last night and, on top of that, the party guests themselves. It would be a big job to track each and every one of them down but he would do it. And he would enjoy it.

Swinging the door shut, he took a small step back and felt something crunch underneath his foot.

'And what's this,' he muttered, stooping down to see.

The glass was cracked and the fine gold surround slightly twisted but the item was instantly recognisable as a lady's earring.

Daniel held the earring in his hand, tossing it gently on his palm. He still felt calm and methodical but inside there was a twinge, a stirring of emotion. It wasn't so unusual that he had noticed that about her – after all, he had noticed everything else about Valerie last night. Why so strange that he had noticed she was only wearing one earring?

He pondered a little more. It was feasible the earring had come off during their energetic lovemaking . . . but their lovemaking had taken place on the desk, quite a way from the safe. So how had the earring found its way to the safe unless it had actually been lost there? He recalled how Valerie had kept disappearing last night, to give him the opportunity to concentrate on his other guests – or so he had thought.

He reflected a little further; Valerie's own words from Ashley's dinner party came filtering back – she was a dancer, between shows. Perhaps in need of cash, he mused. She must have caught a glimpse of the money when he opened up the safe last night. Temptation may have proved too strong. He shook his head – it was too much of a coincidence to ignore; he had found his robber far quicker than he had anticipated.

Still tossing the earring on the flat of his hand, he moved to the desk and picked up the phone. Quickly, he punched in her number.

'Valerie,' he began, his voice smooth and low. 'It's Daniel.'

'Hi,' she said softly. Sleepily, he thought.

'Are you free for lunch today? I'd like you to join me.'

'I'd love to,' she answered, her voice as calm and even as his.

'Good,' he said. 'I'll send a car to pick you up.'

'Fine,' she said. 'I'll expect one then.'

A clever girl, mused Daniel as he hung up the phone. To act so calm, to accept an invitation to lunch, to appear as though she had nothing to hide.

Let's see how clever she can stay, he thought, looking at the earring one final time, then slipping it into his trouser pocket.

Valerie arrived wearing jeans and a T-shirt and a pair of straw-coloured wedges that showed off the gleaming tan of her feet and ankles. Her soft, blonde hair was mussy and carefree and she hardly wore any make-up, just a hint of blush and mascara. Valerie had the kind of even-toned, beige complexion that looked so good on brown-eyed, natural blondes, and the perfect smattering of freckles on the tip of her nose almost seemed to have been painted on.

Daniel took one look at her and felt an immediate sensation in his crotch. Thief or not, he thought, she was one good-looking woman.

He smiled charmingly as she came into the house. 'Hi,' he said, taking a step forward.

'Hello, Daniel.'

Taking her gently by the shoulders, he kissed the top of her head first, then the tip of her nose, then brushed his lips across her mouth.

The maid who had shown Valerie in cleared her throat discreetly.

'Where would you like lunch to be served, Mr Garsante?' she asked.

Daniel looked at Valerie. 'On the terrace?' he asked her.

Valerie nodded. 'Great.'

'On the terrace then, please,' he confirmed to the maid, who smiled and nodded and hurried off.

He led Valerie out to the terrace. Immediately, she walked to the front of the terrace and leant on the low stone wall, looking out at the magnificent, sweeping view. Daniel watched her from behind, noticing appreciatively the way the seat of her jeans hugged her firm buttocks.

'I missed you last night,' he said suddenly.

She turned round to him, a look of surprise on her face.

'After you'd gone home,' he explained softly, turning up the charm factor a tad.

She didn't answer, but she did smile. He sensed she wasn't wholly taken in by the charm, but that she liked it all the same.

'But you did leave me a little something to remember you by.' Would that jolt her, would a shadow of guilt pass over her face?

No, not a trace of anything other than curiosity.

'Did I?' she replied, quite puzzled. If Daniel wasn't so sure of her guilt, he would think her confusion was genuine. 'What did I leave?' she added.

Daniel reached into his pocket, watching every flicker on her face as he produced the crushed earring and held it out to show her. 'This,' he said.

'Oh that,' she said with a careless laugh. 'I knew I'd lost it somewhere. Looks like it met with a sticky end.'

She was a cool, cool customer, thought Daniel. 'Yes,'

110

he said, giving nothing away. 'I apologise for that. I stepped on it in my study.'

'Don't worry,' she laughed. 'It's practically worthless anyway.'

Very cool, decided Daniel. 'Actually,' he went on, 'it was in such a strange place, right at the base of my safe cabinet.'

Valerie shrugged, showing no concern. 'It doesn't matter, really,' she insisted. 'It's worthless. It's my fault anyway, it must have flown off when we were –'

'Something else strange happened to me this morning,' said Daniel, cutting in. 'I found that rather a large amount of money had been taken from my safe, and then curiously I found this earring at the base of the safe, and then, even more coincidentally, I remembered how I had opened the safe last night whilst you were in the room with me.'

Valerie just stared at him. After a few moments, an expression of rising incredulity on her face, she spoke. 'What exactly are you saying?'

'I'd prefer you to do the talking.' Daniel smiled, still charming.

Valerie looked at him, white with anger. 'I don't get this,' she said. 'Are you accusing me of something? Are you accusing me of taking your money?'

'Not at all,' said Daniel softly. 'I'd just like to talk with you about it.'

She shook her head angrily. 'I'm not a whore, you know. I don't want your money. And I don't expect to be paid when I've fucked someone!'

She wheeled furiously away from him. 'Call your driver, please,' she said coldly. 'I want to go home.'

Daniel was truly quite impressed at her display of righteous indignation. But he would match her move for move. 'I'm sorry, Valerie,' he apologised. 'I didn't mean to accuse you of anything. I've had a great deal of money stolen and I was lashing out. Please forgive me.'

'Fine,' she answered crisply. 'But I still want to go home.'

'OK, but please say you forgive me.' Flashing black eyes pleading for forgiveness.

She seemed to calm down. 'OK,' she muttered. 'Just call me a car, will you?'

He stepped towards her, touching her upper arm lightly with his fingertips. He grazed her hair with his lips. 'Stay,' he said quietly.

'No, I want to go.'

'I don't want you to,' he murmured. Quickly, before she could object, he kissed her, pressing his lips to hers. As he kissed her, he felt an immediate kick in his crotch, as strong a response as he had ever known. He pulled her to him, kissing her and kissing her until eventually she began to kiss back, her mouth as hungry and desperate as his, the energy between them something primal and basic.

'Stay,' he said again when they finally broke apart.

'OK,' she conceded, breathless and flushed.

Stay for as long as I want you, Daniel thought to himself.

And until I catch you out, he added, almost as an afterthought.

After lunch, they made love; it was wild and uncontrolled. Daniel sensed that Valerie was still angry with him for his accusation and it excited him more. That, on top of their chemistry, really made the sparks fly.

By evening, he had persuaded her to stay for a few days, assuring her that he would send someone over to her apartment to pick up clothes and cosmetics. Daniel had calculated this as a means to catch her out, to have her relaxed and happy, and when she let something slip about the stolen money, as no doubt she would, he would pounce.

But he had other personal reasons for wanting Valerie to stay. His attraction towards her was mounting steadily and he had already decided he wanted to keep her close for his own private agenda.

With this in mind, he excused himself for half an hour after dinner and made two telephone calls to two close friends. One to Teresa and one to Cara. Inviting them to come over tomorrow for some particular fun and games.

He spoke low into the mouthpiece, explaining his wishes in detail. The two girls giggled as he talked. They said they couldn't wait.

Next day, Monday, Daniel told Valerie he had decided not to go to the office but to spend the day with her. Although she gave little away, he sensed she was pleased and flattered. Her annoyance with him appeared to be a thing of the past. She seemed equally pleased when he told her two close friends were calling by to meet her.

Teresa and Cara arrived together, around mid-morning. Both were in their twenties and very attractive. Teresa had straight, very shiny brown hair which fell bluntly to her shoulders, and gleaming olive-toned skin. Cara was blue-eyed with long, fine, buttercup hair layered round her face and neck, ending just above her breasts. They were casually dressed in short cotton sundresses which showed off long bare legs, and slip-on sandals.

Daniel kissed the women's cheeks in greeting and introduced them to Valerie. Cara and Teresa were so open and amiable and Valerie seemed to like them straight away. If she was at all curious as to the nature of their close friendship with Daniel, she certainly did not show it. Soon the three of them were sitting round the table, sipping chilled drinks and chatting like old friends. Daniel merely looked on.

After a while he turned to Valerie. 'Valerie,' he began apologetically, 'there are a few things I should see to today. How about you and the girls go sit and relax around the pool while I go up to the study and get some phone calls out of the way? There are suits in the poolhouse if you want.'

'Sure,' she said easily.

'Teresa? Cara?' he asked.

'Fine,' they chorused.

'OK,' he said, getting up and pecking Valerie on the lips. 'I'll see you in a while.'

Valerie, Teresa and Cara repaired happily to the pool. Set away from the house, it was in a lush, private area. The pool itself was filled with clear, green water which showed a rich, colourful mosaic bottom. Comfortable-looking, green loungers were dotted round the poolside.

Teresa kicked off her shoes and pushed the straps of her sundress off her gleaming shoulders. Valerie could see pale-lemon straps underneath, presumably of a bikini, and she remembered she had to borrow a swimsuit.

'I'm just going to find a suit,' she called out, disappearing into the large poolhouse in the corner. Virtually straight away, she found several suits hanging on a rack in a cupboard. She picked out a black one-piece that looked to be her size and quickly put it on. It fitted perfectly, clinging nicely to her full breasts and cut high on the leg and very low down her back.

'Great,' she murmured, secretly wishing that Daniel was with them so that she could show herself off. The thought made her hot and she made her way to the doorway of the poolhouse, more than ready for a cooling swim.

As she approached the open doorway, she stopped dead in her tracks, catching her breath in surprise. Cara and Teresa were sitting on the side of one of the loungers, facing each other. They were both entirely naked and Cara was busy playing with Teresa's firm breasts, stroking and squeezing whilst Teresa looked down in rapt observation.

Valerie hovered uncertainly in the doorway, embarrassed by what she was seeing. Yet for some reason that she couldn't make out she was not able to look away.

Both Cara and Teresa were slender with nice, medium-sized breasts. As Valerie watched, Teresa's brown-tinged nipples turned erect and pointy and she was smiling widely as Cara continually squeezed them between her fingers. After a short while, Teresa reached for Cara's round breasts, fingering her small pink nipples as Cara uttered tiny mewing sounds of encouragement. The sight of the two of them fondling each other like that made Valerie feel quite peculiar. She wished she could just withdraw into the poolhouse and leave them to it but something was stopping her – her legs felt like lead and she was hotter than ever.

Teresa began to lean forward, closing luscious lips around Cara's nipples, tugging gently with her mouth. Cara eased her shoulders back, pushing her breasts towards Teresa's mouth. Teresa sucked first on one then the other until Cara's nipples stood out, swollen and red. Then Teresa flicked at the swollen tips with the very end of her smooth pink tongue, Cara closing her eyes and sighing with obvious delight.

Valerie leant against the inner edge of the doorframe, wondering what the hell she should do. She felt heavy and feverishly hot and wished desperately that Daniel would appear to rescue her or that she could slip past Cara and Teresa and go find him herself. Instead her leaden feet were weighted to the floor and she couldn't drag her eyes from the spectacle before her.

Oh no! she thought as she watched.

Teresa had leant back on the bed now, and positioned her legs, straight and close together, up in the air at a perfect right angle to her body. Cara had slipped to the ground and was kneeling at the end of the lounger. Slowly, choreographing her movements almost as though she knew she was being watched, Cara leant forward, towards the backs of Teresa's upright legs. She placed her hands around Teresa's slender ankles and gradually began to stroke downward, caressing

115

Teresa's smooth calves and thighs, and moving with a kind of certainty. Valerie only had a side-on view now and she could only really imagine what Cara's hands were doing as they reached the tops of Teresa's long thighs and settled symmetrically on the fleshy, upraised globes of her bottom. Cara massaged there for several long minutes, a look of rapturous concentration on her pretty, flushed face, and then she eased her face forward, pointed out her tongue and began to lick just above the area she was massaging. First her head nodded slowly up and down then she changed to a quicker sideways rhythm, her fair hair flicking across her shoulders and back. Teresa began to sigh and moan, flinging out her arms to the sides, and, as Valerie realised exactly where Cara was stimulating, she was shocked to find her own sex dampening in the swimsuit and twitches of excitement flicker in her groin. She looked about her for a place to sit down and not see any more but still her heavy legs held her fast.

By the time she looked out again, Cara and Teresa had changed position. Cara was now standing, legs slightly astride, her lovely body fully angled towards Valerie. Valerie was sure Cara would be able to see her looking on, but the unseeing expression of rapture on Cara's face seemed to indicate otherwise. Teresa was kneeling in front of Cara, slightly to one side, her face in three-quarter profile so that Valerie could see a similar expression of delight on her face. This time, Valerie could see exactly what was happening.

Teresa was toying playfully with Cara's tiny patch of buff-coloured pubic hair, tugging lightly and brushing with her fingers. After several moments, she moved her first two fingers lower, delving between Cara's legs. Valerie saw Cara's expression brighten. Seconds later, Teresa began to flicker her fingers gently from side to side and Cara glanced down with a joyous laugh.

'Oh yes, honey,' she urged, coaxing her friend on.

Teresa laughed too. 'Faster?' she asked, smiling up at her.

'Yes!' gasped Cara, lifting up her hair, running her hands all over her own neck and breasts.

Teresa flicked her fingers faster and faster, arousing with increasing vigour.

Cara still seemed to want more, stepping wider apart, thrusting her smooth hips forward, urging Teresa on. She rolled her thumbs roughly over her nipples whilst Teresa worked her fingers between her legs.

Valerie was so caught up in the sight she had no inkling of anything else. That was why she jumped out of her skin when Daniel appeared outside the door, cool, handsome, and with a knowing smile on his face.

Valerie, hot and aroused, was uncharacteristically flustered. She said nothing.

'Come on,' murmured Daniel, grasping her hand and leading her back into the poolhouse. 'Let's leave the girls to it,' he said softly, as he closed the door behind her. The smile on his face told her everything. He had arranged it all, the whole display, the whole shebang. And what was worse, she didn't even care. She was so worked up, so wild for him, that she just didn't care.

She tugged at his shirt, hearing buttons pop as she pushed it off his body. She ran her hands over the hard, dark muscles of his chest, savouring its new familiarity, adoring the way she knew the feel of him now, the way his taut, flat stomach always flickered when she ran her tongue over it, the way he always groaned fleetingly when he entered her.

She grabbed for his trousers. Daniel didn't move to help her. He stood very still, letting her undress him, his eyes and smile watchful. But when she wrenched down his trousers and undershorts, she saw the weight and stiffness of his excited cock, jutting magnificently from his body.

Dropping straight to her knees, she closed her lips around the lovely, smooth end, letting her tongue touch and tease the small slit. Daniel's cock jerked in her mouth and she moved her hands to the rigid shaft, holding it firm as she sucked on the head.

117

He uttered a small groan, placing his hands on the back of her head, twisting his fingers through her hair.

She pushed her mouth further on to his cock, letting it fill her, and then she moved her mouth smoothly up and down until Daniel began gently urging his naked hips back and forth.

For a moment, as she stimulated, she looked up and saw him looking down at her. His dark eyes glowed with voracious desire; she knew how she was already feeling, her tummy churning with excitement, her body taut like a spring, but that look in his eyes drove her on. Desperately, she bobbed her head back and forth, unable to get enough of him. His penis was like rock and she could see the sweat shine on his stomach.

Suddenly he jerked back, pulling himself out of her mouth.

'Here, sweetheart,' he gasped, lifting her up from under her arms. She stood shakily in front of him, still with the delicious man taste of him in her mouth, on her lips. He pulled at her swimsuit, as desperate now as she was. Pushing the straps off her shoulders, he wrested the clinging garment down off her body. Valerie felt gloriously liberated, her full breasts jiggling as he tugged the garment down her legs, then flung it haphazardly to one side.

Her breasts felt swollen and moist and ached for his touch. As he nudged her back to the wall, he covered his hands over them, kneading and feeling, until Valerie's stomach felt scorched with heat.

'God, Daniel,' she urged, backing against the wall, feeling cool plaster meeting her buttocks.

He pressed himself to her, squashing her breasts with his hard, hot chest. She parted her legs. She was wet and swollen and ready, and he pushed straight inside her. Instant relief as he penetrated fully.

He began to move urgently, pumping his hips, giving so much joy and pleasure that she could hardly keep up with it. Her abdomen flared with magical sensations as he thrust his cock smoothly up and down. She pressed herself to him, feeling their flesh stick together, sticky with sweat, and she wrapped her arms up around his neck, stepping up on tiptoe, letting him push her further up the wall.

Her bare back and buttocks rubbed against the wall but it didn't matter. Nothing seemed to matter but the burning pleasure between her legs and the leaping frenzy of her insides.

She climaxed first, digging her nails into his shoulders, shuddering in ecstasy and losing her thoughts in fantastic delirium. Her body pulsated in a rhythmic orgasm while her mind danced with sexual euphoria.

As her climax ebbed away, Daniel still moved within her like a madman, her sex and vagina tingling with hypersensitivity.

'Yeah,' he groaned, as he started to come. He pressed his hands to the wall by her head, grinding his hips against hers.

Determined to intensify his pleasure, she slipped a finger between his hard buttocks, stimulating the sensitive skin of his crease.

His hips seemed to pump with a will of their own. She sensed he was almost there and pressed her finger-pad gently to his bottom.

'Oh baby, yes!' he cried out as he came.

He pressed against her, pushing right inside her. She held him tightly as his climax took control, then they slumped together to the floor, chests heaving, bodies flushed.

'I like sex with you,' murmured Valerie in an understatement.

Daniel was sitting with his back to the wall, knees up and parted. He was resting his forearms on his knees, still catching his breath. He glanced towards her, then reached over and cupped her chin.

'And I like sex with you,' he said softly. 'And I'm going to like it even more.'

'Oh yes?' asked Valerie, intrigued. 'How's that then?'

Daniel got up and held out his hand to pull her up. 'You'll see,' he said as their hands met. 'Very soon, I promise, you'll see.'

Valerie wasn't sure what to make of it. But then she wasn't sure what to make of any of this, this stay at Daniel's. Or indeed Daniel himself. She was more attracted to him than to anyone ever before, she knew that. She was more sexually fulfilled than ever before. She felt satisfied and happy and yet thoughts lingered at the back of her mind – that absurd conversation about stolen money for one, Teresa's and Cara's sexual display for another.

She let him clasp her hand in his strong, firm grip. He pulled her up like she weighed nothing at all. So many facets to this man, she thought, studying his dark, handsome face. So many layers to peel away. What exactly was this new relationship? Was it love? Or something else?

As he laced his fingers through hers, she felt tiny charges run up her wrist. He led her into the poolhouse shower and she shoved all these thoughts out of her mind. Whatever the hell it was, she knew one thing. She wanted more and more of it.

Chapter Twelve

*B*y the time they had showered and dressed and emerged from the poolhouse, it was early afternoon. There were no signs of Teresa and Cara around the pool.

Valerie and Daniel walked hand in hand across the wide lawn back to the house. Valerie's hair was still wet from the shower and she had combed her short bob into the nape of her neck. The sun was at its hottest and, as they walked, she was glad of the cooling dampness of her hair against her skin. Daniel's hair was damp too, combed back and blacker than ever, and there were droplets of water on the shoulders of his white linen shirt. His lean jawline was shadowed with a very faint stubble which made his skin seem darker than it was but, even through that, his face had a glow that bespoke sexual satiety. Valerie was pleased that she was responsible for that. This man is for me, she thought suddenly, and then nearly stumbled at her own shocking certainty.

'Oops,' she giggled, clinging to his hand as she regained her footing.

'Careful,' said Daniel, flashing her a dazzling smile.

'You've made my legs weak,' she joked.

The smile stayed in place but his eyes hooded over. 'Yes,' was all he said.

Valerie noticed. Maybe he had things on his mind, she thought. Maybe business. Or maybe that robbery, although he hadn't mentioned it again to her since their first fractious conversation about it.

'That money that was stolen,' she began.

He shot her a sharp look. 'What about it?' he said.

'I just wondered what the police had said, whether they have any leads?'

'And why would you wonder that?'

'No reason,' shrugged Valerie, wishing she hadn't asked. 'I thought you looked worried was all.'

Daniel was looking so hard at her now that Valerie began to feel uncomfortable. Finally, he said curtly, 'I have the matter in hand.'

'OK,' she replied. And not knowing why, she swallowed with relief. Well, excuse me for asking, she thought. At least I know not to mention *that* again.

They walked on in silence, Valerie feeling slightly miffed. After all, she had only been showing some concern. A few minutes later, Daniel turned his smile on her again.

'Thank you for asking,' he said, his voice smooth and low, like a tool of seduction all on its own.

Valerie shook her head a little. She was baffled. Fortunately, she was saved from having to think too deeply because she spotted Teresa waving at them from the terrace. She waved back automatically and, before she knew it, they were tripping up the steps to the terrace themselves and joining Teresa round the table.

'Hey,' smiled Teresa. 'I wondered where you guys had got to.'

Daniel didn't answer but leant down to kiss Teresa quickly on the mouth. 'Never mind. We're here now,' he said.

'Where's Cara?' asked Valerie.

'Had to leave to meet with her boyfriend,' said Teresa. 'I hope you don't mind if I stay a while?'

'Not at all,' said Daniel. Valerie wasn't positive but she could have sworn that he and Teresa exchanged a kind of a look.

Daniel pulled out a seat for her and she sat down opposite Teresa. Daniel sat opposite both of them and lit a cigarette.

'California law forbids it, I know,' he said, blowing a curl of smoke lazily out of his nostrils. 'But I am at home.'

'And you are a bad boy,' purred Teresa.

'True,' murmured Daniel, tapping ash into a small, glass ashtray.

Valerie studied Teresa, for the first time wondering about her friendship with Daniel. They knew each other quite well, she could tell. She could be an old girlfriend, she mused, there was certainly a suggestion of something more than friendship. Teresa was looking very pretty, she noticed, her teak hair glossy, her face clear and bright with a skilful hint of coral on her lips and cheekbones. All of a sudden, Valerie was conscious of her own damp hair and lack of make-up. Next to Teresa's gleaming dry hair and touched-up prettiness, she felt distinctly unstylish so she scraped back her chair and excused herself for a few moments.

A quick trip to the bathroom put everything to rights. She dried her hair hurriedly, fluffing it up into its usual tousled mass. Her face, as she peered into the mirror, looked fine. To admit she looked radiant seemed too vain, but really she knew that she did. Sex or sun, she thought, attributing the sparkle. Sex. It had to be the sex.

A trace of dewy blush and a smudge of mulberry lipgloss and she was done. Smoothing down her navy mini-dress, she made her way back to the terrace. She saw lunch had been served during her short absence.

'Sorry to keep you waiting,' she apologised.

'No problem,' said Daniel, the gallant host once again. There was not a trace now of the brusque manner she had just encountered on the lawn. 'Champagne?' he asked her, holding up a bottle of Moët.

'Mmm,' she responded.

It seemed like the best champagne she had ever tasted. Cool and fluid and delicious.

Teresa reached forward and clinked her glass with Valerie's and Daniel took a sip of his own, meeting her eyes over the rim of his glass. Boy, was he sexy, thought Valerie as her stomach flipped and the cool champagne eased down her throat.

Valerie picked at her lunch. Exquisite though the food was, she kept meeting Daniel's wicked dark eyes and any appetite she had was quelled by the resulting butterflies in her stomach.

Out of the blue, she felt Teresa's hand settle lightly on her wrist.

'I hope,' Teresa said softly, 'Cara and I didn't shock you at the pool earlier?'

'Shock me?' said Valerie evenly. 'No, not at all.'

'Good,' replied Teresa. 'Because I really believe that when the mood is upon you, you should always give in to it. Don't you?'

Valerie sipped her drink. There were Daniel's eyes again, amused and watchful. 'I guess. Mostly anyway,' she answered.

'I have to admit,' continued Teresa with a little, breathy sigh, 'the mood seems to be coming on me right now.'

Valerie had a vague clue as to where this might be heading. She watched Daniel and didn't answer.

Out of the corner of her eye, she saw Teresa stretch lazily and flick back her hair.

'Another thing I sometimes say,' whispered Teresa huskily, 'is that three's company, two's a bore.'

'I wouldn't like you bored, you're a guest,' said Daniel. He turned directly to Valerie, raising a smooth, jet eyebrow. 'What do you think, honey? Would you like Teresa to be bored?'

She felt hot and heady as she faced him but there

124

was no hesitation in her voice as she spoke. 'No.' She smiled flirtatiously. 'I think we should keep Teresa company.'

'Oh good,' said Teresa.

Daniel had lit another cigarette. He leant with one elbow resting on the back of his chair, smoking nonchalantly. 'Yes, good,' he murmured, blowing out a long plume of smoke.

He finished his cigarette and stood up. Holding out his hands to both Valerie and Teresa, he led them inside, upstairs to his large bedroom. Valerie adored Daniel's bedroom; she had slept there with him last night. Waking up next to him in the morning in this delightful, white-carpeted room had been heavenly. Today, despite the heat outside, the room was fresh and airy and mildy warm. The shades on the windows were half-pulled down, muting the brilliance of the outside light.

Daniel guided them both to the low, luxurious bed which seemed to dominate the room by its size alone. Valerie hovered next to Teresa. Daniel took a seat in a low easy chair nearby. Placing his elbows on the arms of the chair, he leant back casually, not speaking a word.

This was all new to Valerie and yet she didn't feel nervous, although her heart was knocking excitedly at her ribcage and her body felt weak with anticipation. She held her breath, waiting for someone to make the first move. Teresa obliged, sitting down at the bottom end of the bed. With a smile at Valerie, she patted the bed next to her.

'Sit next to me,' she purred to Valerie.

Valerie, glad to do so, settled next to her.

'My two beauties,' said Daniel softly. He was more or less seated opposite them. Valerie, staring across at his cool, lean face, realised her fascination for him was growing by the minute.

'I declare,' cooed Teresa, breaking the charged silence in the room, 'that I'm just so warm and relaxed.' She

125

placed her hand on the back of Valerie's neck, stroking her bare skin in a soothing, plainly seductive manner. 'But you seem a little tense, honey.'

Valerie tilted back her head, enjoying the gentle, sensuous caresses on her neck. 'No, I'm fine,' she murmured and her voice sounded husky even to herself.

Teresa moved her hand down Valerie's back, rubbing her fingers round the top of her spine. It felt so good, Valerie let herself smile.

'Lovely,' she sighed.

'Mmm,' hummed Teresa, moving down to the upper middle of her back. Teresa paused for a moment; Valerie realised she was pulling down the zipper of her dress.

'That's better,' said Teresa, easing Valerie's dress off her shoulders, letting it drop around her waist.

Valerie's senses had been heightened by the soft caressing of her neck and back – now, with her dress fallen to her waist, she felt a tremendous surge of raw excitement. Succumbing to it completely, it was a second or so before she realised what was happening. Without hesitation of any kind, Teresa had pulled down the navy lace cups of Valerie's bra until her breasts had popped over the top.

Valerie took a deep breath, endeavouring to calm herself, to allay these new rampaging feelings of excitement. It was a hard task; she was the only one of the three of them exposing an intimate part of her body, but there were no nerves or inhibitions, just a teasing blend of thrill and expectancy.

With a touch as light as air, Teresa drifted her forefinger across Valerie's smooth nipples.

Valerie flinched, part surprise, part delight. The touch sent immediate, exquisite darts of pleasure through her breasts. Teresa carried on, doing nothing more than brushing her finger across her nipples, scarcely touching at all, but Valerie's breasts felt to herself like islands of pleasure, tingling delectably. As Teresa continued, teasing relentlessly, Valerie began to long for firmer stimulation. She felt shackled by her bra, rendered tighter on her shoulders and beneath her breasts by being pulled down.

Drift, drift, drift, the touch across her nipples. Lighter than a summer breeze. So exquisite, so tormenting. She couldn't stand it any longer and with a deft little movement, she flicked open the fastener and shrugged off her bra.

'That's good,' approved Daniel quietly, his eyes fixed firmly on her naked upper body.

'*Very* nice,' said Teresa, rolling her tongue sensually around each word. Teresa had withdrawn her finger. Like Daniel, she was gazing steadfastly at Valerie's bare breasts.

'How beautiful,' she murmured.

Valerie's heart was thumping; having them gaze at her this way felt so good that she felt the urge to thrust back her shoulders and push her breasts out. And as they studied her, she felt a growing, aching need for actual physical stimulation. Yearning for the kneading and massaging of her tingling flesh, she closed her eyes, locking her arms on the bed by her side. She curled her fingers tight into the bedcover, fearing, if she didn't, her fingers would act with a will of their own.

It seemed like for ever until she felt Teresa's touch again. In reality, it had only been minutes. This time, Teresa cupped her right breast in the palm of her hand, squeezing in a firm perfect rhythm. Valerie opened her eyes and had to look down, had to watch her own breast being elegantly fondled. Teresa cupped her other breast, squeezing that too, then she held her hand flat and began to rub Valerie's nipple against the palm of her hand, round and round, rotating her palm with precious expertise. She alternated systematically from left nipple to right, until Valerie's pink tips stood out like cherries, hardened and pearly, jutting from the full, gold-beige globe of her breast. Her nipples felt as tight and sensitive as nerves.

Suppressing a moan, Valerie flicked her eyes up to

Daniel. He looked transfixed, his eyes glinting as he watched. Seeing his expression, the moan escaped.

'Uh huh,' she moaned softly out loud.

'Oh yes,' responded Teresa in a tinkling voice. She began to pinch Valerie's nipples, pulling gratifyingly on her hard, stiff tips.

'Oh God,' moaned Valerie, her stomach, her sex, tugging in reaction. She began to press her bottom into the bed and, as she did so, Teresa briefly took her hands away, pulled down the top of her own cotton sundress, unclipped her lemon-coloured bra and freed her own breasts. Then she returned her attentions to Valerie's.

Valerie couldn't have stopped herself even if she had wanted to. The sight of Teresa's bare breasts, smaller than her own but just as firm and pert, conjoined with Teresa's ongoing stimulation of her own, was too much, and she reached urgently towards Teresa's chest and fondled her warm flesh. The unfamiliarity of it, the smooth velvet firmness of the other girl's breasts, turned Valerie on even more. She stroked and caressed, growing bolder and bolder and finally dabbing at Teresa's milk-chocolate nipples. Teresa sighed with delight.

'Do that again, honey,' she sighed, and Valerie did, again and again.

They sat on the end of the bed, playing and fondling each other, sighs floating gently in the quiet of the room until, suddenly, Teresa stood up. Quickly, she pushed her dress down her hips and legs and wriggled urgently out of her panties. Then she leant forward to Valerie who was still sitting down.

'Let me help you,' she murmured, hooking her fingers into Valerie's fallen dress, easing it from her body. Valerie lifted her bottom to enable the dress to move. Once the dress was off, Teresa repeated the move on her panties, curling her fingers into the sides and dragging them down her legs.

Valerie could scarcely catch her breath.

'Now . . .' breathed Teresa, letting the word hang. With a smile on her glowing face, she slipped to the floor before Valerie, placed her hands on Valerie's knees, and pushed her legs apart.

'I – !' gasped Valerie, feeling her sex totally, gloriously, exposed to both Daniel and Teresa.

'Shoosh,' hushed Daniel, pressing his forefinger gently to his lips. And as Valerie looked at him, meeting his eyes, she felt Teresa's soft lips touching her sex. Daniel kept his eyes locked on hers all the time.

'Does that feel good?' he asked, his voice thick with passion.

The very core of her sex was being skilfully stimulated, her clitoris enclosed in a warm soft mouth, then teased and thrilled with a darting tongue.

'Yes!' gasped Valerie, flutters dancing up the seam of her sex. 'Yes!' she gasped again, as the enchanting tongue flicked at her bud, driving the warmth to the pit of her belly.

Through a growing mist of pleasure, she kept her eyes on Daniel who in turn was focused on Teresa and herself. She thought of how they must look to him, the image of eroticism they must be portraying. She, perched on the end of the bed, her bare breasts aroused and thrust forward; Teresa kneeling in between her thighs, shining brown hair blunt on her shoulders, naked back and bottom displayed towards Daniel.

And as if to conclude this picture of eroticism, Daniel was now rising, stripping off his clothes, revealing to Valerie his dark flawless body. His penis looked fully erect, projecting magnificently, engorged and rich in its purpled glory. Swiftly, he walked over.

Breathless, speechless, captured by the pleasure of Teresa's expert tongue, Valerie watched his approach in a kind of slow-motion trance.

Daniel knelt behind Teresa, pressing his body to hers. Pushing Teresa's hair to one side, he kissed her neck delicately and whispered in her ear and she stopped what she was doing and smiled. Then she surrendered her position between Valerie's thighs. Daniel edged forward.

The difference was acute. As soon as she knew it was Daniel's mouth between her legs, the scorched sensations of her feelings for him rampaged unchecked through her thighs and body. In place of the warm, teasing build-up she had been enjoying, there were now intense wheeling arcs of delight. He flicked at her clitoris, kissed down the sides, twirled his tongue round the skin of her slit then dipped it inside and licked up her juices.

Teresa was kneeling behind his back, stroking his shoulders and kissing his neck.

Valerie parted her legs wider, beyond inhibition, and Daniel sucked and licked at her swollen roseflesh. The waves began to strengthen, and she clutched at her breasts. She was desperate and wild and she came with a wracking, body-wrenching force, the pleasure like rifling bullets of relief.

It had been so strong, so totally complete, that it took a while for her to come around fully. When finally she did, she heard Teresa speak.

'My turn,' giggled Teresa, tugging Daniel on to the bed.

Teresa lay back flat on the massive bed. Daniel lay on his side next to her, propping his head up on his hand. Lazily, he massaged Teresa's flattened breasts. Then his hand wandered to her slender waist, stroking her gleaming, olive-hued skin. Then he reached lower down, tracing his finger round Teresa's triangle of dark hair, as though drawing lines round the small, curly patch.

Teresa wriggled impatiently on the bed. 'Touch me,' she urged. 'I need you to touch me.'

Daniel stroked down her long, firm thighs. Her skin looked very smooth, like watered silk cloth. As he made his way back to the tops of Teresa's thighs, she lifted her head and shoulders up off the bed, resting back on her elbows. He nudged his hand between her legs and

Teresa's eyes began to smile, then, slowly and casually, he lifted one of her legs one way, the other leg the other way so that her legs were spread wide apart.

Valerie was fascinated – she had never seen another woman's sex so closely and explicitly.

She watched Daniel press his middle finger to the elongated pink nub of Teresa's clitoris and begin to worry the glistening flap of skin gently from side to side. Teresa, still resting up on her elbows, laughed delightedly and almost immediately began to lift and lower her hips in a light lilting motion.

As Daniel continued to stimulate Teresa, Valerie saw a light sheen of sweat break out like a sheer gossamer veil over Teresa's lovely breasts and stomach. Teresa's breasts were moving in a rhythmic jiggle in time with the lilting motion of her hips. Valerie crawled slowly up the bed, aware that Daniel had lifted his eyes to watch her. She reached towards Teresa's jigging breasts and let Teresa's nipples brush lightly against her fingers. Teresa moaned as though frustrated, clearly caught between the teasing torment of Valerie's too-delicate touch and the delicious friction that her touch brought about. Valerie was enjoying this, this exciting blend of teasing power and pleasure-giving.

Between Teresa's legs, Daniel was now stimulating in a different way. Valerie could see him sliding his finger in and out of Teresa's wet body. Spurred on by his actions, Valerie decided to respond, tweaking Teresa's nipples hard.

'God, yes!' squealed Teresa, arching her back and thrusting her hips with increased vigour.

'Come on, baby,' coaxed Daniel, his face suffused with excitement. And he slid his finger faster, in and out, pausing now and again to rub Teresa's clitoris with his thumb. Valerie was getting aroused all over again. Daniel looked so sexy doing what he was doing and so skilled a lover, she thought, watching his movements, seeing Teresa's enraptured responses. Feverishly, she pinched Teresa's nipples which felt hard and swollen between her squeezing fingertips.

Teresa was clearly in a state of intense arousal. She tilted back her head, pushing her breasts up to Valerie, thrusting her hips up to Daniel. She was moaning and laughing and sighing by turns as though she couldn't quite make up her mind what to do.

'Mmmm, yes,' she moaned, 'yes, there, there.'

Abruptly, she seemed to tense her whole body, arching her back, opening her legs wider, pressing her hips down into the mattress. Daniel pressed his whole hand to her opened sex, holding it there as she climaxed as though he was feeling the pulsations of her orgasm.

'Fantastic,' Teresa murmured, dropping her head down to the bed.

Valerie was beside herself again, excitement zigzagging madly through her. She could feel wetness seep to the inside tops of her thighs.

Minutes later, Teresa appeared to have got her breath back. She was sitting up now with her legs curled gracefully to one side. Damp strands of her rich, teak hair clung to the sides of her face. She was looking expectantly from Daniel to Valerie.

Daniel was still lying on his side. Valerie drew her eyes down his lean muscled body and the spasms in her belly leapt through her torso.

'Come here,' he said, crooking his finger to her.

There was a command in his voice, quiet but insistent. Never once in her life had Valerie responded to arrogance, but this man had her well and truly in his grip. And she had never felt so good about anything before.

She went over to him, weak with lust and excitement.

He flipped on to his back and positioned her over his hips. The tip of his cock nudged against the lips of her sex. He had kept his hands around her waist and now he motioned her hips gently back and forth, tickling her swollen clitoris with his cock.

Valerie clenched her inside muscles in response to

his teasing but really she was too aroused to take much more. Just like her old self, she seized the initiative, and clasped her hand around his solid penis. Then she guided the head into herself, sinking down slowly, impaling herself on him.

'Yeah,' she whispered, closing her eyes in utter relief.

'Yeah,' she heard Daniel respond, hoarse and husky.

She started to move, rocking gently, letting his cock stroke her insides. Her bud was rubbing simultaneously against his soft hair and it felt like she was being caressed with a feather. She leant forward a fraction to rest her hands on his chest and opened her eyes as she felt another pair of hands.

Teresa was also leaning over, moving her hands hungrily over Daniel's chest, circling his small dark nipples with the tip of her fingernail. She winked up at Valerie and Valerie leant forward and they laced their hands together, moving all over Daniel's chest.

Valerie needed to move quicker, her hips wanted to thrust and gyrate and press down to him. She bobbed up and down, feeling him inside her, wanting him deeper and deeper within. She moved with such energy, she felt her breasts jiggling and her bottom cheeks quivering.

'Christ, that's so good,' Daniel groaned, bucking up his hips, hitting a magic spot somewhere deep inside her.

'Mmmm,' moaned Valerie, upping her pace.

All of a sudden he reared up, tumbling her over on to her back.

She found herself leaning back against Teresa, her head and shoulders propped up as Teresa's had been before. Daniel had repositioned himself, kneeling in between her legs. He bent her long legs at the knees, then pushed her legs apart and up in the air slightly. Valerie's sex felt stretched and her body throbbed with frustration and Daniel was obviously in a similar state because he wasted no time in sliding in once again. Straight away they resumed a fast rhythm but this time

133

it was Daniel setting the pace. He moved his hips smoothly in sharp, even thrusts and Valerie literally trembled with joy. Behind her, Teresa began stroking her shoulders, the gentle caresses enhancing the fire down below.

Daniel was gripping on to her thighs. His body was gleaming with a sexual sweat. He pumped his hips quicker, the smooth, lean muscles in his arms and chest and thighs defined as he moved. Valerie could not believe it, the depth and intensity of the pleasure he was giving her yet again. Behind her, Teresa was still stroking her shoulders but now she moved her hands forward across her collarbone then down to her quivering, out-thrust breasts. She cupped her hands over them, at first squeezing delicately then more vigorously, more hungrily.

Valerie shut her eyes tightly, surrendering to it all – the searing heat between her legs, the rhythmic thrill of Daniel inside her, the forceful, delicious squeezing of her breasts. She didn't want it to stop – even whilst she craved relief, she willed these feelings to go on and on and on. But of course they would not, could not, and, very quickly, the pleasure began to intensify, to flare from the localised, continuous thrills between her legs and seep to her tummy and bottom and to the tips of her stimulated breasts until every inch of her body seemed to tingle for a moment then explode in a gigantic, overwhelming rush of sheer bliss. Dancing rays of light flashed behind her eyelids; in the distance she heard herself cry out and she heard a lower, deeper groan which must have been Daniel. Their cries seemed remote, far removed, and, for the long precious seconds of her orgasm, she was totally immersed in the hot swirling waters of ecstasy.

Much later that same day, long after Teresa had left, Valerie walked outside to the terrace. She took a seat, watching the early-evening sky grow hazy and shadows lengthen across the lawns. In the distance, a figure came into view. As she watched the figure come closer, she started to recognise the purposeful walk. She saw the dark, swept-back hair, the broad shoulders, the tall, lean physique. It was Daniel.

'Hey,' she said softly, as he tripped up the steps, his two devoted Dobermanns at his heels.

'Hey,' he said back, and walked over, stooped and kissed the top of her head. It seemed a simple, affectionate gesture from a man who had effectively turned her inside out emotionally and sexually and who seemed to oscillate between charm and passion. So far, affection hadn't seemed to figure greatly in his repertoire.

'I feel very close to you,' said Valerie on a whim.

Daniel perched on the arm of her seat, gazing down at her. 'Do you?' he asked quietly.

'Uh huh,' she murmured.

Daniel leant forward, pushing her short, mussed-up hair behind her ear. 'Do you feel close enough to tell me what you did now?'

Valerie looked up at him, nonplussed. What she *did*?

Daniel smiled. 'I won't be angry,' he assured her. 'Just admit it to me now and I promise I won't be angry.'

Valerie felt confused. What on earth was he talking about? That she had enjoyed watching Teresa and Cara by the pool? That she had enjoyed this afternoon's trio with Teresa? 'Admit what?' she said, openly confused.

Daniel carried on staring at her, carried on smiling. He twisted his fingers a little in her hair, a little too hard. It hurt.

'Admit what, Daniel?' she repeated, snatching her hair away from him.

He drew his finger slowly along her jawline, then stood up abruptly. 'I warn you not to play games with me, Valerie,' he said in a cold voice.

He walked over to the French doors. Valerie watched him, entirely perplexed. He looked back at her briefly.

'Because,' he continued, 'whenever people play games with me . . . I always win. It's inevitable.'

Valerie sat on for a while, baffled and annoyed and a tiny bit intimidated. Add another dimension to this man, she thought. To passion and charm and occasional displays of affection, add arrogance. And maybe add danger, she decided as a peculiar, not altogether unpleasant, frisson ran down her spine.

Chapter Thirteen

*T*he desert was a vast, hot, hazy expanse. At some points, it appeared to stretch beyond the horizon and into oblivion, at others, to creep into the belly of the mountain ranges and lose itself in their distant rugged secrets. It was dry and it was empty, with an endless vista of a dusty landscape and far-off mountains. Brilliant blue sky and occasional wildflowers or prickly cacti seemed designed to relieve the arid scorching monotony.

Flat as hell, thought Nadine, gazing out of the car window. Ahead, the road surface had map-like cracks from the heat and wet-looking mirages and shimmering illusions kept rising up from the sun-baked route. Just looking at it all made her hot and, though it was fairly comfortable inside the car, she reached forward and turned up the air-conditioning.

'Go easy,' said Mark. 'It could be miles before we reach another gas station.' He flicked the air-conditioning down again.

'Sorry,' murmured Nadine. 'It just looks so hot out there. So darn hot.'

'It *is* hot out there, honey. So the one thing we don't need is to run out of gas and get stranded.'

'Right,' she agreed. She watched as another shimmering haze appeared in the distance ahead. As it came closer and they drove nearer, it actually began to evolve into a shape and form as though emerging from some kind of filmy chrysalis. A car. The first they had seen since leaving Barstow.

'That's the first car we've passed since Barstow,' muttered Mark, echoing her thoughts. 'It was a good idea to leave the Interstate, no one would have a clue where we are now even if for some crazy reason Daniel did find out it was us who took the money.'

'He won't find out,' said Nadine emphatically.

Mark nodded and squeezed her knee. 'I know, honey, but it was good thinking anyway. From both of us.'

'Yes,' smiled Nadine. It had originally been Mark's idea to leave the Interstate highway but she had agreed and so she was more than willing to take half the credit for the decision.

After leaving Santa Barbara yesterday, they had picked up the Interstate that cut right across the Mojave Desert into Nevada. But amidst the dust-covered heavy trucks which habitually used the route to travel across state, they had felt overtly conspicuous. Mark's sleek, dark-silver Lexus stood out and would be sure to be remembered should anyone, at any stage, care to ask, so they had decided to cover their tracks and transfer to one of the lesser roads, just as fast as the highway – although slightly more hazardous for confirmed city dwellers such as themselves. Nadine had not really felt it was necessary, she was so sure of herself, so sure that she had executed the perfect robbery, but she had agreed anyway. No harm in playing safe. Besides, it was good to be off the highway and out on this remote, empty road.

Last night, they had stayed in a small roadside motel. The greasy little man in reception had tried to play man-buddies with Mark, winking when he saw Nadine and telling Mark that lucky for him the best room in the motel was free. He had shown them to their room, at the end of a wooden walkway. Still winking at Mark, he held the key aloft and opened the door with an embarrassing flourish.

'Is this it?' remarked Nadine, striding in. 'The best room you say?'

'Yes it is, miss,' the man answered proudly, winking at Mark like some sort of twitching maniac. It seemed to take him several seconds to catch on to the fact that Nadine was not favourably impressed.

'Well, it ain't exactly the Ritz, I know,' he muttered.

'I'll say,' snipped Nadine.

'It's fine,' Mark said diplomatically. He slipped several dollars inside the man's breast pocket and ushered him out of the door.

The room had been plain and basic. There was no bath in the bathroom, just a shower. Nadine had really wanted a long soak in the bath and for a brief moment her high spirits had sunk and she found herself hankering for her own pretty red-tiled house back in Santa Barbara. She had had to remind herself that very soon, thanks to Uncle Will, there would be no pretty red-tiled house, no car, no allowance, no nothing. A little discomfort now for a great deal of comfort later, she reasoned and, knowing exactly the tonic that she needed, she headed for their bags in the corner of the room.

Mark had been in the shower when she pulled out the briefcase and peeked at the money. All those snappy bundles packed up in rows. Just one little peek and she was fortified once again, focused and excited. The money had a peculiar way of doing that to her.

'Admiring the loot?'

His voice made her jump. She had not realised he was watching her.

He was leaning in the doorway of the bathroom, a small, apricot-coloured towel slung around his hips. His brown hair, damp from his shower, was slicked back and he was grinning. Strangely, she had noticed the steam from the bathroom behind him was forming a kind of dry-ice backdrop.

'Uh huh.' She smiled. 'And ain't it grand,' she added with cowgirl hoopla.

'Ain't it just,' quipped Mark, playing along.

Nadine switched her eyes back to the briefcase.

'You know,' Mark continued quietly, 'I should be getting jealous. You're paying that money more attention than you're paying me.'

Nadine glanced back at him, at his lean, freshly showered body, at his handsome, smiling face.

'No way, lover,' she murmured, gliding over to him. She reached up and kissed him, curling her forefinger into the towel, tugging it gently from his hips.

The towel was left abandoned in the bathroom doorway. The briefcase lay abandoned in the corner of the room.

The pillows were made out of foam, the sheets were thin, and the bedsprings squeaked as the two of them rolled across the mattress.

But none of that had mattered at all . . .

Now, as she sat in the cool, comfy interior of the car and they cut across the silent desert, another surge of excitement assailed her. She felt high and floaty and free as a bird – she had the money safely tucked away in the back of the car, she had her man at her side, and she was free for ever from her boring old uncle and his fruity money.

She glanced sideways at Mark. He looked thoughtful, one hand on the wheel, the other resting on his thigh. Since his first initial shock at finding out she had taken Daniel's money, Mark had been totally calm and collected. Completely in control. He had believed her when she said it was the perfect crime and that there was no way on earth Daniel would trace the robbery to them. Naturally, she had left out why exactly – she thought it better not to tell him that she had carefully set the scene for Valerie Neiman to take the blame.

Mark had rather a chivalrous side where women were concerned so, why complicate things?

They made a great team, she and Mark, she reflected. Sexually and otherwise.

'Mark?' she said softly.

He flicked his face towards her and grinned. His blue eyes were hidden behind dark sunglasses and his teeth looked very white against the brown-copper tan of his face. 'Uh huh?'

'You're not sorry, are you? Sorry you've gone along with this?'

Mark knocked his sunglasses down his nose and looked at her over the top. His blue eyes were piercing and bright with disbelief. 'Are you kidding?'

Nadine shrugged. 'You seem kind of quiet.'

'Honey, this is the best thing we could have done. We can map out our whole future with this. Sorry? Hell, no.' He shook his head gently.

'That's good,' said Nadine. 'Because I think that too.'

She was silent for a moment or two. But Mark looked so good. So tempting. His brown hair soft and clean, slightly ruffled, his sunshades back in place, his skin gleaming. Despite the cool temperature in the car, she was beginning to get warm, really warm. She wanted his attention.

Smoothly, she reached over, pulled off his sunglasses and dropped them nonchalantly in the compartment between their seats.

'Hey?' he said, startled, glancing sharply at her.

'Mmm?' she hummed, widening her eyes in a look of mock-innocence. 'Something wrong?' she added, hitching up the bottom of her dress. It was a long, light dress and she straightened her legs out in front to hitch the dress up just above her knees.

'Something right,' murmured Mark.

'I'm really hot,' she whispered, her voice cracking softly.

'Don't stop there,' whispered Mark back, flicking his eyes back and forth from her to the road.

141

She hitched her dress a little higher. 'There?'

'Uh uh.' Mark shook his head.

She hitched it higher, to the tops of her thighs. 'There?'

He gestured higher with his hand.

'There?' she teased, revealing a glimpse of the white lace of her panties.

Mark ran his tongue over his lips as though they were dry. 'Higher,' he said.

She lifted her dress higher, just about to her waist. She let the question hang in her bright, shining eyes.

Mark nodded. 'Yeah,' he approved softly. 'That's about right.'

Then with one mighty wrench on the wheel, he swerved off the road and drove for about two hundred yards into the scrubland of the desert.

'Now,' he said, switching off the engine and opening his car door to let in what little air there was. 'What were you saying?'

'I was saying I was hot,' sighed Nadine, fluttering the bottom of her dress at her waist to create a draft. It was like fanning air from a red-hot oven.

Mark leant across, pressing his hand to the fine, pretty lace of her high-leg panties. 'You surely are,' he said. 'Perhaps it might help if we take these off.'

'It might,' giggled Nadine.

She let him hook his fingers into the waistband and ease her panties down, down her hips and thighs and knees and ankles. Carefully, he manipulated them over her light slip-on sandals. He struggled a little as they caught on one of the high heels.

'Sorry,' he laughed. 'Got sidetracked.' And he whisked his eyes up over her nakedness as if in explanation.

Nadine laughed too, stretching out her legs, and twitching her dress just a fraction higher. She glanced down at her exposed lower body, loving herself, loving her body, loving to show it off. Her belly was smooth, with the gentlest of curves, and her legs were slender, perfectly toned. Her pubic hair nestled snugly at the tops of her thighs, trimmed, glossy, fresh, and her golden skin had a lustre which was part perspiration, part glow from within.

Mark was looking at her too, a streak of sweat varnishing his upper lip.

'Open your legs,' he said huskily.

She opened her thighs, letting him look at her, angling her sex just so.

'Yeah,' he approved softly, the laughter gone, his voice pitched low and tense with excitement.

Flutters of arousal cavorted between her legs. She was getting wet. She was getting impatient.

'Now touch yourself,' ordered Mark as though in tune with her thoughts.

Her first touch was light, teasing. She ran her finger lightly down the centre of her sex, from the peeking nub of her clitoris to the sweet, moist skin round her slit. It felt delicious, the smooth, soft wetness beneath her fingertip coupled with the tingling sensation it evoked inside her. She drew her finger back upward and twisted it through her flossy nest of hair.

'Keep going,' coaxed Mark.

'Sure,' whispered Nadine, thrilled by the look of hunger in his eyes.

This time, she played with her clitoral bud, nudging it gently until she could feel it harden and pout from her downy lips. She slipped her finger lower, running it round and round her small opening, teasing herself until her insides trembled with wanting. When her bud was throbbing and her mound was starting to feel tight, she slid her finger inside herself, savouring the slight penetration.

'It's so good, Mark,' she sighed, gliding her finger up and down inside herself, then pulling it out and drifting back upwards, rubbing her juices round her swelling clitoris.

Mark was watching her every movement. The sweat on his neck shone like glass and was starting to dampen patches of his fine cotton shirt. Hurriedly, he began to undo the buttons of his shirt. He slipped it off his shoulders.

'Mmm,' sighed Nadine, raking her eyes down his tan, shining chest. Her lips felt suddenly dry at the sight of him and she let the tip of her tongue linger on her upper lip.

Mark was stepping out of his open doorway, coming around to her side of the car. He opened her door and at once the heat hit her, intensifying the sweat of her passion twofold. As she stepped out of the car, her dress clung to her body and her long hair clung to her neck and shoulders. After a minute or two, the heat seemed more bearable but her sexual excitement seemed heightened.

Fortunately, Mark meant business. His fingers flew at the zipper of her dress, wrenching it down in one urgent swipe. He pushed her dress off her body and it tumbled in the desert dust around her feet. She found herself naked almost before she had stood up.

Mark started to undo his trousers. Nadine reached over to help him, tugging them down to his ankles. She left them there, too impatient to deal with his shoes, and instead pulled at his black boxer shorts, leaving them at his ankles also. They were both more or less naked now. Mark just had his clothes around his ankles. Nadine still wore her stylish high sandals.

Mark's body looked glorious – lean and fit. His clothes crumpled boyishly round his ankles seemed at odds with his rampant, virile masculinity and Nadine found it turned her on even more. She stood behind him, running her hands hungrily over his shoulders and back and then pressing her body to his. The heat between them was immense.

'Let me feel you,' said Mark. 'Really feel you.'

So she pressed herself harder against him, pushing her breasts into his back. His muscled buttocks pressed against the smooth lower curve of her tummy and a dagger-like thrill shot up between her legs.

'How's this?' she asked, swaying her hips.

'Yeah,' murmured Mark.

She stretched up in her high-heeled sandals and began to move her pubis over his buttock cheeks, stroking and tickling his skin with her silky hair, then she started to concentrate on the crease of his bottom, brushing up and down against it.

Mark groaned and tried to turn around.

'Not yet,' whispered Nadine, crouching down behind him, kissing her way down the sleek column of his spine as she did so. She flicked the tip of her tongue across his buttock cheeks, watching him flex his muscles slightly in response. She could tell Mark was tense with excitement and, as she grabbed a hold of his thighs and nuzzled her head in between, he groaned yet again.

'Christ, Nadine,' he groaned, as she licked hungrily at the sensitive skin of his balls.

She didn't reply, dizzy with arousal herself now. She stimulated one then the other, closing her mouth around them, licking and sucking and savouring his taste. Highly aroused though she was, she could not get enough of him, of teasing him, of tasting him. It was Mark himself who stopped her, clearly desperate beyond measure. With strength like a caveman, he put back his hands and hauled her up from behind him.

'Lean against the car,' he urged.

He looked wild. His face was dark and glazed with desire, his chest was heaving as if he had run for miles. Nadine's own pulse was racing, her own chest heaving. Quickly, she positioned herself how she knew he wanted her. Resting her hands against the top rim of the open car door, back arched slightly, legs apart.

Nadine glanced wickedly behind her. Mark, hampered by his clothing which was still around his ankles, was inching towards her. His eyes were glued to her.

She turned her head back forward, closing her eyes. Waiting, waiting for his touch.

His hands circled her waist, moving round to her

hot, moist stomach. He stroked her stomach slowly, sensuously, and then rubbed his thumbs in her navel. Nadine held her breath as his hands drifted down, stroking the fronts of her thighs now, and her hipbones and her stomach again. It was his turn to tease, she realised. His turn to frustrate and tantalise, to make her pant with anticipation.

Finally he was there, pressing his hand between her open legs. He began to massage her with the flats of his fingers, round and round. She was so wet she could hear the slick sounds of his movements and it made her feel woozy, shaky almost.

His other hand was on her bottom, kneading and squeezing her smooth rounded cheeks. As he continued to stimulate both her sex and bottom, she could feel her wetness seep up her bottom crease and, when Mark slipped his middle finger into her crack, he sighed with delight.

'Oh yeah,' he sighed croakily.

He seemed to pause for a moment or two. Then Nadine shivered with delight as she felt him ease the red-hot shaft of his penis along her bottom crease. He squeezed her cheeks around it and began to move up and down, dipping and straightening his knees. His cock slid easily in the wetness, arousing the sensitive, velvet-soft groove of her bottom.

Nadine flicked back her head, clutching desperately at the rim of the car doorway.

She was breathless, hot, aroused almost beyond endurance. She arched her back, thrusting out her bottom. She was highly stimulated there, her crease prickling with tiny burning sparks of sensation but, between her legs, she craved penetration.

She twisted her head back to Mark. 'Now, Mark,' she pleaded.

He nodded, clearly too aroused himself to continue foreplay. He entered her slowly, giving her time to savour the gradual fullness. She held her breath, luxuriating in it all, but as soon as he started to move, she thrust back forcefully against him. He grabbed her waist and pumped his hips against her, propelling her body and mind towards rapture.

They made love frantically, with the sun blazing down on them and the desert all around them. Their urgent moans and cries of pleasure hovered in the empty silence, rose up briefly towards the blue sky, and then floated gently away.

It was quite an adventure and there was a long way to go, but one thing they were both very sure of – they were definitely enjoying the journey.

Chapter Fourteen

There was a single loud knock at the door.

'Come in,' said Daniel.

Bradley Ray entered, as loud and offensive as usual. 'Saw Valerie downstairs.' He winked, glancing meaningfully down at his wristwatch. 'Eight thirty in the morning. You lucky dog, you.'

'Have a seat,' said Daniel, ignoring his remark.

Bradley took a seat opposite, on the other side of the desk. He leant across it. His forehead was glistening with tiny beads of sweat and his tufty, strawberry-blond hair was clumped unattractively over a receding hairline. 'So how about it, Daniel,' he said with a chuckle. 'Valerie as good in the sack as she looks, is she? Best pair of tits this side of the Sierras . . . aside from the wife's, of course.'

Daniel frowned ominously. His mood was already black – Valerie was showing no signs of cracking and admitting to the robbery and he was starting to lose patience. Furthermore, as was his normal custom, he had expected his interest in her to begin to wane after their two sex-saturated days together. That had not happened. It still wasn't happening, and that was annoying the hell out of him too. She was an out-of-work dancer, almost certainly a thief, and he had had his fun with her, so why in hell was she taking up so many of his thoughts?

And now, thought Daniel, staring contemptuously across at Bradley Ray, now he was having to deal with this!

'Bradley,' he said calmly, 'you should thank the sweet Lord in heaven that you are one of the best financiers I have ever employed. Because it's for that reason and that reason alone that I don't haul your ass out of that chair and kick you the hell out of here.'

'What did I say –?' spluttered Bradley. It was the measure of the man that he seemed to be genuinely bemused. He had skin as thick as an alligator.

'In future,' said Daniel quietly, 'show some respect to your wife and her friend.'

'I – !' Bradley was still spluttering.

'And then I won't find it necessary to dispense with your services and blacklist your name from here to New Jersey.'

Bradley looked aghast. 'Blacklist my name? Fire me?' His normally pink hue blanched to a colourless pallor.

'I . . . I apologise, Daniel,' he gasped. 'I didn't mean to be disrespectful to anyone. Really.'

'OK then,' drawled Daniel, feeling much better. Nothing like venting out frustrations on a doughball like Bradley Ray. 'Now, to business.'

'Yes.' Bradley nodded, shifting uncomfortably in his seat, clearly trying to get himself together.

'I called you here today, Bradley, because we need to make some financial adjustments.'

'I see,' said Bradley, tapping his forefinger against his pudgy chin. He looked more relaxed now, regaining confidence quickly as they moved towards his own particular area of expertise. 'What sort of adjustments?'

'I had a large amount, a very large amount, of money taken from the safe sometime on Saturday night or early Sunday morning.'

'Taken?'

'Stolen,' clarified Daniel.

'Stolen,' repeated Bradley with a nod. 'How much are we talking?'

Daniel told him. Bradley whistled softly.

'I see,' he said, still tapping his chin thoughtfully. He unzipped a maroon leather file and plucked out some sheets. 'Well,' he said, after surveying the rows and columns of figures on the sheets, 'it's a hefty sum to cover but I can do it.'

'I know you can,' said Daniel.

'Yep,' continued Bradley. 'I can realign these figures here, here and here.' He circled several figures with a pen and held out the sheets towards Daniel. 'That should free up enough cash to cover the loss.'

'Good.' Daniel nodded, glancing quickly over the figures and then pushing the sheets back to Bradley.

'So,' said Bradley, inserting the papers back in the zip file. 'What did the cops say? Any ideas who took it?'

'No clue,' lied Daniel.

Bradley shook his head. 'Saturday night, big party, outside agencies. Could have been any one of a number of . . .' His voice began to trail off. He stared off into the distance as if a thought had just struck him.

Daniel watched him carefully. 'What is it, Bradley?' he asked quietly.

'Saturday night, you said?'

'That's right.' Daniel nodded. 'Sometime Saturday night or early Sunday morning. What is it?'

'Probably nothing at all . . . only . . .' Bradley trailed off again.

Daniel put his palms flat on the desk and leant across. 'What is it?' he said in a clipped voice.

'Well,' said Bradley, licking his lips and looking uncomfortable. 'Just that on Saturday night, during the party, I think maybe I saw something a little unusual.'

'Go on.'

'Well, actually, I *did* see it, but didn't think much of it at the time. Other than it was a little unusual at a party.'

'Go on,' insisted Daniel, growing impatient.

'As you know I'm a bit of a car buff and there were some real beauties there on Saturday night, in the parking area out front. I was having a mosey amongst them when ... well, when I happened to see a friend of my wife putting some kind of a case into the back of someone's car.'

A friend of his wife, thought Daniel icily. Valerie Neiman was a friend of his wife. There it was. All the proof that he needed.

'The name of the friend?' he asked coldly. A mere formality.

Bradley licked his lips again and looked him straight in the eye. 'Nadine,' he said. 'Nadine Brookes.'

Daniel blinked, but gave nothing away. A bizarre emotion, almost like relief, tugged suddenly at his stomach. It bothered him – it wasn't something he was used to.

So, he thought to himself, he had been wrong all along and she had been telling him the truth. Not Valerie who was his thief at all, but Nadine.

'And whose car was she putting the money in?' he asked quietly, another suspicion already sneaking its way into his mind.

There was a kind of gossipy relish in Bradley's voice now. 'It looked to be Mark Kelton's,' he said.

The suspicion confirmed. Yet Daniel longed for it not to be so. He valued Mark's skills as a lawyer. Moreover, he liked the man. But the bitter fingers of doubt and betrayal were already starting to chill him inside.

'Thank you, Bradley,' he murmured frostily.

Bradley clutched his zip file in his lap but made no move to shift from his chair. 'There again,' he said buoyantly, 'it could be nothing at all. Could all be quite innocent.'

Daniel looked at him like the fool he was. 'Did you see what you just said?'

'Yes, of course.'

151

'No doubts in your mind that it could have been someone else, someone else's car?'

Bradley made himself look insulted. 'No. No doubt at all. I saw what I saw.'

'Then thank you again. I'll take it from here.'

Bradley sat solidly in his chair, licking his liver-coloured lips. He leant forward earnestly, now eager it seemed to play detective. 'Do you think they took it?' he asked in a hushed, excited voice.

Daniel arched an eyebrow sceptically. 'What do you think?'

Bradley's face flushed with excitement. 'I think they prob—'

'It was a rhetorical question,' said Daniel, cutting him off.

'Oh,' muttered Bradley. He still made no move to leave.

'Say goodbye to Valerie on your way out,' said Daniel, making it abundantly clear that the meeting was at an end.

Now, decided Daniel, when he was finally alone in his study. Time for Mark Kelton to make some explanation.

Daniel drummed his fingers lightly on the desktop as he rang through to his offices in town and waited for his personal assistant to pick up her phone.

'Ellen,' he said to her, 'I need for you to locate Mark Kelton immediately. Pull him out of any meetings no matter what and get him to the phone. I'll hold.'

'One moment, Daniel,' Ellen said in her smooth, efficient way. 'I'll speak with his secretary.'

Minutes later, Ellen clicked back on the line. 'Um, Daniel, it appears Mark has taken some leave, gone to see his parents or something. He phoned his secretary, Samantha, early yesterday and told her to cancel his schedule for the entire week. He's back in on Monday.'

'Is he indeed?' muttered Daniel.

'Sorry?' said Ellen.

'Nothing,' replied Daniel.

Got you, thought Daniel triumphantly, knowing it was only a matter of time now. The next time he saw Mark Kelton, it would not be as a friend.

'Any message I can leave with Samantha?' asked Ellen, cutting into Daniel's thoughts.

'No,' he answered quickly. 'But I'd like you to call up Chad Baxter and Lyle Beck instead. Tell them to get to my house pronto.'

'Done,' said Ellen.

'Good girl,' murmured Daniel vaguely. His thoughts raced as he hung up the phone.

'Been a while,' Daniel said to the two men seated opposite.

Chad Baxter and Lyle Beck were both tall, rangy men but there the similarity in their appearances ended. Chad was a crew-cut blond, large featured and cold-eyed. Lyle was his polar opposite – straight, shoulder-length, jet-black hair which he wore pulled back into a tight ponytail. His dark skin was slightly rough-looking but he had even features and a ready smile. The smile was almost certainly an asset, showing as it did a number of remarkably white, albeit uneven, teeth. But when he didn't smile, the thin set of his lips gave a truer insight into his personality, a suggestion that maybe the man was not as affable as the ready smile would indicate.

Both men wore jeans, cowboy boots, and loud check shirts.

Chad nodded in answer to Daniel's greeting. 'It has been a while. Tell us what you need?'

Daniel had time for these two men. They were direct, to the point. They did not waste his time and he appreciated that. At times like this, he used them often. They were professionals, discreet and trustworthy, and they had never failed him in the past. They called themselves private detectives, although all three of them knew this to be a euphemism; they were hard but

153

loyal and they were not afraid to be ruthless. And Daniel knew they would carry out his instructions to the letter.

'I had a robbery,' said Daniel. 'A great deal of money was taken.'

Chad nodded clinically; Lyle leant forward and pressed his chin into his hand.

'Cops informed?' asked Lyle.

Daniel smiled. 'No, the money taken was, shall we say, of dubious origin. I prefer for us to deal with this matter ourselves.'

Lyle flashed his ready smile and eased back into the chair. 'Fire away.'

'I've got a good idea who took it. I'll give you names, addresses, dates, descriptions. Makes and models of cars. The rest is up to you. Talk to people, find out where they are.'

Daniel began to reel off the information.

Lyle slumped casually in the chair, one foot resting on the opposite knee. He had the air of being blasé but Daniel knew he was committing each word to memory. Lyle had a memory like a databank.

Meanwhile, Chad had pulled out a small white notebook. He was jotting down fact after fact. This was their normal practice of teamwork, Daniel recalled. Lyle would remember the facts in his head; Chad would jot them down as corroborative hard copy.

'Fine,' Chad said, snapping the book shut and replacing it in his shirt breast pocket when Daniel had finished talking. 'We'll get on it right away.'

'I want them found red-handed,' said Daniel, his voice menacingly low. 'And I want them found today. They've had a good start but they'll be starting to relax. Hire a chopper, do whatever, but I want them found today. Understand?'

Chad and Lyle nodded solemnly, stood up and shook Daniel's hand. 'Consider it done,' said Lyle, smiling.

The men walked over to the door.

'Boys?' said Daniel.

154

They paused and turned.

'I want my money back,' he warned. 'And I want them found.'

Understanding shone in their eyes.

'No matter what,' finished Daniel quietly.

Chad nodded. Lyle smiled. They closed the door gently as they left.

Valerie was in a quandary. Seeing Bradley visit the house this morning had reminded her that she wanted to call up Ashley and tell her about her stay with Daniel. That in turn had reminded her of Ashley's opinion of Daniel. Ashley's warning voice repeated itself inside her head like a soft, insistent whisper – charming on the surface but different underneath, something steely, something hard . . .

Worst of it was, thought Valerie, was Ashley right?

Deep in thought, she walked along the wide golden sands that ran parallel to the lawns and gardens of the house. Her hands were pushed into the front pockets of her jeans.

Daniel had been tied up with work for over an hour, and the early-morning sun shining hazy on the beach had looked inviting, so she had decided to take herself off for a walk. Tripping down the steps of the terrace, she had seen Daniel's two dogs lazing on the lawn.

'Come on, boys,' she said brightly, patting her thigh.

They had raised their handsome black and tan heads, looked at her with marked indifference, then dropped back to sleep.

'Stay put then.' She shrugged, setting off on her own. Like master, like dogs, she thought. Moody.

She walked barefoot by the water's edge. A smooth wave rolled in, trickling up to her feet. It felt good so she stopped and rubbed her feet in the damp sand. She shaded her eyes, looking out to sea. It was beautiful.

I could stay here, she thought. With him. Even if it were mud and swampland I was looking at, I could stay here. If he asked me to.

But she knew he wouldn't ask, and Ashley's warning voice whispered over and over again. Different underneath, hard, hard, hard ...

Ashley was right. There *was* something underneath. She had seen that in the way the veneer vanished sometimes and he spoke to her in a calculating way. Last night, for instance, that bizarre conversation when he had warned her not to play games. What games? What did that mean? What was he on about? Valerie let out an exasperated sigh. Maybe she would be better off out of it.

And yet there was the passion to think about, the tremendous sexual energy between them. How often did that come along in a lifetime?

Valerie gazed out for several moments more, wondering what she should do. Then she turned on her heel, put her hands in her pockets again and began to stroll back along the beach. She had made a decision.

Daniel had expected to find her on the terrace. She wasn't there. He looked down across the lawns and gardens. She wasn't there either. He walked briskly to the steps that led down to the beach and scanned the long, golden sands. No sign.

The house was quiet when he returned inside. Wondering where she was, he stepped quickly from room to room. He climbed the stairs quietly, moving along the landing to his bedroom. Unusually, his bedroom door was ajar.

Placing his knuckles on the door panel so as not to make any noise, he silently nudged the door open. She was inside the room, over on the far side, with her back to him. Evidently, she had not heard him.

He watched her for a moment, not speaking. The mood of triumph he had been enjoying at having set the wheels in motion to catch Mark and Nadine began to seep away.

'What are you doing?' he said testily.

Valerie spun round, startled. As he had come to

expect from her, she recovered herself instantly. She smoothed her hands over her tousled, blonde hair and smiled.

'Oh hey,' she said breezily. 'Did you get your calls done?'

'What are you doing?' he repeated, ignoring her greeting.

Valerie glanced down towards her suitcase and then switched her eyes back to him. 'Packing,' she said softly.

Daniel looked at her hard. 'Why?'

She laughed. A bit of a brittle, embarrassed laugh. 'You know,' she said, shrugging. 'Things to do. I've been here two days. I figured I didn't want to outstay my welcome.'

'If I had wanted you to leave, I would have said so.'

A shadow of anger passed instantly over Valerie's lovely face. She snapped her fingers in the air. 'That's it!' she said, with that same brittle laugh. 'That's the exact goddamn reason I'm leaving. That arrogance!'

Unfazed, Daniel walked towards her. 'You love it,' he said softly.

'No, you're wrong.' She shook her head. 'I love the sex; I love the passion; I love the chemistry between us. Hell, maybe I even love you. But I do not love the arrogance, and I especially don't appreciate these weird, cryptic things you say to me every once in a while.'

He continued towards her, smiling confidently. 'Then I won't say them any more.'

She looked amazing to him. The flush of anger had heightened her cheekbones and her eyes flashed like jewels. She was holding herself tense and her breasts seemed to strain against her tiny T-shirt. Daniel felt his cock stir at the sight of her. He wanted so badly to push that T-shirt up over her breasts and run his hands over them, feel her nipples stiffen at his touch.

She blinked and looked at him warily. She pushed

her fingers through her hair and then turned back to her packing. 'It's better if I go,' she muttered.

'Is it?' whispered Daniel.

He brushed the nape of her neck with the back of his bended forefinger and watched how she tremored with pleasure. Then he trailed his finger down her back and up underneath her T-shirt. Her skin felt silky and warm.

She twisted round to look at him, her face already softening with desire. 'Daniel –' she began.

He didn't answer, taking her by the shoulders and twisting her fully round until she faced him. Tipping up her chin with his forefinger, he bent to kiss her. He kissed her gently at first, drawing the tip of his tongue flirtatiously along the smooth join of her closed lips. Gradually, he nudged his tongue between her lips, licking her teeth and then meeting the delicious, darting tip of her tongue. She opened her mouth, surrendering, welcoming. They kissed for a while, tongues touching, twirling and eager.

As they eased apart, Daniel noticed Valerie's lips were slightly smudged and rosied from their kissing. The sight made his belly pitch with excitement.

He took a step back and perched down on the edge of the bed. 'Undress for me,' he said. He deliberately didn't say please. He wanted to dominate and he wanted to see her reaction.

Valerie stood demurely in front of him. Excitement all but glazed her features, but he watched her face carefully and he saw the last flicker of resistance fade away. She could not resist him, he saw that. He knew then that she never would.

She undressed slowly, teasing him. She was making him wait but he didn't mind. When she was standing fully naked before him, he decided to return the compliment. He let his eyes linger on every inch of her nakedness and her nipples stiffened by this alone, centring her full high breasts like crimson beads. He drew his gaze slowly down her slender curves, letting his eyes rest on the pretty blonde fluff at the apex of her lightly tanned thighs.

'Pose for me, Valerie,' he said.

'Pose?' she repeated, her voice a little husky. 'In what way?'

'Whatever way you want,' he said easily. 'Show yourself off to me.' She had whetted his appetite with the slow, teasing way she had undressed. He wanted more of the same.

She seemed as if she were trying to control her delight. 'OK,' she whispered.

She lifted her arms high above her head, crossing her wrists gracefully. Her movement was graceful and fluid, every inch the dancer she was, and she struck the pose like a mannequin. She waited a moment, letting him study her.

'You like?' she asked softly.

'Uh huh,' he replied. The movement stretched her stomach and breasts, and accentuated the smallness of her waist.

'Now turn round,' he instructed.

With a quirky smile, she obliged.

'Arch your back.'

Coolly, he regarded her, sweeping his eyes across the fine definition of her shoulders, down the curve of her arched back, on to the firm cheeks of her toned bottom. He looked at her like that for at least five minutes and Valerie must have wondered what he was doing because she turned her head round. When she saw that he was still observing her, she dropped her eyes down her own rear view, as though she wanted to see what he was seeing.

Suddenly, she dropped her arms, resting them sassily on her hips. Daniel liked that. Through her looped arms, he could catch a tantalising glimpse of the flesh of her breasts.

'OK,' he said at last. 'Lie down on the carpet now. On your stomach.'

'What for?' asked Valerie, though her voice contained no reluctance, just interest.

'You'll see.'

She needed no further persuasion, lying down flat on the thick white carpet, resting her face on her crossed forearms.

'Close your eyes,' he said.

She sighed softly as she did so.

'Good,' he murmured as he slipped off the bed and knelt by her side on the carpet. He pressed his lips to the sweet hollow at the base of her head and butterfly-kissed his way down the nape of her neck. When he reached the knobble at the top of her spine, he twirled his tongue around it before resuming the soft light kisses down her spine.

'Mmm,' she sighed happily.

Then he carried on down, brushing his mouth against the uppermost start of her bottom crease and floating his lips down the surface of her intimate line. As he arrived at the fleshy base of her bottom, he nudged her legs apart slightly and continued his kisses down the satin inside of her thigh. When he reached her ankle, he kissed his way back up the other leg, over her bottom again, up her spine again. At the nape of her neck, he pushed her hair back from her ear and whispered, 'I was wrong to say the things I did, those "weird, cryptic things" you mentioned.' It was the closest Daniel would ever come to an apology or an explanation.

'It's OK,' slurred Valerie, apparently lost in the bliss and sensuality of his touch.

He checked that she still had her eyes closed, then he got up silently and went over to a chest of drawers. He pulled out a lilac silk scarf and something else too, then moved quietly back to her side.

'Valerie?' he said.

She opened her eyes lazily.

'Turn over and let me show you how much pleasure I can give you.'

Straight away, she looked at the scarf, excitement sparking like fire in her eyes.

'Hands above your head,' he whispered.

She turned over slowly and held her wrists obligingly above her head. He tied her wrists loosely to the leg of the bed – so loose she could have wriggled free at any time.

'Are you ready?' he asked.

'Yes,' she said breathlessly.

He picked up the long, softly plumed feather he had taken from the drawer and drew it slowly down the underside of Valerie's bound arms. As he directed the feather to her smooth, pale armpits, drifting it luxuriously round and round, a fine line of gooseflesh prickled her skin.

Because her arms were raised above her head, her breasts were stretched up again, slightly flattened by her position. Her nipples, though, were pert and aroused. As Daniel floated the tip of the feather across them, it seemed to perk them even more.

She gasped lightly. 'Oh God,' she moaned, wriggling her arms slightly as he played the white plume to and fro across her tightened nipples.

'No,' she groaned, overstimulated, trying to push up her breasts. 'No more – !'

'Don't you like it?' taunted Daniel.

'I . . . yes, I love it!' she gasped. 'But I can't take it, it's too much. Please Daniel, feel me. Feel me hard.'

And with that, she arched her back off the floor, pushing up her breasts again. Daniel took the feather from her nipples, and brushed it across the smooth flesh of her breasts instead.

'Feel me,' she urged.

'Not yet,' purred Daniel.

He began to drag the feather down her body, watching as she tensed her muscles and pulled her stomach tightly in. He approached the small curve of her mound and began to tangle the plume in her soft fluffy hair. Arrows of excitement shot through his body as he did this, as the white plumage of the feather blended with the short blonde down on her pubis.

Valerie was tilting up her head as much as she could to watch him.

'Spread your legs, Valerie,' he said, his voice thick.

She parted her legs for him.

'Wider,' he coaxed. 'Show me your pussy.'

Valerie shot him a look that pierced his belly. The excitement between them was electric.

'Christ, yes,' he said as she displayed herself to him. Her lips were almost nude, pale shell-pink in colour, and the delicate nub of her clitoris peeked through from the pouting folds. Her sex glistened with silvery moisture and Daniel had to take a moment to collect himself, to try to still the burning frenzy in his groin.

He moved the feather downward, drifting it around her exposed sex, tickling the strained tendons at the insides of her open thighs.

Daniel felt the sweat of sexual desire trickle down the small of his back. Quickly, he shrugged off his shirt before picking up the feather again. This time he drew the downy tip straight up the seam of Valerie's sex. She flinched and sighed in unison.

Daniel continued this for a while, until he could see the slight swelling of her sex. Then, with Valerie's feverish eyes locked upon him, he bent her knees and pushed her legs up and back, until he had exposed her bottom.

Twisting the feather in his fingers, he turned it upside down, holding the long, smooth shaft aloft. He pulled the shaft slowly down her wet sex, until it shone with her sex dew.

'Oh, lovely,' sighed Valerie, closing her eyes.

'Yes,' agreed Daniel, continuing the sensual journey, continuing to drift the smooth shaft downward. As he reached the small pink mouth of her bottom, he began to insert the moistened stem inside.

Valerie flicked her eyes open and tilted up her head again. She caught her breath and didn't speak but the expression on her face told him everything – pleasure, desire, intense excitement. She rolled her hips slightly, letting him slide the stem of the feather in further, and then gently Daniel began to stimulate, wiggling the stem carefully up and down. He moved the fingers of his other hand to her sex and expertly began to massage her.

'Oh God, oh yes,' she moaned, clearly unable to keep quiet any longer.

'Is that good?' asked Daniel, hushed and tense himself.

She writhed on the floor in answer, still with her wrists tied and her knees bent up in the air.

Daniel worked his fingers faster, vibrating her wet sex lusciously from side to side.

'Oh yes, more,' she pleaded. 'More, more.'

He moved his hand quicker, vibrating vigorously, and now and again teasing her bottom with the feather stem.

'Yes,' she moaned repeatedly, each utterance slow and sustained, until suddenly she cried out desperately, arching her back. Her whole body seemed to tremble with rapture. When she gazed up at him moments later, raking her eyes down his bare chest, Daniel saw a mixture of fulfilment and hunger.

Slowly, Daniel moved his hands to the waist of his trousers. He undid the button and pulled down the zipper.

'Still want to leave?' he whispered as he leant across her.

She looked at him steadily, with lust in her eyes. 'No,' she answered, shaking her head. 'Never.'

That suited Daniel fine. For now. Or as long as he wanted. He eased himself inside her, moving quickly, and very soon his mind began to spin along with every inch of his body.

Chapter Fifteen

*T*uesday afternoon in the desert was as sunny and dry as Tuesday afternoon back in Santa Barbara. Only hotter. Much, much hotter. The sun blazed down with relentless intensity.

However, Nadine and Mark were on such a high that they barely noticed the heat. Besides, they were mostly inside the air-conditioned car so they did not really have to deal with it. But if they came across a gas station they made sure they always filled up the tank, aware that the one thing they must not do is run out of petrol. As an added precaution, they were keeping an extra supply of fuel in the trunk of the car.

They were taking their time today. Yesterday, they hadn't seen more than two or three vehicles on the road so they saw no need to hurry. Mark had taken the whole week off work and that was plenty of time to do what they had set out to do.

They had stayed overnight in another small roadside motel, sleeping late and setting off at just before noon. Bit by bit, as time had passed since Saturday night, they both felt more and more sure of themselves, sure that the robbery *had* been perfect after all and there was not a single clue that would lead Daniel to them. Now, more than ever, they felt they were home free.

Nadine stretched out comfortably in the front seat of the car, purring like a contented kitten. Mark flashed her a smile. She smiled back, pushing her sunglasses back through her hair so that Mark could catch the wicked glint in her eye. He did.

'What're you thinking?' he asked, grinning.

'If Uncle Will could only see me now.' She chuckled. 'I'd surely show him how much I need his stupid allowance.'

'Yeah, well,' shrugged Mark. 'He was good to you for a long time.'

Nadine lowered her eyelashes and gazed sideways at him. She was amused. 'So,' she murmured, 'you think Uncle Will was good to me? When he cut off my allowance like that, prepared to leave me without a red cent, you think he was being good?'

'Let's just say no one ever gave me an allowance.'

'Poor baby,' teased Nadine, running her fingertip around the edge of his ear.

'Quit that,' muttered Mark, jerking his head away irritably.

'Oh, is Marky baby being sensitive?' she purred.

'I'll show you sensitive,' said Mark, slamming on the brakes so hard that Nadine had to grab on to the dashboard. She held on tight as the car screeched to a halt.

'Phew,' she gasped, blowing back ribbons of hair that had fallen in front of her eyes. 'Did I hit a nerve?'

'No, I think you hit the dash.' Mark looked as if he was trying to keep his face straight.

'Touché,' snapped Nadine, beginning to feel annoyed herself now. 'Look what you did,' she said plaintively, showing him the reddened mark on her hand where she had grabbed on to the dashboard.

'Let me make it all better,' soothed Mark, taking her hand and pressing it to his lips. When he withdrew his mouth, he smiled at her so beguilingly that she felt her annoyance dissipate at once.

'Let's make friends,' she suggested croakily.

'Good idea,' said Mark, equally croaky.

They leant their heads together, nuzzling each other. Just as their lips met and Nadine was enjoying the smooth texture of the kiss, Mark pulled back. He sat very still in the car.

'What's that?' he muttered.

Nadine was suddenly wary. 'What?' she asked on reflex. She listened carefully. She heard it too – a distant kind of rumbling.

'That,' confirmed Mark.

They listened some more, both alert. Gradually the noise seemed to fade. Mark got out of the car. Nadine watched out of the window as Mark gazed up into the sky. He beckoned her out.

'What do you make of that?' he asked, pointing skyward.

Nadine flicked her sunglasses down from the top of her head and followed the direction of his finger. She saw a darkish object in the distance, getting smaller even as she looked.

'Dunno,' she shrugged. 'A helicopter maybe.'

'That's what I thought.'

They looked at each other in stark silence for a moment. Nadine felt tense and she saw slight furrows in Mark's normally smooth forehead. She looked up into the sky again.

'Whatever it was, it's gone,' she declared.

'Yeah,' agreed Mark.

They gazed at each other a moment more, not speaking.

'Well,' said Nadine eventually, 'what do you think it was?'

'Like you said, a helicopter.' Mark shrugged. 'Probably the military. They have sites and weapons testing in the desert.'

Nadine's face brightened. 'Yes. Or an excursion. They have excursion trips, don't they? For tourists?'

'Yeah,' agreed Mark, his forehead smooth again.

'So it's nothing?' ventured Nadine in a small voice.

Mark scanned the empty sky once again. Then he grinned and nodded. 'It's nothing and it's gone.'

Nadine let her shoulders sag with relief. She walked over to Mark and leant against him. 'Anyway,' she said, 'if it were anyone else, say anyone after us, they wouldn't just fly away, would they?'

'That's right,' said Mark, stroking her hair reassuringly. He leant down and pecked her on the tip of her nose. 'Come on,' he said, nudging her towards the car. 'Let's not get sidetracked.'

'Oh yeah,' chuckled Nadine. 'We were just making up, right?'

'Uh huh. And no bunch of tourists in a chopper is going to do us out of that!'

Some distance away, a dark-coloured helicopter was coming in to land. Two men were seated in the back, one crew-cut and blond, the other dark and ponytailed. As the helicopter landed, kicking up a swirl of dust and sand, the dark man unbuckled his seat belt, leant forward and gave the pilot a rolled wad of $50 bills. He thanked the pilot for his help.

The two men got out of the helicopter. Shielding their faces from the gritty, flying sand and ducking low to avoid the spinning blades, they made their way quickly to a car which was parked close by. Seconds later, the helicopter roared and rose up steadily into the air. As it whirled off through the sky in the direction of Los Angeles, the blond man revved the engine of the car and began to drive fast in the opposite direction.

Mark drove at a steady pace. At the moment the road was so straight that he barely had to steer the car at all. He kept one hand at the base to steady the steering wheel and rested the other on Nadine's warm thigh. Nadine was fast asleep and whilst she slept Mark had been trying to work out how far from the state border they must be.

He first saw the car as a shimmering haze in his

sideview mirror. As it came closer, gradually metamorphosing into a vehicle, he thought little of it. The car appeared to be travelling extremely fast; as they were not, it seemed natural that sooner or later the car would overtake.

But for some reason it did not do that. Some way back the car seemed to slow down slightly. For a while it still maintained enough speed to draw steadily closer, then, at around thirty yards behind them, it appeared to slow again. It kept the thirty-yard distance, trailing constantly behind them, clearly with no immediate intention to overtake. Mark felt the first tingle of unease.

Gently, he nudged Nadine on her thigh. She opened her eyes lazily. Her face had the soft, guileless look of one adjusting from sleep to wakefulness. Mark waited a moment for her to come to.

'What is it?' She yawned. 'Why d'you wake me?'

Mark glanced in the side mirror to check on the car. It was still behind, travelling within its own set distance. Mark exhaled softly. 'Honey,' he said calmly. 'I think we may have a problem.'

Immediately, Nadine sat up straighter in her seat. 'What sort of a problem?'

'We seem to have picked up a tail.' He flicked his eyes up to the rear-view mirror. 'See that car behind. It's been tailing us like that for the past ten minutes.'

Nadine checked her own side mirror. 'Are you sure?' she whispered.

'Oh, I'm sure,' confirmed Mark.

Nadine studied her mirror. 'It seems to be two men.'

'Yep,' Mark nodded.

'Do you know them?'

Mark shook his head. 'Uh uh.'

'Why are they just hanging back like that?' she muttered.

Again, Mark shook his head. 'Beats me. Biding their time. Maybe they're thinking we'll pull in.'

Nadine studied her mirror a little more. 'Who do you think they are?' she asked in a hushed voice.

'Who knows,' shrugged Mark. 'And I don't want to wait around to find out. One thing I do know, we're going to need a plan, and quick, to get rid of them. I think I may have an idea but, first off, we're going to need a diversion. Any ideas?'

Nadine stared off ahead for a minute. Slowly, she began to smile a little.

'What?' said Mark suspiciously. He knew that smile.

The smile began to widen. 'Two men in that car, and what do men like?' She glanced down to her lap and flicked up the skirt of her short summer dress. Her thighs looked sleek, golden, perfect in every way.

'No,' said Mark, his voice short and final.

'Baby,' she coaxed, 'this is dangerous, this could be the end. We have the money large as anything in the back of the car. These guys, whoever they are, even if they're nothing to do with Daniel which by the way I don't see how they can be because I *know* that robbery was perfect – even if they're just a couple of guys out to cause trouble, they're going to find that money if they stop us. And you can bet every dollar in the case they're going to take it. And then, wham, there goes our future.'

Mark seemed unsure. 'I don't know.'

'We have to use whatever resources we've got,' she continued. 'And this,' she swept her hand down her body, 'is one hell of a resource!'

Mark managed a brief smile. 'OK, OK, you've convinced me,' he said, trying to be businesslike. 'So, here's what we do . . .'

They drove on steadily for a while. The car, as they had anticipated, stayed behind, keeping its distance. When Mark saw the approaching bend in the road he knew this might be his one and only opportunity. The looping S-shape would provide a degree of cover for them.

'This is it,' he warned Nadine, pressing his foot hard on the accelerator.

The car surged forward, rounding the bend, even before their tailing car had time to accelerate. They rounded the second bend at maximum speed, out of sight, however briefly, of the second car. Timing was now of the essence.

Mark slammed on the brakes, left the keys in the ignition, and jumped out of the car. He sprinted across the road, crouched down into a trench that ran alongside the road, then lay down flat on his stomach. Seconds later, the tailing car speeded into view.

The second car squealed to a stop, this time stopping about forty yards back. Why? Why stay back? And then suddenly it struck Mark why. These men were professionals; they were not about to hare in unprepared.

Mark kept his body flat and low in the trench, managing to lift his eyes just enough to see what was happening. Nadine had turned off the ignition and was already putting their plan into action. A shiver of pride ran down Mark's spine as he watched her – she was one of a kind, no messing, no baulking, straight on with the job. Thank God he could count on her.

She flounced out of the car, careful to leave her door open. Good. She bent from the waist, peering into the car as if he was still in there.

'*You* can stay in there and boil if you want,' she said to the empty interior of the car. 'But I need to cool down.'

She hadn't yelled or been too obvious, but she had raised her voice just enough for the two strangers to hear if they had wanted. Mark saw they had lowered their car windows. Oh, they wanted to hear all right. But they hadn't left their seats yet and, so far, that was a good thing. He had banked on that. Slowly, Mark began to inch his body forward along the trench, towards the other car.

Meanwhile, Nadine had opened up the trunk of their own car and was pulling out the coolbox. She was careful to close the trunk before she hauled the cooler just a few yards from the car. At no point had she turned towards the other car or indeed given any indication that she was even aware of them. Just as he had told her, thought Mark proudly. The idea was to pique their interest.

Nadine set the ice cooler down on the ground and pulled off the lid. She rummaged in the box for a few moments, before bringing out a bottle of mineral water. Mark was still inching forward in the deep, roadside trench; the desert dirt caked itself to his lips and his eyes felt gritty but bit by bit he was gaining ground and moving towards the strangers' car.

Mark flicked his eyes back to Nadine. She was standing in profile. Her glossy dark hair tumbled round her shoulders and down her back and her short cream dress looked fresh and becoming. Teamed with matching cork wedge sandals which tied up around her ankles, the outfit heightened the smooth even tan of her bare arms and legs.

For a second or so, Nadine rolled the ice-cooled bottle of mineral water against her throat, a look of lazy relief on her face. Then, taking her time, she unscrewed the top off the bottle, tipped back her head and held the bottle to her lips. She sipped the water carefully first of all, before tipping her head back further and drinking thirstily as if craving the liquid. The water began to trickle from the sides of her mouth, running in glistening rivulets down her smooth jawline and neck. Nadine did not seem to care. She kept on drinking, tipping back her head still further, letting the water drench her mouth and neck and the front of her body.

When she had finished, she held the bottle aloft, flicking out her tongue as if to catch the last few drops. Distracted though Mark was, wracked with tension though he was, the sight of her doing that made him pause. Her full lips were shiny and wet and her flicking tongue looked naughty and delicious.

Mark glanced at the two strangers. Nadine seemed

to be having a similar effect upon them. The dark one was smiling and watchful, the blond man equally engrossed.

Nadine was smiling now. She had tossed the empty water bottle carelessly to the ground and appeared to be occupied with the front of her dress which was completely drenched with water. She tugged the sodden fabric away from her body for a moment, laughing gaily, and then she appeared to come to a decision. Without any further hesitation, she swept her dark hair to one side, reached behind herself, and pulled down the zipper of her dress. She eased the dress forward off her shoulders and let it slip to her waist. Then she wriggled it down her body and stepped out of it.

She was naked. Naked and lovely.

The two men in the car exchanged looks, even the blond man's taciturn expression seemed to brighten, Mark noticed. Then they turned back to Nadine, riveted to her. Mark felt a rush of possessive jealousy – he would like to have knocked their gawking heads together!

Nadine was now holding her dress in front of her, wringing the water from it. When she had twisted the garment several times, she wandered to the back of Mark's car and began to reshape the dress and stretch it out across the back of the car as if to dry it quickly. In fact, as Mark knew, she was giving the two men the full benefit of her nakedness.

Her body looked superb. The way she moved as she leant towards the car to arrange the dress showed off her bare, slender back and her rounded bottom. After she had stretched the dress out, it seemed to occur to her that the tie of her sandal needed some attention. She looked down at her ankle, and then crouched to the ground, bending her knees outwards apparently to steady herself and to avoid having to come into contact with the dusty sand.

Mark felt another slight punch in his belly. Nadine's hair fell silkily to the middle of her back and her buttocks were curving out, parting a little because of the position. Mark could even see a tantalising glimpse of pinkness between her legs. She seemed to be redoing the tie around her ankle.

Mark edged forward a little more. He was almost parallel with the other car now. He crossed his fingers, prayed as he had never prayed before, and then he waited.

The two men were still fixated on Nadine. She had stood up again, and turned around as if to walk back to the side of the car. For the first time, she looked directly at the second car. She widened her eyes with fright and dropped her jaw. Her fingers flew to her mouth in simulated alarm. She seemed frozen to the spot. She stood still as a statue, hand across her mouth, nothing to cover her nakedness. Her small pert breasts looked swollen in the heat, her nipples pinker and larger than normal.

The fact that she was staring directly at them, her face a picture of paralysed shock, seemed to galvanise the two men into action. They nodded quickly at one another, then in total synchrony, they stepped out of the car, leaving both doors open. Mark ducked low as they glanced around, and then they started to walk towards Nadine.

Mark watched them carefully. What he saw sent him rigid with shock. A cold sweat of panic broke out on his body. Shoved into the waistband of their jeans, streamlined, smooth and unmistakable, were handguns.

Of course there were, thought Mark, cursing his naivety. They weren't playing in the little league now – these men were dangerous and they meant business, and there was not a shred of doubt in his mind now they had been sent by Daniel. Somehow, someway, Daniel had traced the robbery to them.

In despair, Mark shot his eyes to Nadine – she was acting her part like a trained thespian. There was no time to warn her of the guns, no time to do anything but carry out the plan.

That's exactly what he must do.

The men were staring rigidly ahead as they walked, focused entirely on Nadine. Aware that he must not make the slightest noise now, Mark drew his knees up underneath his chest until he was in a crouching position. Very, very carefully, he climbed out of the trench. Although she gave no indication, Nadine must have seen him because she took her hand away from her mouth and started to reach behind for the back of the car. The move was a perfect distraction, certain to keep the men's eyes glued to her as she pushed out her bare breasts by reaching behind.

With the stealth of a stalking cougar, Mark started to creep across the road. The road looked a thousand miles wide to Mark and each footstep he took seemed to take for ever. His heart thumped against his chest and he could feel the blood pounding in his veins. But he kept on, silently, stealthily, moving towards that open car door.

By now, the men were almost halfway between him and Nadine. They were not hurrying, they seemed so sure of themselves, as if they had no need to hurry. That worried Mark, but he had to keep going, couldn't lose it now. He was almost at the car. Three more steps and he would be there. One. Two . . .

Three! He was there.

Keeping low, he stole into the car. Manoeuvring himself into the driving seat, he felt as though every wish he had ever made in his life had come together then and there – they were the most wonderful set of car keys he had ever seen and they were right there in the ignition.

Now for the tricky part, he thought. The men were getting too close to Nadine, he had to act now. He was staking everything on distracting the two men long enough for Nadine to do her bit. Simultaneously, he started the ignition and grabbed the car door handles

174

to shut them. It worked. The two men wheeled round at once, both grabbing for their guns.

In that instant, Nadine made a run for their own car, slamming the door shut. The engine revved and with a squeal of tyres, she took off.

Mark shoved the second car into gear, pressed his foot hard on the gas, and did the same. The blond man aimed his gun. As Mark sped past, he fired. The glass of the rear side window shattered. Mark's hands shook on the wheel. He gripped the wheel hard to steady himself, instinctively ducking low. Another pop of a gun. This time the rear window shattered. Mark kept going, not really thinking, his survival mechanism kicking in.

Up ahead, he could see Nadine tearing along the roadway. He wasn't that far behind her. He glanced in his rear-view mirror. Both men were standing, legs astride in the middle of the road, aiming their guns with both hands. But the shots were falling short now, lost in the asphalt of the road surface.

Mark straightened up, glancing in his rear-view mirror once again. The two men looked increasingly small as the distance between them and the car grew. They were no longer even bothering to shoot, letting their arms drop down to their sides in defeat. Mark grinned and his body weakened with relief. He was euphoric. They had done it! Goddamn, they had pulled it off!

In front of him, Nadine was starting to slow a little. Quickly, Mark closed the gap until he was hovering on her bumper. Nadine stuck her arm out of the car window, waving gaily. Mark tooted the horn in response, short, jaunty toots of triumph. They drove on in convoy for the next half-hour, putting distance between them and their pursuers, until suddenly Mark spotted something a little distance out, to the left of the roadway. He flashed his lights. Nadine responded, pulling in to the side.

They each got out of their respective cars. Nadine wore only her smile and her sandals. Beaming broadly,

Mark walked towards her and took her in his arms, holding her lush naked body against him.

'You were fantastic,' he said in awe.

'So were you,' she said in a low, passionate voice. 'So calm and brave.' All of a sudden, she seemed close to tears.

'Shoosh,' said Mark, pressing his finger to her lips. '*We* were fantastic. A team.'

'Yes,' she agreed, resting her head beneath his chin. 'Who do you think they were?' she whispered.

Mark was sure of his answer. 'Daniel sent them.'

Nadine drew back her head. 'No,' she insisted. 'That's impossible. I left no clues. He couldn't possibly know it was us.'

'Somehow he does.'

'No.' Nadine shook her head. 'I don't believe it.'

Mark rubbed his hand soothingly on the hot skin of her back. 'Believe it, Nadine,' he said softly. 'I warned you about him, how long his reach is, how you shouldn't underestimate him.'

Nadine looked up at him, her triumphant smile returning. 'Even if it was Daniel,' she said, 'we got away. We beat those guys. We did it.'

Mark felt another surge of euphoric adrenalin. 'I know.' He grinned. 'We did it!'

He pressed his lips to hers and kissed her hungrily. She pulled back a second later with a giggle. 'Pwah,' she said, pulling bits of dust and sand off her mouth and tongue. 'You're kind of dirty, Mark.'

Mark brushed his hand down his gritty face. 'Come here.' He grinned, jerking her to him. 'I'll show you how dirty I can be.'

They kissed again, deep and triumphant, never minding the dirt and the grit. Mark dropped his hands down her back and squeezed the firm cheeks of her bottom.

'One thing,' he said, kissing the column of her neck.

'What's that?' she murmured, tipping back her head.

'Now Daniel knows it was us, we can never go back.'

Nadine looked him straight in the eye, thoughtful for a moment. Then she shrugged and chuckled. 'Who needs to?' she laughed. 'We have everything we need right there in the trunk of the car.'

Mark laughed with her. 'Yeah.'

They kissed some more, their fervour growing. Mark felt the heat of her body through his shirt as she pressed against him. She stood up on tiptoe, pushing her hips forcefully against the hardness in his groin. It hurt a little but aroused him more. Gently, he eased her away – he had something to do before they made love.

'One more thing again,' he said.

'What this time?' quipped Nadine.

'Watch this,' answered Mark with a wink. He walked over to the thing he had spotted earlier, to the left of the roadway. It was the decrepit remains of a disused mine-shaft. Standing to one side, he held aloft the car keys to their pursuers' car and promptly dropped them down the shaft. He swiped his hands against each other in a gesture of completion.

'That takes care of that,' he chuckled.

'Bet that felt good,' said Nadine. Her voice cracked softly in that sexy way it sometimes did when she was worked up and aroused. She crooked her finger towards him. 'Now come here and get a reward.'

And he did.

Chapter Sixteen

M ark and Nadine crossed the border into Nevada later that afternoon.

After their successful encounter with Daniel's men, their lovemaking had been almost cathartic, releasing the tensions of that whole situation. It was only afterwards that they confronted reality. And reality was that Daniel was on to them. They realised they no longer had time to drive at their own pace, linger and make love if they felt like it, sleep in till noon if they wanted. They had had a narrow escape, they knew, and they would be foolish not to learn from it. They may have left those two men carless in the desert but neither Nadine nor Mark was naive enough to think they, and Daniel, would not have a contingency plan. Sooner or later those men would be picked up, and then they would be after them again, madder than ever no doubt.

So, Mark had put his foot down and driven across the final portion of their Californian journey as though he were trying to break the landspeed record. Their plan was to head for Las Vegas and lose themselves in the anonymity of the gambling capital. Once there, they would bank the money and then hire a plane and disappear for a while. The money would stay in the bank, untouched and hidden, until they felt safe enough to transfer it into off-shore accounts.

The plan was a good one and they knew that, the sooner they reached Vegas and carried it through, the better for them. But they would have to appear credible to do that and right now they were exhausted, and Mark was covered with dust and grit from his manoeuvres in the roadside trench. They needed to be off the road for a while and, when Nadine pointed out a signpost to a small town close by, Mark veered off immediately towards it.

'It'll give us a chance to book a room and freshen up,' he said. 'And besides that, we can go through every detail of the plan with a fine toothcomb.'

'Sure,' she agreed, resting back her head a moment and closing her eyes. When she opened them, she saw yet another hazy mirage on the dusty, empty roadway ahead. She blinked to get rid of it.

'Is that something or nothing?' she asked Mark as the mirage failed to disappear.

Mark tipped down the sunglasses he was wearing and screwed up his eyes. 'Er . . .'

They drove nearer. It was not another mirage. It was something. It looked like a sleek, low sports car. As they drew closer, it became clear the car had pulled in to the side of the road. Nadine tensed instantly, wary of everything now.

'It's a car,' she said, her voice taut.

'Yeah,' muttered Mark. Nadine could see the tension in his jawline as he spoke. She put her hand on his arm.

'Careful, honey,' she warned. 'Just drive by quickly.'

Mark nodded. 'You don't think blondie and ponytail have somehow managed to overtake us, do you?' He said it lightly, clearly as a joke, but his voice faltered with tension as he spoke.

Nadine suppressed a frisson of alarm. Although deep down she knew this was impossible, the mere thought gave her the jitters. Somehow she did not think her theatrical display would stall them a second time.

Mark glanced at her reassuringly, covering her hand with his own. 'Don't worry, honey,' he said. 'Blondie and ponytail will still be working on their tans back there.'

Nadine chuckled. 'That, and looking for their car keys.'

Mark winked at her. They were getting closer all the time to the parked vehicle. It looked as if there was someone standing outside the car.

'Hold on,' said Mark, preparing to speed past.

As they shot past, the person outside the car began waving frantically.

'It's a woman,' said Mark, glancing back through his rear-view mirror.

Nadine twisted her head to look back. It was a woman. She seemed distressed, still waving her arms frantically. She looked to be calling out but any words were lost by the sound of their car engine.

Mark began to slow down. 'She looks in trouble.'

'Uh huh,' said Nadine.

The woman had slumped back against her car, resting the heels of her hands despairingly against her forehead.

Mark stopped the car. 'We can't just leave her out here alone.'

'Someone else will come along soon,' muttered Nadine.

Mark raised an eyebrow at her. 'And what if the only people that come along are blondie and ponytail. Do you think they would help her?'

Nadine shrugged. She felt bad for the woman, being stranded out here alone was not something she wanted to think about.

'OK,' she said quietly. 'Go back. But very, very slowly. There could be someone hiding out in the car.'

Mark spread his arm along the back of her car seat and began to reverse. He stopped a short way from the sports car. The woman looked up. Her face brightened and she jogged across the road to them.

'Thank God,' she said breathlessly. There were tear-stains and streaks of sand down her cheeks, but they did not detract from the prettiness of her face. Her light-blonde hair was tied back and her blue eyes shone with unshed tears. 'I've been out here for over two hours,' she gasped. 'I've run out of gas and my cellular phone doesn't work and I just don't know what . . .'

She stopped as her voice became shaky and her shoulders heaved a little.

'It's OK,' said Mark calmly. 'We can help you. Are you out here alone?'

She shot him a look of pure gratitude. Gulping back the tears, she nodded. 'Yes,' she said. 'I live about three miles away. So stupid of me, I knew the tank was low but I thought I would make it back.'

'You live out here?' asked Nadine incredulously.

The young woman nodded again. 'Yes, I bought a place out here about six months ago. I wanted a bolt-hole, a place to come to get away from the city when I felt like it. Somewhere remote.'

'You surely got that,' quipped Nadine.

The woman smiled quirkily, clearly catching the irony. 'Don't I know it!'

Mark tapped the steering wheel. 'Well,' he said, businesslike. 'We have an extra container of fuel in the back. I can fill up your car and then, hopefully, things will be OK.'

The young woman's face shone with relief. 'Thank you so much,' she said, putting out her hand to him in introduction. 'Um . . . ?'

'Mark.' Mark grinned, shaking her hand. 'And it's a pleasure.'

'My name's Anna-May,' she replied, putting her hand out to Nadine to shake her hand also.

'Pleased to meet you,' said Nadine, all charm and radiance.

'Me too,' smiled Anna-May. 'Sorry about the circumstances though.'

'Not a problem,' said Mark, lifting the container of petrol out of the back of the car. 'We were heading into town anyway, we'll fill up again there.'

'I wouldn't call it a town exactly.' Anna-May laughed. 'More of a general store and a gas station.'

'No motel?' asked Mark, carrying the container across the road to Anna-May's car.

''Fraid not,' she replied.

Mark and Nadine exchanged glances. Better they found out now, thought Nadine, than diverting all that way and then not finding a room.

Mark was preparing to fill up Anna-May's car. It was a black, very chic, very expensive-looking Ferrari. He ran his hand lovingly across the edge of the low roof, moulding his fingers to the exquisite contours of the car. 'Some car,' he said, clearly impressed.

'Normally I think so too,' said Anna-May. 'But for the past couple of hours, while I've been stranded here, I've hated it.'

'Yeah, well. She'll be up and running in a moment,' he said, tipping in the petrol. He drained the container of the last few drops. 'There, that should do it.'

'You know, I really can't thank you enough for this,' said Anna-May. She paused for a moment and looked embarrassed. Then she held out the car keys timidly towards Mark. 'You wouldn't care to start it for me, would you? Just to check?'

'Sure,' grinned Mark, slipping into the driver's seat and starting up the car. 'There you go, everything's fine.' He got out of the car again.

Anna-May hovered in the roadway a moment more, still looking embarrassed. 'Er, you were asking about a motel back there, are you looking for a room?'

'Why?' asked Nadine, cutting in smartly before Mark could answer. She had wandered over to join them.

Anna-May smiled and shrugged. 'Just that, like I told you, there is no motel in town but ... I was thinking

182

maybe you would like to come to my house. I have plenty of space and I could cook you a meal. As my way of thanking you both.'

A shower, thought Nadine longingly. Or a sweet, lazy soak in the bathtub.

Mark looked equally pleased. He raised his eyebrow at her in query.

'That,' said Nadine, smiling radiantly, 'would be wonderful.'

'Great,' said Anna-May, clapping her hands against her jeans-clad thighs. 'Follow me then.'

Just as Anna-May had stated, the house was no more than three miles away. It was certainly remote. Hidden from the roadway and set behind ranch-style fencing, it was constructed of red-brown timber and resembled a large, two-floored cabin, faintly rustic in appearance.

There was nothing rustic about the interior, however – Italian tiled flooring and thick, woven carpets, over-stuffed white chairs and sofas and huge pottery lamps. Geometrical Art Deco works adorned the walls.

'My bolt-hole,' explained Anna-May as they entered. She waved her hand around airily.

'It's great,' said Mark, striding inside.

'It's home, I guess,' said Anna-May with mock humility.

Nadine wandered over to a vast picture window on the far side of the room. 'It *is* lovely,' she said, 'but what I'd really like to see is a bathroom. And a bathtub.'

'Of course.' Anna-May smiled. 'This way.'

Nadine and Mark followed her. She led them through a large double bedroom to an en-suite bathroom of cream and coffee-coloured marble luxury.

'I'll just go and freshen up too,' said Anna-May, leaving them alone.

Nadine wasted no time in stripping off her clothes and filling up the bath, pouring in generous quantities of bath oils. As she slipped into the warm silken water, Mark nudged her arm.

'I'm going out to the car and bring in a suitcase, and the briefcase.'

'OK,' she murmured, sinking into the silken luxury.

Mark reappeared five minutes later. He began to shed his clothes.

'Did you get the briefcase?' asked Nadine lazily.

'Sure,' winked Mark, lifting up the case to show her. 'We'll hide it under the bed before we go downstairs.'

'Good,' smiled Nadine. 'Can't be too careful where that money's concerned.'

'Too right,' agreed Mark, stepping into the shower unit. The next thing Nadine heard was the drumming rush of shower water. She sank down further into the bath, closed her eyes, and began to daydream about spending Daniel Garsante's money.

When Mark had finished showering, Nadine was still soaking in the bath; her face glowed and tendrils of her tied-up hair had escaped, sticking to her neck. She deserved some comfort, he thought, recalling her magnificent charade with Daniel's two men that afternoon. Another surge of pride coursed through his body.

'See you downstairs,' he whispered, pressing his lips fondly to her forehead. She mumbled a vague reply.

Pulling a clean shirt and a pair of jeans from the suitcase he had brought in from the car, he dressed quickly. Then he hid the briefcase full of money beneath the bed, before making his way downstairs.

In the open-plan living room area, he sank down gratefully into one of the overstuffed armchairs. There, he relaxed, shut his eyes, and began to think about spending Daniel Garsante's money.

'Care for a glass of wine, Mark?'

He turned his head quickly. He had been miles away, lost in a land where he never had to look at a price tag.

Anna-May was holding up a bottle of white wine. Mark could see a condensing mist on the outside of the bottle from where it had been chilled. He had not realised until then how thirsty he was.

'Please,' he nodded.

He watched her turn slightly to pour wine into three glasses. Another thing he had not realised properly until then was how lovely Anna-May was. Washed clear of tears and desert dust, her skin had a soft, dewy luminescence. Her blonde hair was thick and buttery, worn in a single plait which fell to the middle of her back. She had changed from her jeans and shirt into an ankle-length, floaty white dress – he could see just enough through the light, sheer fabric to tell that her body was slender. She was barefoot.

She walked over to him. Her fingers brushed lightly against his as she handed him a glass of wine. Then she sat down on the sofa opposite, curling her legs beneath her and nursing her own glass of wine against her chest.

'I really can't thank you enough for helping me out back there,' she said softly. 'I don't know what I would have done if you hadn't stopped.'

Mark shrugged his shoulders in a self-deprecating way. 'It cuts both ways. We have to thank you for all this hospitality.'

'It's nothing,' she said, taking a small sip of her wine. 'Actually, it's my pleasure.'

Mark smiled his thanks, she smiled back. Then her gaze travelled up to the galleried landing behind Mark. Automatically, Mark glanced back. Nadine was walking along the landing. She began to glide down the stairs. She was dressed in a short, yellow towelling robe, her long legs bare. Her hair was still tied up messily, long damp ribbons trailing down her neck. Her face looked fresh and lovely, glowing from her long soak in the bath.

She picked up the third glass of wine from the table, sipping it slowly.

'Hope you don't mind,' she said to Anna-May. 'I borrowed this robe.'

185

Anna-May turned to smile at her. 'I don't mind at all,' she said. 'It looks great on you.' Her eyes lingered a little on Nadine.

Nadine pressed the chilled wine glass to her cheek, looking back at Anna-May then switching her gaze to Mark. Her clear green eyes were bright with something; Mark felt himself stir slightly. He was aware of an undercurrent, a certain excitement in the room. He placed his wine glass carefully on the side table and sank back into the chair. Anna-May was looking at him too now.

'You know,' she said quietly, 'I would really like you to enjoy yourselves here. Tonight.'

Mark was silent. Nadine was too. She was running her finger slowly around the rim of her glass.

Anna-May waited a few moments, then continued. 'And I would really like to enjoy myself too.'

'Or rather three,' she finished softly.

Although he had thought – hoped – as much, Mark's cock leapt at the idea. Nadine's eyes were shining brighter than before. She had stopped toying with the rim of her glass and was putting the rim to her lips. 'Mmm,' she sighed, letting the wine moisten her mouth. 'I like the sound of that . . .'

'I do too,' said Mark, his voice low.

Nadine put her wine glass down and then stepped forward on to the soft carpet rug between him and Anna-May. Her tongue darted flirtatiously to the corner of her mouth at the same time as she moved her hands to the tie of the towelling wrap she was wearing.

'How about I break the ice?' she murmured.

Her elegant hands undid the tie first of all, then she moved them to the upper edges of the garment and pushed it off her smooth shoulders, letting it slip to the floor.

'Oops,' she whispered, standing perfectly poised between them.

Mark ran his eyes down her naked body. Out of the

corner of his eye, he was aware of Anna-May doing the same thing.

Clearly, Nadine was enjoying showing herself off. She was drawing the backs of her fingers lightly down the sides of her small, pert breasts as though highlighting their prettiness, moving them similarly down the sides of her body.

Anna-May sighed. She uncurled her legs from beneath her and stood up. Bending low, she reached for the hem of her ankle-length dress and then drew the dress slowly right up her body and over her head. With a giggle, she flung it carelessly over the shade of a lamp.

Like Nadine, she was totally nude.

Also like Nadine, she was lovely. Nadine's skin tone was slightly more golden, Anna-May had a tan of light, even butterscotch. Her breasts were firm and jaunty and she cupped them in her hands, turning to Mark with a naughty little smile. Mark dropped his eyes appreciatively to the smooth, slender curves of her waist and hips then to the small, dark-blonde triangle of curls lower down.

Jeez, he decided as he looked back and forth from Nadine to Anna-May, he had discovered Utopia. 'Well,' he muttered, 'I guess the ice is well and truly broken.'

Chuckling lightly, they moved closer together until they were standing directly in front of him, superbly nude. Anna-May reached towards Nadine, and traced her fingernail down Nadine's bare upper arm. Nadine looked at Mark, smiling.

'Do you want to watch us, Mark?' she whispered.

'First,' added Anna-May, meaningfully.

Mark grinned, wondering what good deed he had done to deserve this. 'Uh huh,' he said. His voice was already croaky.

Anna-May and Nadine turned to face each other, their breasts almost touching. They were of a similar height and, as they took a step closer, their nipples skimmed against each other's. Mark watched, entranced, as they pressed the twin velvet tips of their breasts together. Both girls caught their breath. Mark's stomach did a cartwheel. They were pushing their shoulders back and pushing their breasts forward. In an unspoken pact, they began to sway their chests from side to side, brushing their nipples against one another's. It looked so erotic that Mark felt weak.

They continued to stimulate each other in this way and their smooth nipples began to harden and, as their pointy tips met, they both began to sigh softly, almost underneath their breath.

After a while, Nadine dropped to her knees, tugging Anna-May down with her. Now they were both kneeling, still facing each other. Anna-May lowered her eyes to Nadine's breasts. Without speaking, she reached forward and began to fondle them, cupping the firm golden mounds and toying gently with Nadine's stiffened nipples.

Nadine stretched back her neck in obvious delight and let herself be played with. When she straightened her neck again minutes later, her face was a little flushed and her eyes were dancing with desire. With a strained little moan, she reached reciprocally for Anna-May's bare breasts, touching and caressing her lovely, firm flesh. For a while, they stroked and fondled each other, sighing with pleasure, now and again letting the very tips of their tongues touch and tease in mid-air between them.

Mark was enthralled. He could barely move, and his eyes were glued to every movement they made. Anna-May was now stroking Nadine's stomach, drifting her fingertips lightly downward. At the same time as she let her fingers roam between Nadine's thighs, Anna-May cast a wicked glance towards him.

Mark nodded his encouragement, watching closely as she patted Nadine's nest of trim, silky hair and then moved her fingers down further.

Nadine gasped with joy, opening her kneeling legs.

188

With gentle, stroking gestures, Anna-May began to fondle her sex.

'Mmm,' murmured Anna-May, feeling Nadine.

Nadine was breathing faster – shorter, sharper inhalations. She was still toying with Anna-May's breasts whilst Anna-May's attentions were between her legs. Anna-May's fingers were swirling gently now, stroking Nadine's soft, wet sex.

Suddenly, Nadine dropped her hands to Anna-May's kneeling thighs and urgently pushed them apart.

'Oh yes.' Anna-May jerked, as Nadine pressed her whole hand in between and began to stimulate.

It felt like a shot to Mark's groin. How sexy could it get. These two beautiful women, kneeling face to face, their thighs apart, touching and stroking each other in the way they were, having him watch them like this. Minutes before, he had not felt able to move; now, he could not keep still.

Leaning forward on the chair, he reached down to them both, stroking the small of their backs. They each turned to look at him, their eyes shining, their faces aglow. He dragged his hands down their backs and then cupped the cheeks of their firm bottoms.

They had not stopped arousing each other's sex but, as Mark cupped their buttocks, their urgency seemed to grow. Their fingers fluttered faster between each other's legs and Mark squeezed their bottoms hungrily, his own desire sky-rocketing.

He could not stand it any longer. His cock was so swollen, it strained against the front of his jeans. With a groan, he stopped what he was doing and began to undress. Immediately, the girls moved to help him. Giggling, they tore at his clothing, tugging off his shirt and jeans.

'Magnificent,' breathed Anna-May, clasping his swollen penis between her hands.

'Isn't it,' breathed Nadine. She grabbed his wrist and tugged him down to the rug with them.

He felt better now that he was naked, no constraints at all on his body.

'OK, girls,' he grinned. 'Carry on where you left off . . .'

Nadine smiled knowingly at him, then turned to Anna-May. Anna-May was sitting up with her arms locked slightly back from her sides. Her breasts were thrust outwards and Nadine reached out and rolled Anna-May's nipples between her fingertips. Anna-May moaned softly, instantaneously arching her back and parting her long legs slightly.

'Oh yes,' muttered Nadine, slipping her fingers between Anna-May's legs once again. She flicked her middle finger rhythmically over the other girl's clitoris until, soon after, Anna-May opened her legs wider. Nadine knelt lower. As Mark looked on in rapt silence, Nadine eased her head down and stuck out the tip of her tongue. Daintily, she began to lick Anna-May, flicking her tongue over her nude, swollen bud.

Anna-May tilted back her head, sighing softly. 'That's so good,' she sighed. '*So* good.'

Nadine swung her head gently from side to side, holding on to Anna-May's wide-open thighs. Nadine was more or less on all fours now, her head was down low, her bottom in the air. Too much for Mark to resist.

He manoeuvred himself behind Nadine. Placing his hands on her pert golden bottom, he drew his tongue with teasing slowness down her silken crease. Nadine wriggled with delight and he did it again and, as he watched over the length of her back, she began to move her own tongue faster between Anna-May's legs, more driven, more impatient.

Anna-May's sighs of pleasure were getting louder. She was arching her back, pressing her sex desperately to Nadine's active mouth. Her nipples were tight and erect.

With a drawn-out, gentle sigh, she climaxed. She closed her eyes. Her body moved in smooth undulations and a faint, pretty flush warmed the skin of her neck and cleavage.

Nadine lifted her head from between Anna-May's legs, a rapt expression on her beautiful face.

After a moment or two, Anna-May opened her eyes again. They were as blue and clear as a mountain lake. A post-orgasmic glow made her skin more luminous than before. She looked utterly radiant.

Nadine was still positioned on all fours, the twin peaches of her buttocks poised in the air. With a wink at Anna-May, Mark nudged his tongue down Nadine's sleek crease once again. Anna-May gazed on, obviously fascinated.

Mark nudged his tongue a little lower, tasting Nadine's sugary wetness.

'God, yes,' moaned Nadine, swaying her hips round slightly.

He moved back upward, stimulating her crease again.

Anna-May's face looked animated. She was playing the tip of her tongue teasingly across her top lip. Curling her legs underneath her, she knelt to Nadine's side, reached underneath her and began to fondle Nadine's small perfect breasts.

'Yeah!' gasped Nadine, stretching and swaying her body like a cat. Mark was teasing her from behind, Anna-May was teasing her breasts. It was clear she could not keep still.

'I have to stand up,' she said, her voice slurry, syrupy with desire.

As she stood, Anna-May edged round, kneeling in front of her, placing her hands on Nadine's svelte thighs. With teasing little motions, she licked at the tendons at the inside tops of Nadine's thighs. But not for long. She seemed as desperate to stimulate as Nadine was for stimulation and, moments later, she drew her tongue hungrily along the seam of Nadine's sex.

Nadine juddered with unbridled joy. She glanced

back at Mark who was still kneeling behind her. 'Lick me, baby,' she pleaded. 'I need you to lick me.'

'Try and stop me,' muttered Mark, his body hot, his groin burning.

He drew his tongue up and down her bottom crease, now and again pausing to tickle the plump, swollen flesh of her sex. He was aware of Anna-May, kneeling in front of Nadine, teasing Nadine's bud with her tongue. That heightened his own level of excitement almost to a fever.

'Uh huh,' coaxed Nadine, as he began to knead her buttocks. Her skin was silken with the sweat of passion and she was moving her hips in a lilting rhythm, little by little getting faster, nudging her sex towards Anna-May then thrusting her bottom back to him.

Suddenly, she stopped. She bent her knees right out. She was silent for less than two seconds, then, as her body trembled superbly, she let out a cry of pure ecstasy. Mark gripped her tightly, savouring the bucks and tremors of her orgasm.

'Oh my Lord,' she murmured, dropping down to the carpet between them.

Mark was as hard as concrete now. The sight of Nadine and Anna-May, both luscious and rosied from sex, made the coil of desire twist tight in his stomach.

He lay down on the rug on his back. Soft, female hands floated on his body, parting his legs, drifting in between. Warm, smooth lips closed around his penis and balls, lapping, inciting, till he could not take any more. Quickly, he sat up.

Nadine sat to the side of him, running her hands over his shoulders and chest. Anna-May climbed into his lap, straddling his hips. Holding his cock firmly in one hand, she eased the tip back and forth along the moist, pink seam of her sex. It was teasing where he could no longer stand to be teased and, with a groan, he put a stop to it, hauling her down on to his lap and sliding himself inside her. Relief. It was relief and pleasure and boiling excitement.

Anna-May gasped delightedly. 'Mmm,' she moaned, sinking down for full penetration. She rocked gently in his lap, the slight friction within sending disproportionate thrills along the length of his cock.

Nadine's hands were still on his shoulders. She was gazing avidly at him and Anna-May. Her hands started to move again, stroking his body hungrily. She leant across to kiss him, devouring his mouth, and Anna-May began to rock faster. Mark blinked for a moment, and lay down flat, succumbing to the indescribable pleasure of it all.

Anna-May bobbed rhythmically upon him. He could feel the smooth cheeks of her bottom jog against his balls.

'Christ,' he groaned at the blistering heat between his legs, in his belly, in his thighs.

Anna-May leant forward, brushing her lovely, jigging breasts on his chest. He glanced sidewards to Nadine. She was looking on raptly, the tip of her tongue moistening her top lip. Anna-May bobbed and writhed, increasingly urgent, and Mark was losing control. The delicious pressure was mounting, rolling towards that sexual peak. Excitement pervaded every nerve that he had, dominating his body and mind. He exploded on a crest of scorching energy, aware only of an exquisite tide of bliss.

As the tide subsided to a gentle wave, he tilted up his head. Anna-May was still astride his hips. She was leaning forward slightly, resting her hands on his chest. She looked exhilarated, exhausted, and sexually fulfilled.

Nadine was nuzzling against his ear. 'Honey, that's made me so hot. I'll give you ten minutes to recover.' Her voice was tight with excitement.

Mark took one look at her. 'I'll only need five.' He grinned confidently, his body charged once again.

Chapter Seventeen

*L*ater on that evening, Mark, Nadine and Anna-May sprawled lazily on the cushions and sofas in the living room area of Anna-May's house. Anna-May had set a fire going in the grate to ward off the chill of the desert night. After the glorious excitement of their energetic lovemaking, they were now content to lay around, relaxing, sipping wine. There was a pleasant, quiet ambience in the room. They talked together in soft voices with the flames crackling gently in the background. Occasionally, the keening wail of a distant coyote broke into their insular tranquillity.

Nadine and Mark found out a few things about Anna-May: she ran her own jewellery design business and worked both in LA and Las Vegas. When she had finished telling them about herself, she regarded them both silently, tilting her head on one side.

'Your turns now,' she said, after several moments of contemplation. 'Do I dare to ask what you are both doing way out here in the desert? Running away from something, I presume.'

Nadine and Mark exchanged a surreptitious glance.

'Why would you presume that?' asked Mark, thinking on his feet.

Anna-May shrugged and gave him a secretive smile.

'We're all running away in one way or another. I know I am – I come out here to run away from the city.'

'We could just be tourists,' said Nadine, looking lazily into the fire.

Anna-May chuckled. 'No, I don't think so.'

'Why not?' enquired Nadine.

'Because, for one, you don't act like tourists, for another you don't dress like tourists. When you passed me by first time, back on the road, you drove like people running away from something or someone.'

Mark and Nadine were both silent. Anna-May took a tiny sip of her wine, moistening her lips. Her mouth looked smooth and inviting. After a moment or two, she looked up. 'Of course,' she said softly, 'it's really none of my business. I didn't mean to pry, I just thought maybe I could help you out in some way.'

'OK,' said Nadine, turning to look at Anna-May directly. 'What if I told you we *are* running away –'

'Nadine!' cut in Mark.

Nadine held up her hand. 'No, Mark. We should tell her. We should tell her all about those two guys after us. I'm divorced, you see, and not only that, my ex-husband was also my business partner.'

Mark palmed his hand down his face to cover his surprise. He took a deep breath. He had actually thought for one scary moment that Nadine was going to spill all to Anna-May. He should have known better, he thought, admiring Nadine's cool, unruffled, yarn-spinning demeanour.

'Anyway,' continued Nadine, 'I have some important business documents I have to get to Las Vegas. For reasons of his own, my ex-husband does not want me to get these documents to Las Vegas, so he's sent two men after me to make darn sure I don't do that.'

Anna-May was listening, unblinking. 'I see,' she said quietly. 'Do you know what these men look like?'

'Oh yeah,' nodded Mark. 'We know. They were following us this afternoon. We finally lost them back there in the desert, but for how long . . . who knows?'

195

Anna-May looked thoughtful for a moment. Then her face brightened. 'But what if we were to alter things so these men didn't know what *you* look like?'

'What do you mean?' chorused Mark and Nadine.

'What if you left your car here and borrowed my car to drive to Las Vegas. It would throw them totally off track, wouldn't it? They think they're following a silver Lexus, not a black Ferrari.'

Nadine and Mark looked at each other, their eyes alight. Mark whistled softly. 'It's a great idea,' he said.

'A fantastic idea,' agreed Nadine.

Mark looked Anna-May straight in the eye. 'You would trust us with your Ferrari? You only met us this afternoon.'

'But since then we've gotten to know each other pretty well.' Anna-May smiled. 'Besides if it wasn't for you both, I could still be stranded out there in the desert.' She shivered involuntarily. As if to emphasise her point, a single coyote howl pierced the night.

'It's very kind of you,' murmured Nadine. 'So generous.'

'I like to be generous,' she shrugged. 'Please let me do this for you.'

Once again, Mark and Nadine exchanged looks. There was no doubt whatsoever they were of the same mind.

'OK,' said Nadine.

'OK,' said Mark.

'OK,' said Anna-May, holding up her glass for a toast. 'Here's to a successful trip to Vegas.' They all clinked glasses, smiling together.

'Besides, I do have an ulterior motive,' added Anna-May in a low voice.

'What's that?' muttered Mark. He knew there had to be a catch.

'Because when you bring the car back – after your successful trip – we can celebrate. Really, truly celebrate. All together.'

'We don't have to wait until then.' Nadine smiled,

her voice already tightening with desire. 'We have the rest of the night.'

'Exactly,' agreed Mark huskily. He drew both women down to the fireplace and, in the warmth and the firelight, they began to move their bodies, pressing, touching, loving every moment.

They rose early next morning, refreshed and revitalised by their energetic night of sex.

Wanting to come across as two professional people in business, they dressed accordingly. Mark wore dark trousers, a crisp white shirt and a blue and grey patterned silk tie. Nadine decided on a simple, black linen dress, short enough to suggest seductiveness, long enough to look businesslike. More inclined to play up the seductive angle, she chose strappy black sandals to go with it. To complete the look, she wound her long, dark hair up into an immaculate French twist.

The high narrow heels of her shoes clicked on the tiles as she followed Mark to the doorway. Anna-May, wearing a white, wispy robe, accompanied them out to her car. Nadine slid into the passenger seat. Mark passed her the briefcase which she placed carefully at her feet. From here on in, she did not want that briefcase out of her sight.

'See you later on then,' said Anna-May.

'You bet,' nodded Mark.

'Good luck!' she said.

Mark grinned and blew her a kiss. He stepped into the car, revved the engine and then they were off.

The drive in Anna-May's car was smooth and luxurious. Mark was loving it, Nadine could tell. Under other circumstances, she would be too, but right now she had one thought and one thought only. To get the money intact to Las Vegas.

The city itself was amazing. Rising from the Nevada desert like a breathtaking illusion. High-rise structures, hotels, casinos, cars, people. And then more people, more cars, more casinos. After the vast emptiness of the desert, it took several moments to acclimatise.

'We made it,' breathed Nadine triumphantly.

'So far, so good,' agreed Mark. 'Now we have to play our parts and get the money to the bank.'

'Uh huh,' murmured Nadine, looking around.

They were cruising down the famous Las Vegas Strip, centre of the gambling universe. Casino after casino lined the Strip, resplendent, eccentric, excessive. As Nadine looked on, she began to feel curious. Something deep inside seemed to be compelling her.

'Mark,' she said quietly. 'Let's go inside. Just for a moment.'

He glanced at her. She could read the same blend of curiosity and compulsion in his expression as she was feeling. 'OK,' he said simply. 'And *then* we'll find a bank.'

'Uh huh,' she murmured. 'Then we'll find a bank.'

They left the car with a valet parking attendant. Mark held the briefcase down by his side as they walked into the casino. Even at this hour of the morning, the place was teeming with people. Mark and Nadine looked as unassuming as everyone else, meriting glances only because of the startlingly attractive couple they made. No one gave the briefcase a second look.

They wandered around the huge interior, taking in the excess of it all, the blackjack tables, roulette wheels, slot machines, the endless ways to win or lose money. Mark chuckled wryly as a chubby, middle-aged man lucked out on a slot machine, coins gushing forth like a waterfall.

'I guess he's happy,' Mark stage-whispered to Nadine as the large man whooped and chortled with glee.

'I guess,' said Nadine, seeing the look of pure triumph and elation in the chubby man's eyes. At that exact point, she realised something. She wanted that look herself. She wanted to play and she wanted to win. Lord, how she wanted to win.

Tense with this strange new excitement, she walked over to the roulette table.

A good-looking young man with gelled-back hair stood back from the wheel. His white shirt, black bow tie and waistcoat reminded Nadine of a maître d'.

'Make your bets, please, ladies and gentlemen,' said the young male croupier.

He set the roulette wheel in motion. It spun around in a blur of speed. As it began to slow, the ivory ball bobbed teasingly from number to number, red compartment to black, black to red.

'Final bets now, ladies and gentlemen,' said the croupier, as the rotations of the wheel dramatically lessened.

'The betting is closed,' he announced seconds later.

The wheel turned slowly round and round and then, finally, stopped. The ball settled snugly in a black compartment and the croupier called out the winning number.

As the croupier began to rake in the losing bets, Nadine looked around the table. A petite blonde woman with bird-like features was an obvious winner – her face had that same look as the man at the slot machine, that look of greedy bliss. And, as she regarded the woman, Nadine was overwhelmed by a desire to play the table. She simply had to do it, whatever the consequences. Win or lose.

She turned round looking for Mark. He was already at her shoulder.

'Mark,' she began. 'How about we try our luck, just once, just to see? We could buy a few chips –'

'Pre-emptive strike, honey,' he grinned, handing her some casino chips. He moved his lips close to her ear. 'I changed two bundles of one-hundred dollar bills. We can afford to lose that and get this gambling thing out of our system.'

Nadine twisted round her head and pecked his cheek happily. 'What a guy!' she quipped.

'Hey, I know it!' he shrugged with a grin. He turned her back to the table, standing behind her and holding her gently at the waist. The croupier was once again preparing to take bets.

'Go on,' Mark whispered. 'Make your bet.'

Nadine made her choice, staking the entire number of chips.

'Here goes,' she murmured as the wheel began to spin. Excitement sliced through her body as she watched the wheel turn and, as it began to slow, she found herself gripping the edge of the table. Likewise, Mark's fingers were tightening at her waist.

The wheel slowed down. The ball stopped spinning. She leant forward.

'I think we won,' she said to Mark in disbelief.

Mark was staring at the wheel too. The croupier announced the winning number. 'We did,' Mark said in a muted voice. 'We won!'

She gazed up at him. 'Let's play again,' she said, her voice shaking with elation.

Mark needed no persuasion. Clearly, he was riding the same wave of compulsion as she. 'Yeah,' he agreed quickly.

This time they doubled the stake – their winnings and the original stake.

'You choose,' said Nadine.

'Sure,' said Mark, making the bet.

The wheel began to spin again, blurred rotations that seemed endless. As she watched and wished and waited, Nadine felt the incredible charges of tension and excitement that she had felt the first time. It was unlike anything she had known before, tandem emotions of highs and lows, excitement and apprehension.

The wheel slowed, the ball came to a stop. She and Mark leant forward in unison. They stared at the wheel then at one another. Twin expressions of incredulity.

'We did it again,' whispered Mark.

Nadine exhaled a long, shuddery breath. 'I know,' she said tightly, completely caught up by these new feelings, new sensations.

'Incredible,' laughed Mark softly. 'Absolutely incredible. We won twice in a row!'

'You know what's happening, don't you?' she whispered. 'We're on a run, a winning streak.'

'Can't argue with that,' chuckled Mark.

Nadine's mind felt blurry, intoxicated. Some faint link with reality reminded her that what she was about to suggest to Mark was the height of stupidity and yet she was powerless to stop herself. It was as though she was drugged, as though she needed to feed this new addiction. She needed to experience the excitement one more time. She needed the ultimate high.

'We won twice already, we're on a winning run, it's got to be third time lucky,' she said, her voice so taut she thought it would snap. 'Let's stake the lot, all of the money!'

Her safety net was Mark – the cool-headed lawyer, the voice of reason. Mark was her safety net, Mark would refuse.

He had not yet answered. She looked up at him. His eyes were glassy with gambling fever. She could see that he was not about to refuse.

He simply nodded.

Hands clasped lightly, with a pretence at nonchalance, they made their way over to the cashier. The cashier's deadpan expression faltered a little when he saw the amount of money involved. He was slightly deferential when he handed them their chips – after all, here were people who had the odds stacked against them, who had walked into the casino with a small fortune, who more than likely would walk out of there with nothing. Nadine flashed him a dismissive smile. What did he know? she thought, laughing inside. They were on a winning run, they could not lose . . .

Back at the roulette table, the young male croupier proved his professionalism. He did not even blink as they placed their stake and made their bet.

The game began. The roulette wheel began to spin, round and round and round. Nadine watched so avidly that she began to feel dizzy, compounding the nerves that wracked her body. She began to feel a little nauseous. A simple rebound of the ball one way or another and they would lose everything. She gripped Mark's hand nervously. Suddenly this didn't feel so good, the excitement, the nerves, the tension. A slight inclination of the tiny little ball the wrong way and they could lose it all. *Lose it all!*

'Mark,' she gasped, unintentionally digging her fingernails into his hand. 'I think we're making a mistake.'

Mark jigged her hand reassuringly. 'Don't worry, Nadine. We're on a winning run.'

'No,' she said urgently, trying to get him to see. 'It's just two wins. We can't stake it all on the basis of those. We can't. We should withdraw –'

'We can't,' said Mark.

'The betting is closed,' announced the croupier at the same time.

Nadine froze helplessly, and looked on, watching the final few turns. There was nothing else she could do. The ball bobbed from black to red, black to red, tumbling lazily. It was almost over, she couldn't stand to watch. Shutting her eyes tightly, she felt a rush in her head, noises and voices crashing around until she could not distinguish one from the other. She knew the croupier must be announcing the winning number but try as she might, she couldn't hear him.

'Nadine?'

It was Mark's voice, quiet, concerned.

She opened her eyes.

'You OK?' he asked softly.

'Is it over?' she mumbled.

He nodded solemnly.

'Have we . . . Did we . . . ?' She couldn't bring herself to say the words.

He nodded again.

'Did we win?' she whispered in a tiny voice.

He pulled her close to him. She could feel his body trembling with emotion. Then he began to smile and to smile and to smile. 'Yes, baby. We won. Un-fucking-believable. We won!'

Nadine felt weak. 'We won,' she repeated vaguely. It would not sink in.

Mark pressed his lips to her ear. 'A goddamn fortune,' he murmured over and over.

A discreet cough from the croupier reminded them where they were. 'Sir, ma'am, if you care to move this way, this gentleman will escort you to the casino bank to cash your winnings.'

Coolly, Nadine regarded the gentleman in question. A wrestler in a tux was an appropriate way to describe him. She didn't fancy having him escort her anywhere.

'No thanks,' she said to the croupier, her voice light and tinkly. 'We'll make our own way.'

'As you wish,' replied the croupier in such a way that implied he thought they were mad. Clearly, if he had won the amount they had won, he would want the escort around.

Minus the wrestler, they set off for the casino bank. Mark circled Nadine's waist loosely with his arm and neither of them spoke. It was as though they were in a dream world, and if either of them spoke or reacted in any way, the dream might shatter and reality take a hold.

But as they came within sight of the casino bank, reality took hold in a big way. Reality was a familiar cold-eyed, blond man hovering near the entrance. An equally familiar dark-skinned man with a ponytail was loitering at an adjacent booth.

'Shit,' muttered Mark.

Not breaking stride, he manoeuvred Nadine into a half-turn. 'Keep walking,' he said calmly.

Nadine glanced back.

'Don't look back,' snapped Mark. 'Do you want them to spot us?'

'I was just checking it was them,' Nadine hissed back defensively.

'It's them all right.'

They continued to walk, checking their pace so as not to stand out. Nadine spotted an exit sign and they veered towards it.

Out on the street, the heat hit them with shocking intensity.

'We've got to get to the car quickly,' said Mark, tugging her by her wrist along the street.

'Wait up,' she moaned, tottering unsteadily on her heels.

'Sorry, honey,' he apologised, slowing down a little. He shook his head distractedly as they walked. 'How in hell did they track us here?' he muttered, seemingly more to himself than to Nadine.

'How in hell did they make it out of the desert?' she piped up.

Mark shrugged his shoulders. 'We knew that they would . . . eventually. But here?' He glanced back at the casino in disbelief. 'How'd they track us here?'

'Maybe it was just coincidence,' she ventured. 'Bad, bad coincidence. After all, they didn't see us, did they? So maybe they just reckoned we would be heading for Las Vegas and now they're just going from place to place, casino to casino, looking out for us.'

'Right now I'd believe that, I'd believe anything,' said Mark, shaking his head again. 'First off, we beat virtually unbeatable odds in the casino and win an absolute fortune. Then blondie and ponytail turn up and prevent us cashing in that fortune.'

Nadine stopped in her tracks. She held up the velvet sack of casino chips. 'How are we going to cash them in, Mark?' she whispered.

'I don't know,' he muttered, sounding really worried. 'But we can't stay here, it's too dangerous.'

They started to walk again.

'We'll have to figure out something quickly,' said Nadine.

'We will,' Mark assured her. 'Just give me a few moments.'

They had reached the parking area. They stood in

subdued silence, waiting for their car to be brought around.

Several moments later, the car appeared, gliding towards them, smooth and sleek. And borrowed.

The thought hit them both simultaneously. Mark snapped his fingers in the air; Nadine jerked up her chin excitedly.

'Anna-May!' they exclaimed to one another.

Anna-May was their answer. She had wanted to help them before; she would want to help them again. Anna-May was how they would cash in the chips.

They reached the dusty track that led to Anna-May's house.

'Do you think we can trust Anna-May?' asked Nadine.

'Do you?' answered Mark ambiguously.

She stared out of the car window. 'I think the truth is we don't have a choice. She's our only hope right now.'

'Exactly,' said Mark.

'It will mean we have to split the money with her,' Nadine said.

'We'll have to give her a cut, sure,' replied Mark.

Nadine had the velvet sack of chips on her lap. She stroked it possessively. 'Damn Daniel and his stupid men,' she murmured.

Mark glanced at her. 'Don't worry, baby,' he soothed. 'Even after we give Anna-May a cut, we'll still have more than enough.'

Nadine gave him a brave smile. 'I know, honey. And besides, I like Anna-May, I really do.'

'I like her too,' grinned Mark. 'And I like that you like her, it makes for a happy threesome.'

'Mmm,' she chuckled wickedly, jigging the casino chips in her lap. 'And I'm just about in the mood for that.'

'Uh huh,' said Mark, as they drew up to the house. 'Fun first, favours later.'

Stashing the velvet sack of chips back into the briefcase, they wandered up to the door. Mark had barely tapped once before the door opened.

'I heard the car,' explained Anna-May, looking lovely in the doorway. She was wearing brief khaki shorts, a clingy striped T-shirt, and dazzling white plimsolls. The outfit showed off acres of her smooth, toned flesh.

Mark leant forward and kissed her cheek. He handed her the keys to her Ferrari. 'Thanks for the loan of,' he grinned.

Anna-May dangled the car keys in the air. 'My pleasure,' she smiled.

'*Our* pleasure,' purred Nadine. 'It's one hell of a car.'

Anna-May nodded, then followed that with a mock type of frown. 'So,' she said, leaning against the door-frame, 'are you guys going to tell me how it went or do I have to drag it out of you?'

'On the whole it went well,' answered Mark. He held up his thumb and forefinger in an itsy-bitsy gesture. 'There was one, tiny little hiccup but we'll talk about that after.'

'After?' teased Nadine, shooting up a perfect eyebrow.

Anna-May joined in the tease. 'Yes, after? What exactly is after?'

'After is after,' he grinned, nudging them both inside.

Anna-May and Nadine tripped up the stairs, giggling like schoolgirls. Mark locked the front door and then, still carrying the briefcase, followed them up the stairs. His stomach rolled in a riot of sexual anticipation.

As he walked behind them along the landing, both girls began to peel off their clothes. Nadine turned round, letting Anna-May pull down the zipper of her dress. She shook off the dress, leaving it where it fell, then she carried on walking, undoing her bra as she went.

Anna-May criss-crossed her arms at the base of her T-shirt, wresting it over her head. She wriggled out of her tight, khaki shorts, then, like Nadine, continued on her way.

Mark followed the trail of discarded clothing. He saw Nadine's black lace bra flung over the banister. Two steps further along, he found her panties tossed across a vase. Anna-May's minuscule white panties, he found abandoned just outside the door.

'Now, this is what I call a homecoming,' he cracked, as he stepped into the room, greeted by the sight of the two nude young women.

Anna-May curled her finger seductively, beckoning him towards them. He walked over, loosening his tie as he did so.

'Let me help,' murmured Anna-May, lifting the circle of his loosened tie up over his neck and face. She stepped up on tiptoe to pull it over his head and Mark watched her full, high breasts jiggle delightfully as she pulled the tie off.

He began to unbutton his shirt. Nadine stepped behind him, helping him ease the shirt off his shoulders, then she looped her arms beneath his, running her hands slowly over the skin of his chest. He could feel the light, teasing touch of her nipples on his back and it made him feel leaden with desire.

Anna-May knelt down in front of him, pulling off his shoes and socks. She began to work on his trousers, dragging them, along with his boxers, down his legs and then flinging them to one side.

'Mmm,' she sighed, her eyes on a level with his swollen cock. She glanced up fleetingly at him before moving her face forward. Mark felt her hand encircle his shaft, then the warm, moist velvet of her mouth on the head. She flicked her tongue expertly along his slit, sending shivers of pleasure up along his penis and into his balls.

With her head bowed in his groin, Mark could only see the top of Anna-May's head, her butter-blonde hair, her thick plait lying down her slender, naked back.

'Christ,' he groaned joyfully, as she ran her tongue lightly over his balls.

Nadine, still behind him, still stroking his chest,

brushed her nipples deliciously against his back. It was all so good, so perfect, but at this rate it was also going to be far too quick for him. Mark wanted to slow it down, take his time, savour Nadine and Anna-May to the full.

Garnering his will power, he placed his hands on the top of Anna-May's head and gently eased her back.

'What is it?' she asked, sounding puzzled.

'Nothing,' Mark answered huskily. He held out his hand and lifted her to her feet. Stepping back from in between them, he circled their tiny waists.

'On the bed, please, ladies,' he instructed with a grin.

Exchanging looks of anticipation, they turned and waltzed over to the large double bed, swaying their bottoms emphatically, clearly for his benefit. Stretching out on the white, Egyptian cotton sheets, they tilted up their heads and regarded him seductively, like two exquisite temptresses. Volleys of excitement shot through his belly.

He crawled on to the bed, in between them, feeling the heat of their warm supple bodies. Kneeling up on his heels, he feasted his eyes upon them, letting them show themselves off to him. Like mirror images, they lay on their backs, heads still tilted up off the pillows. Nadine's small golden breasts looked pert and hot, her pink-brown nipples smooth with inner heat. Anna-May's breasts were slightly fuller, although just as jaunty as Nadine's, but her nipples were already aroused, rosy and erect.

Nadine reached up to her hair and began to uncoil her French twist. Shining dark tresses fell to her shoulders and over the tops of her breasts. Anna-May left her hair as it was, but pulled her thick plait round until it coiled around one side of her neck, resting on her front. The smooth, unplaited end dusted the fine outline of her collarbone. They were both so sexy and lovely that Mark's breath caught in his throat.

He resumed drawing his gaze down their bodies. When he reached their hips and thighs and the tantalising triangles on their tiny mounds, his groin began to ache so badly that mere observation began to feel totally inadequate. He had to touch them, feel them, stimulate them until he could see the rich, plump swell between their legs and the growing rapture on their faces, and hear their climactic cries of joy.

He could not wait a moment longer to begin doing exactly that. He reached out to both girls, and cupped their small venus mounds simultaneously. He pressed down hungrily, feeling their soft fluffy hair tickle his palms, and when they opened their legs obligingly, his fingers found the moist intimacies of their sexes.

Nadine sighed gently, still tilting up her head to watch him.

Anna-May moaned in a soft sweet tone. 'Yeah, Mark,' she murmured as he nudged her clitoris, 'right there. Oh God, yes.'

'Touch your breasts,' urged Mark, continuing to stimulate them both simultaneously between their legs.

Eagerly, Anna-May cupped her own breasts, squeezing her roseate nipples between her fingertips. Nadine was less urgent, dabbing lightly at the tips of her nipples, teasing herself. Mark was incredibly aroused, seeing them pinch and flick their nipples with elegant fingers and perfect polished fingernails. Nadine had started nudging her sex up against his hand whilst Anna-May was pressing herself hard against him. Withdrawing his hands for a moment, he held his breath at the erotic sight before him.

They had both opened their legs wide. Nadine's trim dark nest of hair contrasted wonderfully with Anna-May's neat blonde triangle. Lower down, their smooth, delicate lips were moist and plump, parting lusciously to expose their hardened cores. Mark groaned with blistering desire.

Nadine sat up quickly, as desperate as he. She rolled over on to her stomach, then raised her thighs and bottom in the air. She looked glorious, angling her cheeks towards him, revealing her wet, pouting sex.

'Fuck me, Mark,' she said, her voice soft yet urgent.

'Mmm,' he answered, kneeling behind her. Straight away, he entered her, guiding himself in with his hand. The bliss was indescribable. He pushed in further, briefly pausing to savour the sensations, then, almost immediately, he began to move. He nudged his hips back and forth. With each gentle thrust, Nadine's buttocks quivered wonderfully and she arched her back, pushing back against him.

Mark looked directly down as she did this, entranced by the golden flesh of her buttock cheeks which were pressed to his blazing groin. Gently, he slipped his finger between her cheeks, feeling the slippy, smooth skin of her crease. Then, with the pad of his fingertip, he began to rub up and down, savouring her satin seam.

'Yes,' she sighed joyfully, tossing her head so her hair cascaded across her back and shoulders.

Seconds later, she stretched out to Anna-May, running her hands over Anna-May's smooth stomach. Bending her face to Anna-May's breasts, she stuck out her tongue and began to touch her nipples with tiny, darting flicks.

Anna-May pushed up her chest, sighing delightedly and Nadine flicked and teased continuously. Mark watched this and had to quicken his pace, thrusting fast and deep inside Nadine. She moaned responsively, and curled her tongue hungrily around Anna-May's tips.

Nadine had been resting her hand on Anna-May's stomach whilst she licked at her nipples, but as Anna-May writhed in joy, Nadine's hand started to wander downward. She rested it for a moment on Anna-May's mound, plucking playfully at the tidy little nest, then she moved her hand boldly between Anna-May's thighs. Deftly, she began to massage Anna-May.

Mark was beside himself. Seeing Nadine now stimulate Anna-May was almost too much for him and he pumped his hips furiously, slapping Nadine's bottom as he moved.

Nadine glanced round at him, her face lustful and gleaming. 'Oh yeah,' she coaxed. 'Faster, baby.'

She bucked back against him, simultaneously moving her hand quicker between Anna-May's legs. Anna-May caught her breath and opened her legs wider. As Nadine's skilful fingers fondled and massaged her, she pressed her body down into the bed and her moans got louder, more intense. Mark gripped Nadine's hips, thrusting inside her, shorter now, sharper now, quicker now, faster, faster, faster . . .

His body took control.

He came with such a force, it seemed to wrack his whole being. A thrill swept initially from the backs of his knees and, just as it began, he saw Nadine thrust up her buttocks and jerk back her head and cry out with rapture of her own. Then, with astonishing speed, his orgasm consumed him entirely. In fact, it was all he could do to close his eyes and surrender and let the pleasure engulf him completely.

It seemed strange to be sitting on a covered back porch slap bang in the middle of a desert. Admittedly, it was a very stylish back porch, built from beautiful, red-brown wood and looking out on to a garden entirely comprised of desert flora – huge yucca plants, varying kinds of cactus and unusual green-leaved shrubs with bulbous, yellow blooms. There was a highly efficient rotating fan affixed to the ceiling above which lifted the scorching air into a pleasant, hot breeze and that, coupled with the shade of the roof, made the heat bearable if not exactly cool. But it still seemed strange and barren and Nadine had another of those quirky yearnings where she wished she was back in her pretty white house with its sparkling blue pool and Jacuzzi out back.

When they had this thing sorted, she decided, one of

the first things she would insist on would be a house with a pool.

She leant forward to the table and picked up the jug of iced tea, filling three empty glasses.

'Thanks,' smiled Anna-May as she handed her a glass.

When she handed Mark a glass, she gave him a fleeting look of encouragement then she slipped into the chair next to him. On the way back from Las Vegas, they had discussed the story they would tell Anna-May. Now Nadine waited for Mark to begin.

Mark scratched the side of his nose and cleared his throat. Then he looked directly at Anna-May. 'Time for us to come clean,' he said with a shameful smile which only enhanced his handsome features. 'About the reason we were really heading for Las Vegas.'

Anna-May widened her pretty blue eyes. 'Would this have something to do with the little hiccup you mentioned?'

'Yes,' replied Mark steadily.

'Just how clean have you got to come?' she asked quietly.

Nadine leant forward. 'The ex-husband part was real,' she lied. 'And the bit about being in business with him. And the part about the two men he sent after us.'

'But we were not entirely honest about what was in the briefcase,' Mark joined in. 'It wasn't business documents at all; it was money.'

Anna-May didn't speak but her eyes shone with curiosity.

Nadine continued quickly. 'It was *my* money,' she explained. 'My ex-husband had been stealing from the business – and me – for years, so I was only taking what was mine. I cleared out the accounts and Mark and I took off, but he found out quicker than we anticipated and sent these two hired thugs after us.'

'What kind of business were you in?' asked Anna-May.

Nadine was caught off balance. She hadn't anticipated that question. Her mind raced.

'Property,' Mark answered promptly.

Nadine exhaled softly. Thank goodness for Mark and his sharp lawyer's mind.

'I see,' murmured Anna-May.

Mark picked up the reins. 'Anyway,' he continued. 'We went to Las Vegas with the intention of banking the money somewhere safe. But the hiccup I mentioned to you was that we both got an attack of gambling fever in Vegas.'

Anna-May seemed unsurprised. 'You wouldn't be the first. How much did you lose?' she asked sympathetically.

Mark leant forward, resting his wrists on his knees. 'That's exactly it,' he explained. 'We didn't lose at all. We won. We defied every statistic there is and we hit three total wins!'

Anna-May looked at Mark, then at Nadine, growing disbelief on her face.

'It's true,' Nadine confirmed softly.

'Wow,' breathed Anna-May. 'But how is that a setback, shouldn't you both be ecstatic?'

'We were,' said Nadine, 'for all of ten minutes, the time it took us to walk to the casino bank and spot the two men my ex-husband hired right by the entrance. For obvious reasons, we didn't get to cash the chips.'

'Ah,' said Anna-May, enlightened. 'So that was the hiccup?'

'Uh huh,' said Mark. 'And you know what? Right now we're going to ask you for one hell of a favour.'

'What kind of a favour?'

'Well,' said Mark, carefully laying the groundwork, 'we'd like to offer a three-way split with you . . .' he paused a moment to let that be absorbed, 'if you would cash in the chips for us.'

The silence was absolute. Anna-May looked astonished.

'Why me?' she murmured eventually.

'We can't go back there ourselves,' answered Mark. 'Those two guys know who we are. And they look like pretty determined guys, they're not going to give up until they're told to. But they don't know you. You could walk in there and cash the chips as bold as anything and they wouldn't know a thing about it.'

It was clear Anna-May wasn't happy. Nadine intervened.

'We need you, Anna-May,' she appealed, making her voice quaver slightly.

'It's not that I don't want to help you,' said Anna-May, her voice soft. 'It's that I don't want to be entrusted with that amount of money. What if something went wrong? What if I lost it? How can you trust me with something this big?'

'You lent us your car,' reminded Nadine. 'That was trust.'

Anna-May shook her head in confusion.

'We trust you, Anna-May,' said Mark earnestly. 'And you have nothing to lose, only to gain. Think of it, a third of the money!'

A flush warmed Anna-May's cheeks. 'It isn't the money. It's –' She cut herself off, shrugging her shoulders helplessly.

Mark and Nadine sank back in their chairs.

'OK,' said Mark, sounding exasperated. 'If you don't want to help us, we'll leave it at that.'

No one spoke after that. After a while, Nadine got up and walked to the front of the porch. Resting her hands on the wooden railing, she stared out at the barren, baked horizon. The late-afternoon sun seemed as hot as at noon.

'My sonofabitch ex-husband has won again,' she murmured, play-acting defeat. 'I suppose deep down, I always knew he would.'

'We tried, honey,' said Mark. 'At least, we stopped him getting the money.'

Nadine turned round, nodded and flashed a brave

214

smile. Then she turned back to gaze out at nothing. Minutes passed by in empty silence.

A quiet voice broke the silence. 'OK,' whispered Anna-May.

Nadine wheeled around. Mark leant forward. Both of them gazed hopefully at Anna-May.

She lifted up her chin and then nodded decisively. 'I'll do it.'

'You will?' said Nadine. 'You really will?'

Anna-May nodded again, smiling shakily. 'Uh huh.'

'Oh, you sweet darling,' cried Mark, jumping up from his seat and planting a kiss on Anna-May's mouth.

Nadine was more restrained. 'Thank you, Anna-May,' she said sincerely. 'Thank you so, *so* much. I knew we could count on you.'

'You *can* count on me,' stressed Anna-May. 'And I want you to know that, so I've thought of a way we can establish some kind of trust between us.'

'Yeah?' asked Mark.

'Wait here,' said Anna-May, with a secret little smile. She pushed back her chair and strode into the house, reappearing within moments.

She placed a small case on the table. It looked like a flat, leather make-up case. Instinct told Nadine that it wasn't.

Nadine was right. When Anna-May opened the case and displayed the interior, the nature of the case was revealed. It consisted of three rows; each row was divided into several compartments, each compartment was lined with midnight-blue velvet, and inside each compartment was an item of jewellery. Sparkling, exquisite items of jewellery.

'My work,' said Anna-May proudly. 'My designs.'

'They're lovely,' purred Nadine, picking up a diamond wristwatch. 'But how are they relevant to what we're discussing?'

'I want you to keep them with you when I go to cash

in the chips. Think of them as a kind of security. I trust you with these, you trust me with the money.'

Nadine listened carefully. She liked the sound of that. It made a whole lot of sense.

Mark began to speak. 'No, Anna-May, there's no need. We do trust you with –'

'Just a moment, Mark,' cut in Nadine. She covered his hand affectionately with her own to lessen the impact of her interruption. 'I think that if Anna-May feels she wants to do this, we should let her.'

Mark looked Nadine hard in the eye. His sky-blue eyes seemed to reach right inside her and read her mind.

'OK,' he said finally. 'We do it that way.'

'Great,' said Anna-May. 'This way we all get to lose something if we break our trust.'

'Also,' added Nadine, 'it would be a good idea to swap cars again. Mark and I would be too obvious a target waiting for you in Mark's car. But you would have to park Mark's car well away from the casino in case it was spotted. We don't want them to see you in Mark's car.'

Anna-May thought for a moment. Then she smiled widely. 'Good thinking.'

'So we're all agreed?' said Mark.

'Agreed,' sang Nadine, holding up her glass of iced tea in a toast. She looked at it and laughed. 'Iced tea doesn't quite cut it. Do you have champagne?'

'Yes,' said Anna-May, and chuckled.

The champagne was brought out and poured, and they all toasted each other. And then the finer details of the plan were discussed.

Daniel Garsante sat back, propping his feet casually on the desk in front. He considered the latest report filed by Lyle Beck and Chad Baxter.

They had traced Mark and Nadine to the Mojave Desert. Therefore, Mark Kelton was certainly not en route to visit his folks as he had asserted to his secretary

– Daniel knew for a fact that Mark's parents lived in Wisconsin. Moreover, the incident mid-desert had removed any vestige of doubt as to the guilt of Nadine and Mark.

According to Lyle and Chad's investigations, Nadine and Mark had been seen in Las Vegas. Lyle and Chad had a successful manner of interviewing, slipping $100 bills to their interviewees tended to jog people's minds and, in keeping with this theory, a certain young male croupier in one of the major casinos had furnished them with some interesting information. It would appear that Mark and Nadine had had some very good luck on the tables.

But good luck invariably ran out, thought Daniel with a slow, hard smile. Not long now, he murmured to himself.

Chapter Eighteen

*T*hursday dawned as any other day, but for Mark, Nadine and Anna-May it was special. Thursday was the day they were all going to get rich.

A plan had been formulated in minute detail. Firstly, they would drive in tandem to a rendezvous point in the desert-land within sight of Las Vegas. Anna-May would then continue on into the city in Mark's car, with the gambling chips in her possession. Mark and Nadine would sit and wait in Anna-May's Ferrari, her collection of jewellery safely locked away in the brief-case which formerly held the gambling chips.

Upon Anna-May's return, they would hide out at her house. After a day or two, Anna-May would charter a plane for Mark and Nadine – a midnight departure – for Florida, whereupon they would set about dispelling any trace of their whereabouts. That accomplished, they would head for the Cayman Islands, bank the money off-shore and forget all about the name Daniel Garsante.

They set off mid-morning. Mark felt relaxed as he drove Anna-May's car. Nadine, in the passenger seat, seemed just as relaxed. By the end of the day, they were certain they would be rich.

As they approached the designated meeting point,

Anna-May, driving in front of them, began to slow down. She braked, waiting in the road. Mark pulled over to the side and parked, then with three beeps on the horn, Anna-May began to move off. Her hand appeared from the window, waving jauntily. The car accelerated. Within a short while, it was nothing but a dust speck in the distance, heading for the hazy sprawl of the city. En route to riches.

Nadine flashed Mark a smile. She leant over and brushed her lips across his mouth. 'We deserve this, baby,' she purred. 'And when we've got the money, we're going to enjoy every cent, you and I.'

'Too right,' answered Mark, cupping her cheek in his hand. 'Too right, we deserve it.'

Gently he stroked her cheek, soft and smooth like a rose petal. Her clear green eyes shone with excitement, her full lips were parted slightly in wondrous anticipation.

'We're nearly there,' she said, her voice tight and low.

'Uh huh,' he agreed, the very thought making his stomach lurch with adrenalin. 'Nearly there.'

Mark realised with a start that it was no longer merely a question of the money. This game of cat and mouse, keeping one step ahead of Daniel and his men, had unleashed something inside him. The money was important, of course it was, but right now, uppermost in his mind, was the idea of beating Daniel Garsante. Beating him at his own game.

It was a while before Mark realised Nadine was staring at him.

'Something on your mind, Mark?' she said softly.

He turned to look at her. 'You could say,' he replied. 'Winning.'

'We've already won,' she answered. 'Three times over, at the casino.'

He nodded. 'I'm talking about *this* game. Winning at this game. Getting away with it.'

Nadine spoke emphatically. 'We will get away with it.'

'I know. And won't it be sweet. I've never known Daniel Garsante to lose at anything before.'

Nadine giggled. 'It'll be a new experience for him.'

A victorious chuckle bubbled up into Mark's throat. A feeling of warmth swirled in his belly. As he looked at Nadine, at her smooth skin and inviting lips, the warmth got warmer. Nadine's eyes glinted knowingly.

'We've got a couple of hours to kill,' she said lightly, glancing at her wristwatch. 'What can we do for two whole hours, I wonder?'

'Beats me,' grinned Mark, already leaning towards her.

He bunched her dark hair behind her neck and pressed his lips to hers. Her lips were warm, quite dry, and as he played his lips across hers, she opened her mouth slightly, giving him a teasing taste of her hot, moist tongue.

'Maybe I can think of a few things,' she murmured, her teeth scraping his.

'Maybe I can do a whole lot more than think,' announced Mark, reaching into her dress and cupping one fine, pert breast.

'Mmm,' she sighed, arching her back as his fingers squeezed her nipple. 'Suits me . . .'

A burning sensation scorched the calf of his right leg. Mark jerked awake and looked down.

His leg had eased into a patch of direct sunlight through the open car door. The sun had already burnt a small area of his naked skin. It hurt like hell, he thought, snatching his leg into shade and then rubbing at the sunburn.

Next to him, Nadine stirred. They were both lying on the reclined passenger seat, their hot, gleaming bodies close. Nadine had thrown one long, tan leg across his thighs, virtually pinning him to the seat.

'Hey, baby,' she said, her voice lazy with a mixture of sex and sleep.

Mark played his fingers in the small of her back, tracing the lower curve of her spine. 'Hey,' he answered drowsily.

He lay still for a moment, enjoying the hot closeness of Nadine, every inch of her naked body pressed to his. He could smell the heady scent of her body fragrance and he found himself getting excited all over again. It was several minutes before he tilted up his head to look at the time.

'Nadine,' he said, still stroking her back.

'Mmm?' she hummed sleepily.

'Come on, baby. Wake up, it's almost time. Anna-May will be here any moment.'

Nadine lifted her head off Mark's chest, held his wrist whilst she checked his watch and then eased herself over him, straddling his lap. 'So she will,' she answered excitedly. She dropped her eyes to Mark's erection and chuckled wickedly, clasping her hand possessively around it. 'Looks like we've both got some excess energy to work off.'

'We should get dressed,' murmured Mark without conviction.

'We have a few minutes,' said Nadine.

'Right,' he agreed, running his hands hungrily over her smooth, flat stomach. He circled her waist, lifting her up from his lap slightly, then let his hands wander round to her bottom. Feverishly, he began to squeeze each perfect cheek.

'Yes,' sighed Nadine, drawing out the word. She started to work her hand delightfully up and down his hard shaft.

Mark needed a quick release. His sexual arousal was acutely heightened by a feeling of tension – had everything gone according to plan, had Anna-May been successful, had they finally, ultimately, outwitted Daniel?

221

'Touch me, baby,' pleaded Nadine, her urgency mirroring Mark's.

He pushed his hand between her legs, cupping her moist core. She felt delicious as he fluttered his fingers over her sex, rubbing in the essence of her sex dew.

'Oh God, yes,' she moaned, moving her body in superb undulations, stimulating Mark at the same time with her hand.

They touched and caressed, massaged and stimulated, both aware of the other's urgent need. And as each brought the other to a swift sexual peak, their cries of ecstasy seemed to crack the silence of the surrounding desert.

'Lovely!' gasped Nadine, slumping forward on to Mark, cushioning her head on his shoulder.

He gathered his breath for a short time, stroking Nadine's damp back. The time, he noticed, had moved forward ten minutes.

'This time, we get dressed,' he said decisively.

'OK,' whispered Nadine and he could detect in her voice a kind of nervy excitement.

They dressed quickly. Nadine rummaged in her handbag, pulling out a water spritzer, a hairbrush, and a slim, silver tube of lipstick.

'A quick fix,' she laughed, brandishing the items.

She spritzed her face with water, pulled the brush back through her long, dark layers, then applied a light coat of mauve lipstick. She looked fresh, dewy, beautiful.

'I feel like a million dollars,' she quipped, dropping the items back into her bag and resting the bag up on the top of the dashboard.

Mark chortled. 'In less than five minutes, you can actually feel your own million dollars, and more.'

'And so can you, my darling,' she smiled. 'A million and more.'

Mark put on his sunglasses and leant back comfortably in the car seat. The minutes ticked by, slow as anything. Time was the strangest entity, he reflected.

Five minutes could feel like for ever if you weren't careful. He made a conscious decision not to stare at his watch. Beside him, Nadine was quiet.

Time went by. A bug flew in and settled on the steering wheel. Mark flicked it off with his fingernail.

Next to him, Nadine uncrossed and recrossed her legs. He could hear the faint rustle of her dress as she did so. Behind his sunshades, he closed his eyes, fighting the urge to glance down at his watch. There was no need. Any moment now, Anna-May would turn up, a smile on her pretty face, a stash of money in the car.

Another bug flew into the car. Slowly, it began to crawl up the windscreen. Once, it fell down, landing on the dash; doggedly, it began its journey all over again. Mark watched it closely, admiring its persistence.

'Darn insects,' muttered Nadine, reaching over and swatting it with the back of a book of road maps.

Mark shut his eyes again, listening to silence. He prayed for the rich, familiar sound of his car engine.

Nothing. Only silence. And the queasy instinct of time passing.

'She's late.' Nadine's voice was steady, matter-of-fact.

'Yes,' answered Mark. Finally, he glanced down at his watch. 'Forty minutes.'

'Yes,' said Nadine. 'Something's gone wrong.'

'*Very* wrong.'

'What do we do?'

Mark looked at her solemnly. 'Wait it out. If she's coming back, she'll turn up. If she's not here by nightfall . . .' He shrugged, letting his voice trail off.

'We assume she's not coming,' Nadine finished for him.

'I guess,' said Mark.

Neither one of them stated the obvious. Whatever suspicions they had went unsaid. Instead, they laced their fingers through each other's, kept their thoughts to themselves and continued to sit there. Waiting for Anna-May.

Ten more minutes went by. Mark eased forward on the car seat. His shirt was sticking uncomfortably to his back. He plucked the clinging cotton away from his skin.

Fifty minutes late.

He took a deep breath, trying not to think of that. Next to him, Nadine sighed, a small, damaged sound. It hurt him to hear it.

'Be calm, honey,' he said.

'Oh sure,' she said. A note of sarcasm blended with her anxiety.

Another five minutes passed by. The minutes seemed eternal.

Mark's unease was growing by the second; and a bizarre new feeling began to seep through his body, so new to him that he could barely define it. Rarely, if ever, had he felt something this raw. The feeling was a kind of desperation, fading hope, panic.

So when he saw something appear on the horizon, he thought, at first, it was his mind playing tricks.

Nadine's fingers gripped his. 'Look!' she gasped excitedly.

'You see it too?' rejoiced Mark.

'Yeah,' she sang, craning forward as if to see better. 'Yeah, I do.'

Mark screwed up his eyes behind his sunglasses, focusing on the horizon for all he was worth. The distant vehicle was moving in a camouflage of dust and exhaust fumes – but undoubtedly it was heading their way.

'Thank God,' breathed Nadine. 'I won't tell you what I was thinking.'

'Me too,' said Mark, his spirits soaring.

Obviously travelling at great speed, it steadily grew closer. Within moments, Mark got an inkling that their relief was a little premature. He was not sure when it hit him exactly, but very quickly he realised they were not witnessing the approach of his own car. What they were seeing was the approach of a motorbike.

'What the hell – ?' he cursed, twisting the key in the ignition, ready to move on.

'Wait,' stalled Nadine. 'It could be nothing to do with us. Just be ready to take off if we need to.'

The motorbike was almost upon them, slowing down. The rider was clad in a heavy leather jacket, black jeans, black boots, even the visor of his helmet was tinted. He braked opposite their car but remained on his own side of the road. Mark was poised for a getaway.

The rider lifted off his dusty helmet and cradled it against his body. Mark felt slightly easier: the rider was a boy, no more than eighteen, nineteen tops. His face had the flushed, chubby-cheeked look of a cherub and he had short, thick fair hair which stuck out in parts and stuck to his head in others. He did not look threatening in the least and Mark found himself increasingly at ease.

'Looks can deceive,' warned Nadine, as if in tune with Mark's relief.

The boy jerked his chubby face towards them. 'You guys waiting on out here for Anna-May?' He spoke with a pronounced, Southern drawl which made his voice seem as soft and harmless as his looks.

Nadine leant across Mark to speak out of the car window. 'Did she send you?'

The boy shrugged, noncommittal. Then he revved up his bike, rounded in the road, and shouted above the revs of his engine. 'I got me a message to give you from Daniel Garsante, kind of like a rhyme.' The boy chortled. 'If you trust a girl called Anna-May, a heavy price you'll have to pay!'

With that, the boy unzipped a pocket in his jacket, threw something to the ground, replaced his helmet and then gunned his bike and began to speed off. He raced along the roadway, back the way he had come just moments before.

They remained in the car, stunned into silence, frozen in shock. After a while, Mark palmed his hand down his face. His legs felt leaden as he stepped out of the car and walked across the road. Stooping to pick up the item which the boy had dropped, he tossed it casually on the palm of his hand.

'What is it?' asked Nadine, sounding strained.

Mark laughed dryly. 'A $1 casino chip. A nice little insult from Daniel Garsante, I reckon.'

As he wandered back to the car, Mark felt his shock give way to anger, a tight, cold anger that dragged on his insides. Damn Daniel Garsante. Goddamn him to hell.

'What are you doing?' he asked Nadine, as he stepped back into the car. She was reaching into the back, hauling the briefcase on to her lap.

'Checking on something,' she murmured, flicking open the clasps of the briefcase. Carefully, she lifted out the jewel case given to them by Anna-May. When she opened it up, it was empty.

'That bitch,' hissed Nadine, holding the case upside down, shaking it out.

'No use doing that,' remarked Mark in a resigned, prescient monotone, 'it's empty.'

'How did she do that?' hissed Nadine. 'I locked it away in the briefcase the moment she gave it to us yesterday.'

Mark shook his head. 'I don't know. She's one crafty lady, she must have swapped the jewel cases at some point, a full one for an empty one. Christ, we should have known it was a set-up. It was all too neat, far too coincidental. We should never have trusted her.'

'I never did trust her,' snapped Nadine. 'Why do you think I got her to leave her jewellery with us?'

'Oh and a whole lot of good that did, huh?' rejoined Mark. 'See, that's an empty case you've got in your hand, honey.'

'Don't get wise with me, Mark. It was you who stopped to help her in the first place. I would have driven right by her. It was you, Mark. You and your goddamn chivalry. Your fault!'

'Whoa,' he winced, putting his hands up defensively in front of his chest, 'I won't let you lay this on me. We made our decisions together. All the way, baby.'

'Face it,' snarled Nadine, her voice like acid. 'You're a soft touch and you got us into this mess. So tell me, Marky, honey, sweetie, how are you going to get us out of it and get that money back?'

He threw up his hands in despair. 'We've lost it. It's over, Nadine, don't you get it? Over.'

She looked at him hard. 'For you, maybe. Not for me, I don't give up so easily. I need to think. I need some space.'

She flounced out of the car, walked a few paces and then stared out into the vast, empty space.

Mark banged his hands down on the steering wheel. He was furious, with himself as much as with Nadine's reaction. Maybe she was right, maybe he was a soft touch, but admitting that sure as hell didn't make himself feel any better. He had just kissed away his whole future. Shit, he fumed, banging down again on the steering wheel.

Looking out at Nadine, her flawless face dark with temper, Mark experienced another surge of anger. Yes, maybe he had been taken in by Anna-May, but she had been too, he thought, glaring at Nadine. And she had no call to blame him for it all.

He drummed his fingers angrily on the steering column, looking for something to vent out his anger on. Nadine's handbag was perched jauntily on the dash. That would do, he decided, and lashed out viciously, swiping the handbag on to the floor of the car. It was a stupid, infantile gesture he knew, but it worked, releasing at least some of his fury.

Calmer now, he let out a sigh. Nadine's bag lay lopsided on the passenger side, the contents spilling out over the car floor, the lipstick she had used earlier, the hairbrush, the spritzer of fresh spring water. Feeling more like himself, Mark leant down and began to replace the contents in the bag. As he dropped in the items that had fallen out one by one, his fingers brushed against a package, secreted in the bottom of the bag. It caught Mark's eye because a corner of the tissue paper was torn and a whitish sparkle gleamed through.

Now, ordinarily, Mark would not have looked further. He would have respected Nadine's privacy. But today was not ordinary and Mark was not himself and he was in no mood to respect anybody's privacy. He tore at the tissue paper, his heart pounding in his chest. The tissue paper was soft and came away easily; a good job as it turned out as Mark's fingers were shaking like crazy as he worked.

He stared down into the bottom of the bag, the tissue paper ripped open. Rip out my heart as well, he thought, his whole world crashing in that instant. For there, in the centre of the shredded paper, lay what looked to be Anna-May's entire collection of jewellery designs – a diamond wristwatch, diamond rings, diamond necklaces . . .

How could she do this to him? he despaired, glancing out at her. Doublecross him like this.

In a day where betrayal was being heaped upon betrayal, this one really hurt. It stung like hell, in fact. The money was never really his in the first place and neither was Anna-May. But Nadine? Nadine was his lover, his partner. He trusted Nadine. He had risked everything for Nadine.

Carrying the handbag, he got out of the car and walked to her. She looked deep in thought, gazing outwards. She did not turn to look at him as he approached.

He threw the bag at her feet.

She looked down. 'What's this?' she asked, picking up the handbag.

Mark stood away from her, his hands on his hips. He ignored her question, responding with his own. 'Why, Nadine?' he asked softly.

'Why what?' she asked, her jade eyes wide like saucers.

'Quit with the pretence,' said Mark. 'Look inside.'

She did, and Mark watched the realisation dawn. When she lifted her eyes back to him, guilt glistened within their guarded loveliness.

'I had to,' she answered calmly. 'I had to take the jewellery. I needed a safeguard, I didn't totally trust Anna-May.'

'That does not answer my question,' said Mark. 'Why the little act back there in the car? Why try and double-cross me?'

Nadine stalled, moving backwards. 'Like I said before, Mark,' she answered quietly. 'You're a soft touch. You fell for the whole deal with Anna-May. I didn't think I could count on you any more.'

Mark shook his head in disbelief. 'You didn't think you could count on me, huh? After I risked everything with you.'

Nadine edged back again, as though wary of him. 'We can forget this, Mark,' she whispered. 'Put it behind us, and start again. Please.'

Mark wagged his forefinger at her. 'Oh no, honey, no more chances. We're through, you and I. Here's what we're going to do – as soon as we get to Vegas, we sell the jewellery, split the money, and then go our separate ways.'

'OK,' purred Nadine. 'Whatever you want, baby.'

Mark recognised too late what was happening.

The entire time they had been talking, Nadine had been steadily edging back to the car. In the instant it registered, he moved, his reflexes sharp. But Nadine had the head start. Clutching her bag, she raced the short distance to the car, jumped in, slammed the car door.

Mark covered the ground like a track athlete. He was almost there. The car engine purred into life. He stretched forward to the door, straining every muscle in his arm; his fingers scraped against the hot paintwork as he clutched at anything he could . . . stretching, stretching out . . .

His hand slipped from the door. As the car moved forward, he stumbled, and whilst he struggled to regain his footing, he was somehow aware of the Ferrari hovering some way down the road.

Nadine was peering through the car window, a triumphant smile playing on her beautiful lips. 'Like I said, Mark,' she purred. 'You're a soft touch.'

And then she accelerated, driving off towards the city.

Mark straightened up, dusting down the thighs of his trousers. Numb with incredulity, he watched the Ferrari glide into the distance, until, like the motorbike messenger and Anna-May earlier, it was nothing but a dusty dot on a hostile landscape.

Daniel took the call in the office of his Santa Barbara home. He listened carefully until Lyle Beck had finished speaking.

'Well done, Lyle,' said Daniel quietly.

He held the phone away from his ear for a minute and let himself savour the moment of success. Though it was a feeling Daniel was used to, he never seemed to tire of it and this particular achievement was especially sweet.

Daniel pressed the phone back to his ear. 'And congratulate Anna-May for me,' he relayed to Lyle Beck. 'She did a great job.'

Daniel could hear the smile in Lyle's voice as he replied. 'I will,' said Lyle. 'She's worth her weight in gold bullion, that girl.'

Daniel considered Lyle's remark. It was not an overstatement. Recruiting Anna-May into the project had been Lyle's idea and nothing short of genius. Lyle knew Anna-May from way back – she was a consummate actress, a former Las Vegas showgirl who preferred the thrill and financial rewards of 'undercover' work to the exacting grind of kicking her way through two shows a day. And there was no doubt about it, she excelled in her new career. She had been the linchpin of the entire set-up and she had played her part to perfection. The set-up had worked like a dream, right down to the redwood house they had rented in the desert as Anna-May's 'home'.

Furthermore, triumphed Daniel, his money had been tripled. Nadine and Mark's flutter on the casino gaming tables had been entirely fortuitous. For him, that was.

'There will be a bonus in this for the three of you,' said Daniel. The combined elements of good planning and good fortune made him feel magnanimous.

'Thanks,' said Lyle, characteristically economical with his words. Lyle made a sound down the telephone as if clearing his throat, and then he proceeded to talk. 'Daniel,' he began, 'what about payback for Mark Kelton and Nadine Brookes? What action do we take regarding that?'

Daniel thought for a moment and smiled a cold, hard smile. 'I'll figure something out. Give me an hour, Lyle.'

The conversation over, Daniel pushed back his chair and stood up. Not a bad start to the afternoon, he mused. He felt good, extremely good, and he wanted to celebrate. With that in mind, he made his way out of the house and down to the pool area.

Valerie was lying on one of the green sunloungers by the poolside. Her tousled blonde hair was scrunched into a knot back from her face, and she had a pair of small round sunglasses perched on the bridge of her nose. The lenses were so dark Daniel could not see her eyes behind them.

He felt a knock in his groin at the sight of her. She wore a minuscule black bikini, the top consisting of two patches of fabric, the bottoms little more than a tiny, matching triangle. The bikini top actually exposed more of her breasts than it covered, offering a tantalising exposé of the full, smooth globes.

Silently, Daniel walked towards her. He knelt down

next to her. She did not move at all – obviously she hadn't heard him. There was a bottle of sun milk down by the side of her lounger. He picked it up, emptied a generous amount into the palm of his hand and then pressed his hand gently on to her navel.

Her stomach flickered slightly at the contact.

'Hello,' she said lazily, pushing her sunglasses up on to the top of her head.

'Hello,' he said, flashing an even white smile. He began to massage the cream into her navel, enjoying the moistened, slightly tacky texture of her skin.

'That's nice,' she sighed. She was sitting with the top of the bed raised so that her upper body was tilted up slightly. Consequently, she was able to watch his ministrations simply by lowering her eyes. After several moments of watching him, she spoke. 'You seem happy.'

'I am happy,' murmured Daniel. 'I've recovered that money that was stolen.'

'Oh good,' chuckled Valerie. 'So now you know I'm not your thief.'

'I already knew that,' he responded, massaging the milk towards her ribcage.

'But you *did* suspect me?' she asked, sounding a tad annoyed.

'No,' lied Daniel. 'Never.' Why rock a boat when the storm had passed, he reasoned.

His hand moved steadily upward. He reached the flimsy cups of her bikini top and deftly manoeuvred them down beneath her breasts. Her bared breasts looked glorious – smooth, high swells of flesh, centred with perfect, rose nipples. Not lifting his eyes from them, he felt around on the ground for the bottle of sun milk. Once located, he held it high above her chest, squirting down a fine line of cream.

'Ooh!' She giggled. 'That tickles.'

As he began to massage it into her breasts, caressing her rich flesh, cupping each mound, Valerie stopped giggling and started to gasp instead.

'Who did take the money?' she managed to ask between gasps.

'Just a couple of losers,' murmured Daniel, toying with her cream-moistened nipples.

'Oh,' muttered Valerie, her interest clearly waning. She seemed far more interested in what was going on with the sun milk.

Daniel's hand felt slick. He moved it easily over her hot skin, caressing her collarbone, squeezing the malleable flesh of her breasts.

'That feels so good,' she breathed, watching his movements in a kind of trance.

He traced his hand down to her navel again, then smoothed the remains of the sun milk into the front of her long, supple thighs.

'*This* feels so good,' he purred, patting her venus mound through the fine elastine of her bikini bottoms. 'And this is even better,' he continued, pushing his hand inside, coiling his fingers through her soft hairs.

After a moment or two, he hooked his thumbs into the side strings of the bikini and dragged the bikini bottoms down. Valerie did nothing at all to resist, merely watching with a look of growing excitement. When he reached her ankles, she wriggled them together, manipulating the bikini until it fell to the ground.

She lay back, naked but for her bikini top which in any case was pulled down in such a way as to expose her breasts. She looked relaxed, at ease with her nudity in spite of the fact a member of his housekeeping staff could come down at any time. In the five days she had spent with him, Valerie had shed her inhibitions. Her eagerness to do so pleased him. Actually, most things about Valerie pleased him, and that fact continued to surprise him.

Daniel enjoyed the hold he knew he had over her. He enjoyed watching how her face would cloud with a veil of lust and arousal whilst his hands and fingers would drift on her flesh. He enjoyed leading her to a level of excitement where she was feverish with the need to climax, where he could choose to tease or show mercy, where she all but begged him for release.

He carried on stroking her stomach and thighs. Gradually, he edged around until he was kneeling at the base of the sunlounger, directly in front of her.

'Lift up your knees,' he murmured.

She bent her legs up at the knee. The position of her knees shielded the lower curve of her stomach and below from his eyes.

He nodded, pleased. Making himself wait to see her in full.

'Now . . .' he murmured, reaching forward and easing her knees apart. 'Ah, yes . . .' he breathed. Now he could see, all that he wanted – the satin gleam of her stomach, the silky moss of her pubes, the delicate shell-pink seam below.

She looked at him playfully and then let her knees drop outwards, displaying herself fully. Her sex looked delicious, an enticing light down feathering her outer lips, her clitoris soft and sleepy.

Daniel pressed his middle finger to her nubby bud and wiggled it gently, coaxing it from its protective folds. Soon it began to swell. Satisfied, he parted the pretty pleats of her lips. Then, enclosing her nub between two fingers, he vibrated it softly.

Valerie sighed, lifting her feet out to each side of the lounger, spreading her legs even wider.

Her sex was wet now, glistening deliciously.

Daniel felt his belly flip with excitement. He leant up on to the lounger and moved his face down. With a slow, luxurious movement, he pressed his tongue to her and drew it up the length of her clitoris.

'Oh God,' she gasped.

He took a moment to savour her taste, then he repeated the movement very slowly, exerting just enough pressure to make her gasp again. He teased her for a while with these long firm strokes, before curling his tongue around her clitoris, and then licking at her pouting lips.

She writhed on the lounger, lifting her legs up. Daniel stopped what he was doing to push her legs up higher and wider.

'I like that,' he purred, stroking the backs of her thighs right down to the start of her buttocks.

Valerie wriggled a little more. Her eyes were bright, feverish. 'Please, Daniel,' she pleaded. 'Don't stop. Please.'

He ducked back to her, lapping her sex urgently with his tongue, stopping every now and again to keep her on the edge of ecstasy.

'Oh, yes,' she kept saying, strained and yet joyous.

He flicked and teased her clitoris, then dragged his tongue down around her plump, moist roseflesh. Expertly withdrawing before that crucial peak.

'I can't take much more,' she groaned.

He fluttered his mouth over her.

'Mmm,' she yearned, arching up her hips.

He withdrew yet again, master of the tease.

'No, don't!' She jerked herself up to him.

'Ssh,' he whispered, thinking how superb she looked, her legs widespread and high, her hips nudged up, her stomach pulled in, tight with tension.

Her face was gleaming with a sheen of perspiration; wisps of blonde hair clung to the edges of her flushed cheekbones. 'I need you,' she pleaded, struggling to sit up, staring covetously at his swollen crotch.

'Not yet,' he chided.

He clasped his hands around her waist. She felt as light as a pliant doll as he turned her over on to her hands and knees. She glanced back at him eagerly, frantic with desire.

'You want me like this?' she asked croakily, arching her back, thrusting her hips and bottom up high.

'Oh yeah,' he answered, his voice thick.

She kept her head half-turned around, watching him whilst he surveyed her. He drew his eyes across the straight perfection of her shoulders, then down her slender back, following the precise curve of her spine. Her toned bottom, arched upward before him, gleamed wonderfully. His mouth went dry at the sight of her.

'Lean forward,' he instructed.

She leant forward a fraction.

'More,' he insisted.

She leant forward a fraction further, until her nipples skimmed the surface of the lounger. As though she could not help herself, she began to sway her upper body slightly, brushing her nipples against the fabric.

'Yes,' approved Daniel, moving forward.

Gently, he eased her buttock cheeks apart, admiring the dark-pink nudity of her crease. Her damp sex, perfumed with arousal, beckoned beneath, tempting every sense he possessed. Moving forward, he pushed his mouth against her once again, inserting his tongue inside her small slit. He heard her sigh and felt her push back against him.

He made his tongue rigid, digging it in and out, loving the pulpy, fruity feel of her inside, the peach-skin softness of her feathered outside.

Valerie swayed her nipples to and fro as he tongued her, pushing her hips back forcefully against him.

'Oh God, more,' she urged, bucking back rhythmically.

Roughly, he clasped her buttocks, holding her steady whilst he poked his tongue within. The fact that she could no longer move her hips seemed to make her groan more loudly. She pressed the side of her face down on to the sunbed, lifting her bottom as high as she could. Daniel pushed in further until his tongue was buried deep inside her sex and his lips pressed hard against her roseflesh.

Suddenly she froze, a moan evolving into a drawn-out sigh. He could feel the beating contractions of her orgasm, squeezing round his tongue in mini, rhythmic spasms; and then she began to react, her back and shoulders juddering with pleasure.

She collapsed on her stomach for a while, not talking nor moving.

'Incredible,' she sighed eventually, turning over.

Daniel, rampant as a stallion, didn't answer.

It *had* been incredible. Valerie's body tingled from head to foot. She took one look at Daniel in front of her and charges of desire fizzed anew. The air between them was electric.

Daniel stood up. His eyes smouldered, blacker than ever, and his face was set, his lean features drawn in a familiar expression. The expression signalled just one thing; Valerie went weak at the thought of it. She was lost, she thought, lost in this man, and no matter how often she had him, it was never enough. Never would be.

He mystified her. There were things about him she would never know. Part of her didn't want to. As Ashley had warned her, there was something beneath the charisma and good looks, something hard, maybe even dangerous. But Valerie did not give a damn. The excitement, the passion, the sex, even the mystery – so long as it all continued, then she did not give a damn.

His eyes never left her face as he unbuttoned his shirt and let it slip to the floor. His body was perfect, each lean brown muscle, each millimetre of smooth unblemished skin.

She sat up on her knees and reached forward. His taut belly flickered as she drew the back of her finger-nail across it. Her own tummy swirled as she moved her hand down, moulding it to the magnificent, upright swelling in his trousers. She gripped it firmly, watching his reaction.

'Unzip me,' he murmured.

She did, pulling the zipper down slowly, releasing his cock. He took a stride forward, bracing his legs either side of the sunlounger. The muscles in his thighs bunched through his trousers as he held his own weight. He glanced fervidly at her exposed breasts. Valerie knew what he wanted and she reached behind her back, pulling the tie of her bikini top and then throwing the top off altogether. Her breasts were totally bare now, full for her frame, high and perky.

Holding the shaft of his penis in her hands, she leant back slightly and then guided his penis in between her breasts. Daniel cupped her breasts in his hands, pushing them together, enclosing his penis. He murmured appreciatively and then began to move, sliding his cock up and down her cleavage. Her skin was moist with a mix of sun milk and perspiration and his cock moved easily, stimulating the inner sides of her breasts.

She held his cock at the base and he slid up and down with increasing vigour, rolling his thumbs over her nipples as he continued to squeeze her breasts together.

He was so hard, and her breasts felt glorious – hot, stimulated, aroused.

'Christ,' he groaned, thrusting back and forth, squeezing her breasts, teasing her nipples.

Her nipples stood out like pearly beads, almost too hard, too sensitive.

He pumped his hips in an urgent frenzy, his leg muscles bunched with the strain. She held on firmly to the base of his penis, willing him forward, experiencing a strange, novel thrill through her breasts. Droplets of sweat spotted on his stomach, trickling into the waist of his trousers. He was approaching orgasm, she could tell, and, with a final, jerky nudge, he climaxed, spilling on to her cleavage and neck.

His legs gave way and he slumped down, still straddling the sunbed with his legs. He was still cupping her breasts, and Valerie was torn by a whole new sensation. She covered his hands with her own, pressing them down, crushing her nipples beneath his palms. She rotated his hands round and round, pressing down, hard, hard, squeezing, feeling her nipples hard and sore ... and suddenly a climax tore through her upper body, tugging at her breasts and nipples and shoulders and back.

She thrust out her chest as far as she could, glorying in the magical thrills shooting through her.

'That's never happened to me before,' she gasped to Daniel in astonishment. 'It was fantastic. But strange, kind of strange.'

His confident smile made her woozy. 'There's nothing strange about pleasure, honey. In my opinion, you can never have enough.'

'Never have enough of you,' she murmured. But she did so under her breath so that Daniel could not hear her. Better that way, she thought intuitively, brimming with her own kind of confidence.

Chapter Nineteen

A wind had got up. It had a hollow, melancholy sound as it howled in the vastness. It was a warm wind. Despite that, the currents of air seemed to cool the skin and it relieved the baking domination of the sun. But the wind was short-lived and, in a way, Mark was glad. Its howling emptiness gave him the creeps.

He walked slowly along the roadside. After a few steps, he stopped and screwed up his eyes, squinting into the distance. A droplet of sweat worked its way down the edge of his forehead and trickled into the corner of his eye. The salt stung his eye and made his vision blurry. Nothing to see anyway, he thought, blinking the sweat away and attempting to focus. Nothing but a hazy skyline miles in the distance.

Another bead of sweat followed the first. This time, Mark pressed his finger to it. A third droplet followed and Mark started to worry. Christ, he thought, at this rate he was going to dehydrate. She hadn't even thrown out a bottle of water.

He looked down at his watch. It had been half an hour since Nadine had driven off and left him and it was only in the last few minutes that it had actually started to sink in. She was not coming back for him. She *really* was not coming back.

He sank down on the side of the road to rest for a while, to conserve what energy he had. He knew that anger was futile but he could do very little about it – he was seething with it, with a fury which attacked his guts in almost agonising waves. Besides, he reflected, it was this anger that would give him strength and keep him focused and make goddamn sure he reached civilisation.

How in hell did he get himself into this? Stranded in a desert on the outskirts of Las Vegas. He pulled his trouser pockets inside out – and with the grand sum of five bucks and seventy-five cents to his name.

Mark held the few dollar bills and coins in the palm of his hand. Plain old-fashioned greed, he reminded himself, looking down at the scant collection, that's how he got himself into it. A briefcase full of money was how he got himself into it. That, and a green-eyed seductress named Nadine.

Not to mention that other blue-eyed betrayer, Anna-May.

Not that difficult really when you thought about it, to end up stranded in a desert, broke, jobless, career in tatters.

Mark shook his head, disbelieving his own gullibility. Man, he took the prize for that one. How had he not seen it coming? With Anna-May, he had had little choice – it was either take a risk on her or take a risk going back to the casino and running into blondie and ponytail. But Nadine was a whole other matter: he truly had not seen that one coming. He had thought they were in this thing together, all the way.

Some lawyer's instinct, he told himself dryly.

He shook his head again, picked up a stone and hurled it mindlessly across the road. It landed in a heap of desert dust. Mark chuckled ironically. Like my career, he thought, landing up in a heap of desert dust!

The sun blazed down, burning the top of his head – he felt perspiration gather on the back of his neck.

Jesus, he realised, he had better get moving. Or heat-stroke could really be a problem.

He got up and started to walk along the side of the road again. He kept his eyes fixed firmly on the distant skyline. He would make it, he told himself grimly. Just to see the look on Nadine's face when he found her. His mouth felt dry but he swallowed anyway, to try to rid himself of the acrid taste of bitterness. It was a taste he was beginning to get used to.

Mark felt a surge of relief. Some way back he had reached a fork in the road. Which to take, left or right? Instinct told him to go left and so he had gone right. To date, his instincts had let him down badly.

And now he saw that he had been right to go right. About a hundred yards ahead, there appeared to be a gas station. Mark walked quicker, a sudden hopeful spring in his step.

The place was badly in need of repair. A rusty, flipover sign indicated an outdated price for fuel and the gas pumps looked old and dilapidated.

'Hello,' said Mark, walking up on to a covered, wooden porch. 'Anyone around?'

No one answered. A lone gust of wind blew the rusty sign and it creaked for a second, then settled.

'Hello,' repeated Mark, a little louder. He took a few careful steps forward on the porch, noticing that the wooden floorboards were rotten. The door to the small, flat-roofed building was hanging off its hinges. Mark was getting a strong feeling that the place was deserted.

He twisted the doorknob and pushed the door. It creaked a little, scraping on the floor, but it opened.

'Hell-oo,' he called out, knocking on the outside of the door, then going inside. 'Anyone around?'

The place was most definitely deserted. Shutters were closed in the room, but the light from the opened doorway revealed a sparsely furnished room strewn with cobwebs. Silver-lit particles of dust hung in the air and there was a musty smell of age and abandonment.

242

There was a broken shop counter and a cash register at the rear of the room, a door at the back which had obviously once led through to a living area, and an ancient sagging sofa to the side. And, to Mark's amazement and delight, there was a dusty, old-fashioned drinks machine in the corner.

'Oh you lovely lady,' he crooned, feeding in a couple of quarters and praying for a miracle. Nothing happened, and yet he could see the lines of soda cans stacked teasingly behind the discoloured glass.

'Shit,' he cursed. 'Take my money like every other goddamn person today.' Landing out an almighty punch, he thumped the side of the machine, and with a comical, heavy belch from the machine, a soda can tumbled into the tray at the bottom.

'Thank you,' Mark muttered sarcastically, snatching the can. Bad-tempered, he kicked the machine for good measure. Another can of soda landed jauntily in the tray. At any other time than right then, Mark would have seen the funny side.

The soda was flat and warm and tasted like cardboard, but Mark poured it down his throat like it was an ice-cold beer. He felt a kick of energy, an instant fix of sugar and water.

He took the second soda, peeled back the tab and sipped it more slowly. Then he walked over to the door, kicked it shut to close out the sunlight, carried the soda over to the couch, stretched out flat on the relative comfort of the lumpy cushions, and closed his eyes. He meant to relax for only a minute or so, but within that minute or so he was asleep. Betrayal, heat and thirst made a man weary.

It was a sound outside that woke him. The gentle click of a car door. Mark sat up and listened. He was certain he could hear footsteps.

A clammy coldness crawled down his spine. He told himself to keep calm – it might just be a passing motorist; there was even a chance it was Nadine, stricken with conscience, come back to pick him up. Or, he realised, it could be something or someone rather more sinister.

For all that had happened to Mark that day, he was not a fool. Daniel Garsante may have outwitted him and got his money back. But Mark knew that it was a job half-done. Daniel Garsante was not a man to betray; all along Mark had known that. Daniel would want his revenge and his henchmen were still out there somewhere. More than likely hunting him down.

He heard another sound, a crunch of stony gravel, then a faint, creaking of the rotten porch floor. Despite the heat, the skin on the back of his neck prickled into gooseflesh.

Delicately, he placed the soda can down on the floor. His eyes scanned the room for a weapon of some kind. There was nothing.

But he was not about to go down without a fight and he had an idea. Reaching to his waist, he unbuckled his black leather belt and pulled at one end. Like a silent snake, it slid from his trouser loop-holes. Mark wound the ends of the belt round his wrists, and then clasped either end with both hands. He yanked the belt out to both sides, testing its capability. Perfect, he thought. From behind, he could use it to crush the air from somone's throat like a python.

Outside, the rotten floorboards creaked again.

Mark stood up. Stealthily, he crept across to the door. The door would open inward, so he positioned himself behind it. Surprise was everything. That much he knew.

He pressed his ear to the wall and listened. There wasn't a sound, not a creak, not a rustle, but instinct told him someone was there. This time, he was prepared to go with his instincts. He tightened his grip on the ends of the belt.

Then he heard something. He glanced down, locating the sound. The doorknob was slowly moving. Someone was turning the doorknob.

Mark tensed his whole body, poised for attack.

The door was being pushed open, it was scraping on the floor. A sliver of sunlight entered the room, patterning the floor in a distorted triangle. Mark concentrated on the triangle, watching it grow and change shape as the door opened a little more. He gripped the belt tightly, stretching it straight. He ran his tongue over his lips: they felt as dry as parchment paper. His whole mouth felt dry; he barely had enough saliva to swallow. Adrenalin was coursing through his entire body, heightening his senses, his reflexes. The door opened wider. He balanced on the balls of his feet. He bunched the muscles in his arms as he held up the belt.

A gloved hand appeared, leather-clad fingers curling round the edge of the door.

Mark held his breath. Ready. Ready to kill.

He heard the brush of clothing against the other side of the door. Someone was entering.

Mark took a deep breath. Waiting. Biding his time. Choosing his moment.

It happened so quickly.

He saw movement, the shadow of a figure, and he pounced. Springing from behind, throwing over the belt with the primeval instinct to survive.

Realisation only dawned after several seconds – the squeal, the coughing, the uneven contest of strength. Mark stopped as soon as he realised, instantly loosening his grip and releasing the struggling, terror-struck intruder. He took one close look at her and almost wished he had carried on.

He backed off, flinging the belt in disgust over on to the sofa. He exhaled softly.

'So,' he said, grim-voiced. 'You're back.'

'Yes.' Her voice was hoarse, a little shaken. She held her hands gently to her neck.

Mark looked at her and shook his head. 'I had you by the throat. I should have carried on.'

Her lovely eyes flickered. Other than that she did not react to his words.

Mark studied her for several moments. He wandered

over to the drinks machine, kicked it twice and retrieved two sodas. Then he walked over to the door and stepped outside.

'Goodbye,' he called out, without turning back.

Outside, the car was parked askew. He supposed he could go back in there and take the keys off her by force.

Nah, he thought, strolling on by. He still had some integrity. He could not knowingly attack a woman. Not even Anna-May.

Strangely enough, he felt refreshed, invigorated, as he walked along the roadside. The city skyline did not seem to be getting any closer, but he was not that bothered any more. He would make it eventually, he knew, and he felt unnaturally calm and surreal about his situation.

He had pushed the two soda cans into his trouser pockets. A moment ago, he had reached for one of them and peeled back the tab and now he stopped to take a sip.

As he held the can to his lips, he was aware of the car's approach behind him. It was *his* car after all, and he would know the sound of the engine anywhere. He ignored it, casually resuming his roadside walking.

The car drew up level with him, and then crawled alongside at his walking pace. Despite himself, Mark glanced sidewards. Anna-May was leaning right across, out of the passenger window.

'Jump in,' she invited.

Mark continued to walk, steadfastly ignoring her. He sipped his soda as he walked.

'Mark,' she pressed. 'You'll never make it. Jump in.'

'I'd rather take my chances on foot,' he muttered, 'than jump in the snakepit with you.'

To his surprise and extreme annoyance, Anna-May chuckled. 'I'm not such a snake really,' she laughed. 'In fact, I'm not bad at all, once you get to know me.'

'I don't want to get to know you.'

She chuckled again. 'Aw, come on, don't be that way. You had your belt wrapped round my throat a few minutes ago. That must have relieved some of your animosity.'

It was the laughing that did it. And the smart-alec words. Mark felt his new calmness dissipate and his anger resurface like a red-hot tide. He stopped in his tracks, glaring at her. 'You're a double-crossing bitch, Anna-May.'

'I know it,' she admitted. 'Talking of which, where's Nadine?'

Mark shook his head, disbelieving his situation all over again. 'Another double-crossing bitch. I seem to have an affinity for them.'

Anna-May did not seem surprised. 'Face it,' she said softly. 'Life's like that.'

She sounded almost philosophical. Mark softened his tone a little, suddenly wanting some answers.

'Why did you do it, Anna-May?' he asked. 'All that money. A third of it yours. There was no way Daniel paid you that much.'

She nodded. 'No,' she agreed. 'No, he didn't. But you don't cross a man like Daniel Garsante. Not if you're sensible and want to stay healthy, you don't. Besides, he hired me to do a job and I did it. It's called professionalism.'

'It's called betrayal is what it's called.'

She shrugged. 'Funny thing, betrayal is the exact same word Daniel used when I was hired. Once upon a time, so he said, he had in his employ a brilliant young lawyer; a man he trusted and liked – you could almost say a friend –'

'OK, OK,' cut in Mark. 'Save the storytelling. I know what I did.'

She shrugged again. 'Anyhow, the way I see it, you've kind of struck lucky on two counts.'

'Oh yeah?' he countered, squinting up into the sunshine. 'I'm stuck in the desert. No money. A career in the dirt. And Daniel's crazy men still on the lookout for me. Real lucky!'

Anna-May smiled prettily, coiling her thick blonde plait round her hand. 'You and Nadine turned a generous amount of money into a fortune, Mark. In a way, Daniel is grateful.'

Mark raised a sceptical eyebrow.

'OK,' conceded Anna-May. 'Maybe he's not grateful exactly. But he is satisfied. Satisfied enough to leave you both be.'

Mark thought about this. 'Considering our recent history, why should I believe you?'

'Because I'm here, telling you. I came back to find you and tell you. I found out a short while ago from an associate of mine, one of Daniel's – what did you call them – "crazy men". Daniel has called them off, Mark. You're safe.'

He wasn't quite sure why he believed her, but he did. He palmed his hand down his face and found it was shaking with relief. He took a moment, letting the news sink in.

A few minutes later, he nodded, scuffing his feet in the dirt. 'You said I was lucky on two counts. That was obviously one. What's the second?'

Anna-May winked. 'Me.'

He stared at her. 'You?'

She stared back steadily. 'I like you, Mark. I want what I like.'

He continued to stare at her. She smiled. She had a very pretty smile. And very pretty eyes. A beautiful face, in fact. And a body –' he let his eyes travel down her neck and cleavage and he felt a wicked stirring in his groin.

'Well?' she murmured.

Mark turned his head slightly, glancing at the long empty road ahead. He turned back to Anna-May. Her blue eyes sparkled, clear as alpine water. So clear you could dive right into them, he thought. So long as you remembered to put on a life-jacket!

'Well?' she repeated. 'What do you think?'

He pulled open the car door and slid in. 'I think I like what you want,' he grinned.

Anna-May leant across and kissed his dusty lips. 'I guess that makes us compatible.' She smiled, thrusting the automatic into drive and speeding off into the hazy sunshine.

Chapter Twenty

*S*ince arriving in Las Vegas, Nadine was feeling a lot better. The drive to get there had not been so easy for her – she actually felt a little sad about what she had done to Mark. But a girl had to look out for herself, she reflected, and if it took a few pangs of sadness to do that, well then, she would deal with them.

She would get over Mark, she consoled herself. Especially when she had around a hundred thousand dollars from the sale of the jewels all to herself. Besides, Mark would make it out of the desert. Of that, she was convinced. Mark was a survivor. A soft touch, but a survivor.

And she was too. More than that, she was a winner.

And now that she was in the city she had an agenda to follow and no time for remorse. The first thing she needed was a private phone booth. Within moments of cruising down the busy thoroughfare, she had spotted one. She pulled up in front of it.

'J for jewellers,' she murmured, flicking through the pages of the phone book. She traced her fingertip down the page, stopping and tapping the page when she found the one that appealed to her. Maurice, Jave & Co. Specialist Jewellers. Perfect.

Jotting down the address, Nadine stepped back into

the car and consulted a city map she had had the foresight to buy a few moments ago. Then she knocked down her sunglasses from the top of her head. Glancing in her rear-view mirror, she reversed out on to the thoroughfare once again, and headed into town.

It did not take her long to find the jewellery store. Maurice, Jave & Co. were located on a quiet side road. The street was very clean and the shops looked exclusive, with potted palms and miniature trees strategically placed outside sparkling glass doorways.

Nadine parked in the shade at the end of the street. She took out her compact and checked her make-up, pouting her lips and grazing her fingernail over her fine eyebrows.

Her tummy was fluttering excitedly as she got out of the car. She smoothed down her dress, swung her bag over her shoulder, and began to walk.

As she sauntered down the quiet street, she caught sight of her reflection in a gleaming shop window. A tall, slender young woman, exuding sensuality from every perfect pore. Her shining dark hair tumbled in flattering layers across her bare shoulders and upper back; her long, mauve dress skimmed the subtle contours of her breasts and hips, revealing a hint of golden ankle between hemline and high, strappy slip-ons. Nadine smiled serenely. She looked every inch a woman who should own diamonds like these, she thought, patting the package inside her handbag. With a wicked little wink at her own reflection, she rang the bell to Maurice, Jave & Co. and smiled radiantly as she was led inside.

Mr Jave made himself available. Nadine had noticed a man glance down from a first-floor gallery as soon as she walked in. The next thing she knew, the man was at her shoulder.

'I'll serve this lady, Suki,' he had said to the immaculate, platinum-blonde assistant who had been preparing to serve.

251

Mr Jave had led Nadine through to a private rear room. She was now sitting opposite him as he picked up Anna-May's jewels, piece by piece, and held them up, studying them through an eyeglass.

'Lovely,' he kept repeating.

Mr Jave had a peculiar, hushed manner of speaking, as though he were in awe and did not want to raise his voice. Nadine wasn't sure whether it was she he was in awe of, or the jewellery.

He was a broad-shouldered, stocky man, with jet-black hair and eyebrows. He wore an expensive dark suit which fitted his sturdy frame flawlessly, and Italian shoes which were polished like mirrors. His eyes, when he was not screwing them up into the eyeglass, were big, brown, puppy-dog eyes. Honest eyes, thought Nadine, congratulating herself on her choice of jeweller.

Mr Jave examined the last item of jewellery, then laid it out reverently alongside the others.

'Beautiful pieces,' he said quietly. 'Exquisite craftsmanship and design.' He kept touching the jewels as he spoke.

Nadine smiled calmly. Inside, she simmered, thrilled by his words. Selling these would, in some very small way, make up for the fortune Anna-May had stolen from her.

She reached to her neck and toyed with the pretty diamond pendant she had decided to keep for herself.

'I'm selling the entire collection, Mr Jave,' she said, twisting the pendant between her fingertips as she spoke. 'Are you interested?'

Mr Jave looked down at the jewellery, fluttering his fingers from piece to piece. 'Well,' he said thoughtfully. 'It is not our usual practice –'

'Are you interested, Mr Jave?' persisted Nadine, growing a tad impatient with his waffle.

He glanced at her patiently, picked up the diamond wristwatch and ran his fingers slowly over the bracelet. Clearly, he was not to be hurried. Not wishing to appear desperate, Nadine bit back her impatience.

Mr Jave sat back and exhaled a soft breath, 'Yes,' he said decisively, 'I think under the circumstances I can make an exception. Yes, Ms . . . er . . . ?'

Nadine saw that he was waiting for her name. 'Duvalle,' she thought up quickly. 'Ms Duvalle.'

He nodded. 'Yes then, Ms Duvalle, I'm interested.'

Nadine leant forward. 'How much will you offer me, Mr Jave?'

Mr Jave considered the items before him. Nadine tapped her foot underneath the table. After several moments, he looked up. 'Taking into account the exquisite craftsmanship and design,' he beamed, 'I feel I can be generous and offer you two thousand dollars.'

Nadine blinked. 'Pardon me?'

Mr Jave smiled benignly. 'Two thousand dollars.'

Thoughtfully, Nadine twirled the pendant at her throat, back and forth through her fingers. 'Mr Jave,' she began, making herself curl her tongue seductively around her words to curb her impatience. 'I appreciate a joke as much as anyone, but I am in rather a hurry.'

Three deep furrows creased Mr Jave's forehead and his thick dark eyebrows knitted into one. He looked genuinely affronted. 'I can assure you, Ms Duvalle, that I never, *never* joke where jewellery is concerned.'

Nadine felt a little short of breath.

'And I can further assure you that two thousand dollars is a very generous offer. As I was saying, it is not our usual practice in this store to purchase imitation jewellery, but in view of the exquisite craftsmanship and original designwork and high-quality materials, I am prepared to . . .' Mr Jave let his voice trail off as he gazed at Nadine in concern. 'Ms Duvalle,' he said earnestly, 'are you all right? You look a little flushed.'

Nadine felt like she was burning up. She pressed the inside of her wrist to her forehead – her skin was like a furnace. 'Fine, thanks, Mr Jave,' she murmured. 'Just a tad warm in here. Did I hear you say the word "imitation"? Did I hear that right?'

Mr Jave regarded her, his brown eyes flashing with sudden comprehension. 'Oh my,' he said softly, sympathetically. 'You didn't think they were – ?' He stopped as if he could not bring himself to finish. 'Genuine?' It seemed he pushed the word out with an effort.

She looked at him like he was mad. 'Of course they're genuine. I'm not stupid, I know diamonds when I see them.'

Mr Jave pursed his lips, shaking his head gently. 'No, Ms Duvalle. I can assure you these stones are not diamonds.'

Nadine frowned at the jewels. 'But they're so beautiful,' she said, 'so fine, . . . so real . . .'

Mr Jave nodded sadly. 'I know, my dear,' he said. 'As I said, the craftsmanship is superb and the materials exquisite. Whoever made them is truly an expert. Most people would think them to be genuine.'

'I don't believe these aren't diamonds,' she muttered, running her thumb over the sparkling stones. 'It isn't possible.'

'Glass and zircon,' explained Mr Jave.

He sat there mutely, whilst Nadine looked gloomily at the jewels, picking them up one by one, inspecting them closely, trying to see the simulation for herself. She could not see it. She simply could not see it. Nadine was no stranger to diamonds; she felt sure she was able to differentiate between the real thing and a fake. Why else would a woman as smart as herself have fallen for such an obvious ruse?

But, no matter how closely she looked, to her they looked as real as they had done before.

Mr Jave, a kind man by nature, spoke up: 'In this instance, it would take an expert such as myself, Ms Duvalle, to see the difference. If you did not already know they were replicas, it would take an expert.'

His words were clearly meant to comfort, but Nadine wished he would shut the hell up. What use were words to her? She wanted diamonds.

But Mr Jave seemed intent on consoling her. 'Fortunately,' he said brightly, warming to his solicitous role, 'there is a small market for items as well made as these.'

He smiled across at her as if to say that all was not lost.

Nadine wanted to scream. Everything was lost. Her money was lost; a fortune in casino chips was lost; and now, goddammit, the jewels were lost.

But she did not scream. Instead, she smiled back radiantly at kind Mr Jave, unclipping the pendant from round her neck and placing it down alongside the other items. 'If I add this to the collection, Mr Jave,' she said sweetly, 'will you throw in an extra one hundred dollars?'

Mr Jave leant across the table and patted her hand. 'I think I can do that, Ms Duvalle.' He smiled. 'Would you prefer cash or a cheque?'

'Cash would be fine,' she replied.

She sat in a quiet corner of the bar, staring down into her empty glass. A piece of lemon lay crumpled in the bottom, looking as listless as she felt.

For a while, after she had left the jewellery store, she had sat in the car, railing wildly against Daniel and Anna-May. The detail of the setup astounded her – they must have planned and covered for any eventuality, she realised, right down to an opportune collection of fake diamond jewellery.

Alone in the car, she had seethed with fury, incredulous that she had been outsmarted, incredulous that anyone could go to the lengths Daniel had. She twisted the facts over and over in her mind – the money she had stolen originally must have been mere pocket change to a man as wealthy as Daniel. Why go to such extraordinary lengths to pursue them, she thought, why? And the more she twisted it over in her mind, the more Mark's cautionary words came back to haunt her. Daniel Garsante was not a man to cross; his reach was legendary; he would never give up . . .

Nadine stared miserably into her empty glass. What was she going to do now? The $2,100 she had in her purse was all her money in the world. She had blown it with Mark: he would never take her back. She had blown it in Santa Barbara: she could never go back there. The $2,100 would only last so long, and finding a job was out of the question.

A remorseful return to Uncle Will's fruit farm in San Bernardino and humble pie with Uncle Willem seemed like her only prospect. Nadine felt weary at the thought.

She pushed her glass to the back of the table. Breathing out a deep, empty sigh, she glanced up, gazing reluctantly at the doors to the bar. Her only option was to go out of those doors, get back in the car, and then head on back to goddamn fruit country.

Suddenly, the door to the bar opened and a man walked in. Nadine stared. The man was in his late twenties, tall and fit-looking with a rugged outdoor tan. He was dressed in jeans and a T-shirt, and wore sturdy workman's boots which were covered in dust. His dark-blond hair was longish, curling at the ends into the nape of his neck.

Cute, thought Nadine. But that was not the reason she was staring. The man reminded her of someone, someone handsome, fit and wonderfully virile. Someone who lived and worked in San Bernardino. Someone whom she knew for a fact could make her insides dance and her stomach twirl.

Jake, she thought triumphantly. Jake, Uncle Will's hired hand.

She edged out from her table and sauntered over to the door. All of a sudden, she felt brighter. Jake, she repeated softly to herself. Jake would make life on the fruit farm bearable. Jake would even make it fun.

Maybe San Bernardino wasn't such a bad prospect

after all, she thought, pushing open the doors and stepping out on to the street.

What was more, she thought cheerily, glancing at the sleek, low vehicle in front of her, she still had Anna-May's car!